BOOK 2
THE CURSED HERALD

A NOVEL BY

RINA S. MAMOON

ISBN: 978-1-7752440-8-0

Author Website: rinasmamoon.ca

Acknowledgements

Thank you, Mom, for your love and support. Dad, who spread the word around when I released my debut novel, *The Lost & Cursed*. And my brother, Michael, for taking an interest in this project of mine.

I would also like to thank those who congratulated me via Dad sharing the news, including Aunt Danielle and Uncle Sikander; and Aunty Farida. I also extend this thanks to Millie, Murray, and Phyllis. My cousin, Jillene, and her boyfriend, Mitch. And my cousin, Matthew.

Thanks to all the friends who congratulated me on my first release, including Jamie, Chris, Shane, R. J., and Melissa. I also extend this thanks to colleagues such as Jaro, Cheryl, Michael, Justin, Andrea, and Dave.

And thank you, dear reader, for taking the time to read the second instalment to *The Dark One* series. I hope you enjoyed reading it as much as I enjoyed writing it.

Table of Contents

Chapter One

Waking Nightmare

The sun was setting as Mara Ashwood walked home on a cold and snowy December afternoon. Not many people were around, which was odd because the city was often lively during the Winter Festival. Wreaths and holly decorated the street lights illuminating her path.

She took extra care with each step, for a layer of ice covered the ground.

Mara frowned. The recent agreement to not celebrate her birthday left her sour, for it was her twenty-fifth. There was no time to throw a small celebration due to the fast-approaching wedding. Even the grand ceremony she kept hearing about did not alleviate her disappointment.

As she reached her home, a very ornate carriage strolled by and stopped before her. She glanced over, recognizing the wooden carriage decorated in gold. She knew its owners.

"Miss Ashwood," called a familiar man from within the transport.

Peering inside, Mara identified the short and round man by his bright blue eyes, greying hair, and matching beard and moustache. Mr. Arthur White was one of her professors at the College of Ardana. He wore a thick dark coat over his suit and tie, making him appear rounder.

Gazing at the other occupant, she immediately recognized the handsome young man. Her fiancé, Karl White, was three years older than her. He also wore a matching coat over his black suit but kept his fit physique. Karl often had his shiny brown hair combed to the right. He owned a thin, pale face with a proportioned nose. His narrow chin possessed some stubble, as well as a tuft of hair under the bottom lip. His groomed eyebrows sat above bright green eyes.

Every time Mara saw Karl, she could not help but think of him as a prince. Not only was he handsome, but he was also rich and powerful. According to Mom, the Whites were distinguished nobles throughout the land. Mara sometimes wondered why he chose her because she was a commoner. Karl could have chosen any other woman within his social class.

Karl gazed in her direction, his eyes drawing her in. She began to approach the carriage.

"What's going on?" Mara asked.

"There is a ceremony we must perform before the wedding," Mr. White replied. "It is custom to the Faith."

"A ceremony?"

The two men nodded.

"It is like a test." Mr. White gestured to his ward. "We shall summon the Goddess, Kallisto. If Karl truly loves you, he can resist her beauty. She will bless your marriage, granting you two a long and happy life."

Mara took a step forward, but stopped and looked back at the wooden house—her family home. "I should let Mom and Dad know."

"We must leave immediately," Mr. White insisted. "We shall let your parents know once the ceremony is complete."

Mara grew uncertain. She never heard of this ceremony before. What if Karl failed? According to legend, Kallisto's beauty could enchant any man who gazed upon her. How could Mara compete? What if the wedding got cancelled? Mom would be upset, though Dad might be thrilled by the news. He never liked Karl, let alone trusted him or his father. Mom was always in favour of the wedding since she introduced the two.

Even Allen and James Moen, the twin brothers she met in college, were wary of her relationship with Karl. Allen disliked the nobleman because he made their lives miserable. But Mara chose to forgive Karl, and the two grew closer much to the brothers' disappointment. If the wedding never happened, Allen would be overjoyed. No, she should not be thinking this way, for she loved Karl. After Mara entered the carriage, the three departed for Golden Mountain.

While leaving the City of Mirahyll, Mara remained unsure about doing this behind the backs of her family and friends. She gazed at Karl. He looked out the window with a blank expression on his face. It was hard to tell if he was worried. Never once did he look at her. She switched her attention to Mr. White. The older man frowned as he gazed out the window on his side. The looks on their faces confused her. One appeared indifferent while the other was full of dread. Maybe they knew this ceremony would end in misery, but none had the heart to tell her.

* * *

The carriage finally reached the Temple of Kallisto, located on the mountain. Once the coach stopped, the three got out. The snowy path was lit up by gold and ivory pillars of fire. According to history, this temple was part of the grand palace the gods ruled from until the cataclysm one thousand years ago.

Mara stared up at the temple and froze. Deep down, she did not want to do this ceremony. None of her family and friends would be there to comfort her if it failed. She was alone. Her unwillingness to move caught the attention of her two companions. Her fiancé stepped before her and gave a reassuring look.

"It will be okay," Karl said softly.

Seeing his green eyes made her fears melt away. She had to believe in him because she loved him. He turned around and walked up the path. Both Mara and Mr. White followed him up to the temple.

Entering the gold and ivory building, she saw a large group of people also attending the ceremony. They all watched her in scrutiny, making her feel nervous. Not many approved of their relationship—a noble and a commoner. It was as if their love was some unholy union. She ignored them and watched the priestess at the top of the stairs.

High Priestess Alena, who led the Faith in Ardana, sat on her golden throne. Mara could not see her face, for the veil hid the woman's features. From head to toe, Alena wore a dress of white and gold with many jewels adorning her. She gripped the armrests before rising to her feet. The priestess descended the stairs and came closer to them.

"No, I will not allow this," the woman boomed.

Alena removed her veil, unleashing a bright flash of light that filled the room. The light faded, allowing Mara a glimpse of her face. The woman was beyond beautiful with flawless pale skin and long blond hair. Her nose and lips were thin on a heart-shaped face. The woman had perfect proportions on her feminine frame, being a little more on the slender side. Her golden eyes were familiar to Mara. It was Kallisto.

Everyone sank to their knees, enthralled by Kallisto's radiant beauty. Mara, who remained unaffected, saw Karl on his knees, gazing at the goddess' loveliness. Kallisto approached him with fluid and grace. She reached out and stroked the side of his face. Karl closed his eyes as her hand caressed him.

"Come," Kallisto commanded.

Karl opened his eyes. He kept looking at the goddess as he rose to his feet. The more he watched her, the more Kallisto's intoxicating beauty drugged his senses.

Mara watched as he went to the goddess' side. She reached out her hand and called to him.

"Karl! No!"

Her cries fell on deaf ears. Kallisto had bewitched him, making him blind to his fiancée's existence. The goddess continued to hypnotize him, pulling him deeper under her spell. Kallisto then pressed her lips to his own. Mara grew horrified. Her prince was not pulling away. Instead, he deepened in the kiss while holding the goddess in his embrace. Mara needed to do something, or else she would lose him.

3

"Leave him alone—"

All of a sudden, Mara was struck down by a powerful force. She hit the ground. Every inch of her body throbbed in pain. Looking at her hand, she saw her flesh turn grey. Her nails turned into sharp black claws. Decay spread throughout her body as black scars formed on her face. Her heart pounded out of fear and dread. What was happening to her? Lifting her gaze, Mara noticed the dark stares of the followers. Even the goddess and Karl gave a malicious glare. Seeing her fiancé's face made her feel something was wrong. It was as if he became a different person.

"I had slain you thirty years ago," Kallisto addressed her, "because you dared to stand in between our love!"

Remembering what happened, intense rage began to fill Mara. She clenched her teeth as she glared at her murderer. Her canines grew longer. Looking back at her claws, she wanted to tear Kallisto apart. She lifted her gaze to the goddess again, revealing glowing yellow eyes. Mara suddenly dashed at her, wanting to kill Kallisto. But Karl stood in the way.

Acute pain drew her attention down to her stomach. A well-crafted sword had impaled her. The black and red grip with strips of gold was familiar. The golden pommel possessed a ruby gemstone. Black ooze stained the double-edged straight sword, also known as the Hand of Kratés.

Mara looked up at Karl again, but no longer did she see her prince. Commander White stood in his place, gripping the sword that penetrated her abdomen. He wore his commander's garb, which consisted of a dark grey overcoat, and golden plates on the left shoulder and bicep. A red cape, cascading the right side of his body, was held together by a brown leather shoulder pad. Brown leather gloves with blue fingers covered his forearms, with the left adorned in the same metal plating. He also wore white pants with brown knee-high boots. Brown leather armour protected his thighs, while golden plates covered his knees.

She stared into his eyes, wondering why he would do this. Mara opened her mouth to speak, but only blood poured out. He pulled the blade out of her body. She cried out in pain as she hit the ground with a thud. No one moved a muscle to help her. Nobody cared. She watched as the commander rejoined Kallisto and held her in his embrace. The goddess caressed his face and kissed him. Mara tried to get up, but the sword had sliced through some vital organs and arteries, making her bleed internally. She was drowning in her blood. Everything faded to black. The last thing she saw was the goddess and the commander.

* * *

Mara jolted awake to a cold late-fall morning. Even though it was just a dream, she checked her injury. The wound had already healed, yet a notable slice in her black Silver Thorn armour remained.

Gazing at the morning light, Mara felt the warm sun on her face. At least a day had passed since escaping from her captors. The frozen air killed off the remaining embers from the campfire she made last night. The tattered black cape she used as a blanket offered little warmth. Mara groaned as she sat up. Her body ached from lying on the icy ground. She wished she was home, sleeping in a warm bed.

She found herself alone in the wilderness of Terra. The snow covering the trees and ground silenced her surroundings. Mara wondered if the Holy Blades were aware of her escape by now. The stolen long sword remained in her possession, though its durability was wearing down. It was inferior to the straight sword Talon forged for her. She needed to see the blacksmith as soon as she arrived in Mirahyll. She took a deep breath and rose to her feet. Her home was less than a day's travel, but the growls of her stomach put her mind on other things. She made some snares with tree branches last night, thanks to Dad's teachings. It was time to check them.

On the way, she found a small body of water which remained unfrozen. She approached it. Looking at her reflection, she pulled down her dark brown mask to reveal a gaunt face. Black vertical scars decorated her greyish skin. Her lips were a darker grey colour, and her eyes had dark scleras. Only her irises appeared normal until they glowed yellow. She was one of the undying—a victim cursed with immortality, yet not invincible. Dread plagued her mind as she remembered how she ended up in this predicament. At least the healing stone from Khan could restore her, but she only had one, and now was not the time to use it. At least her black hood concealed her inhuman visage. She pulled her mask back up and moved away from her reflection.

Approaching a snare, she discovered a hare. The adorable critter struggled to break free, though it was no match for the huntress' trap. Mara felt guilty, but her growling stomach demanded sustenance. She approached the rabbit with glowing eyes. The huntress crouched down and grabbed the animal with her right hand. Even the creature's squeals would not change her mind. She took the hare by the neck and picked it up. With her other hand, she pressed her palm against the creature's chin and pushed its head back. The undying took a deep breath and kept pushing until the animal's neck broke. The hare stopped struggling and went still. Mara looked at the rabbit's limp body before lowering it and returning to her campfire.

She took some fresh wood and restarted the fire. The flames grew stronger while she turned her attention to the animal. The huntress needed to prepare it for cooking. She used the sword to cut through the underbelly. After putting down the blade, she began to pull the hide off. As Mara skinned the rabbit, her navy blue gloves became stained in blood. Once she removed its fur, she cooked it over the flame.

Mara took the time to clean her gloves while waiting. She rubbed some snow on them. The blood came out, revealing the pale blue fur and feathers lining them. Even the brown leather straps with gold buckles became like new. She glanced back at her cooking. It had to be ready by now.

She never ate rabbit before but had little choice. Mara pulled her mask down, then took a piece. Her fangs pierced the meat, tearing off pieces and swallowing. Thanks to her dulled sense of taste, it was not too bad. As an undying, she could only taste flesh or meat. If restored, she could appreciate the taste of milk, cheese, bread, and vegetables. Once she finished her meal, she put out the campfire, then left for Mirahyll.

Mara needed to be cautious because she remained within enemy territory. She glanced up at the gold and ivory temple sitting on the higher elevation of Golden Mountain. The huntress hoped she did not have to return anytime soon. At least it appeared quiet. Also nearby was Ozin Village, which she avoided since the incident with Saskia. With Holy Blades swarming the place, she would do best to keep a distance.

Drawing closer to home, Mara spotted the large tree she used to sit under while taking a break in her travels. All the leaves had fallen to the ground, leaving the branches bare. Regardless of the season, she felt drawn to this tree. Some small birds took residence, flitting from one branch to another. Black-capped chickadees spotted her and chirped in alarm. Mara watched as they flew away. The air became cold. She saw her breath while a single snowflake fell. Mara was not aware of snow today. At least the roads were quiet. She wrapped her cape around herself while heading north.

* * *

Much of the day had passed by the time Mara reached Mirahyll. Unlike her dream, the city was much more lively. Although the street lights had no decorations on them. That often signified the Winter Festival, which spanned from December 21 to the end of the month.

Many people walked the streets, taking note of her raggedy appearance. They kept a distance. Mara figured it was her rough appearance or that she smelled. The last few days had taken a toll on her attire.

As long as the hood cast a shadow, and her mask concealed her face, she did not draw much attention. The snow increased. The snowy city reminded Mara of her travels to Hemal with its similar gothic architecture. Heading to her parent's home, she noticed a crowd gathering before a gold and ivory cathedral.

The Grand Cathedral was the second home of the Faith of Kallikratés, the ancient theocratic order responsible for her predicament. She was unsure about investigating, but something was going on. Most of the people in the front wore fancy attire. Nobles from the upper quarters came to attend the meeting. Not too far from the cathedral were the towering houses they inhabited. The manors could be mistaken for castles.

Mara remained inconspicuous by staying in the back with the middle and lower-class citizens. They did not seem to mind her presence.

A priest in gold and ivory robes stood before the podium. Mara had seen the middle-aged man before. The fair-skinned priest appeared to be overweight. Some greying strands of hair were present under his cap. His eyes were blue. The look on his face was dismissive and arrogant. The huntress knew what the man was like based on her previous interaction with him.

"The time of the Dark One's awakening is nigh," Father Vernon announced. "The prophecy looms, but our salvation has arrived. The Great Lord Kratés has been reborn!" He gestured to a figure next to him.

Mara glanced over to the man beside the priest and froze. Commander White approached the podium as Father Vernon stepped aside. He stood proud with his hands behind his back, giving a stoic expression. Only he showed up. Her murderer likely remained in her temple in Golden Mountain. At least he had not noticed the huntress. Seeing his frozen face reminded Mara of the ill-fated attempt to slay the goddess. She reached for the spot where he stabbed her. Even though the wound had healed, the pain of betrayal remained.

Surprised reactions and murmurs of excitement flowed through the crowd.

"As the reincarnation of the Great Lord Kratés, I shall stand by my Goddess," announced the commander. "Together, we shall defeat the Dark One. Peace will reign for all eternity!"

People began to cheer. Mara glanced around, seeing how in awe they were of the prophecy coming to pass.

The commander then warned, "However, there is something you must know—the truth spoken from our Goddess!"

She gazed back at him. *'He wouldn't, would he?'*

Commander White raised his right hand before him, tightening it into a fist. "One thousand years ago, a wicked girl awoke the Dark One and allowed it to destroy our nation. Because of her, the Cursed Herald, the Golden Age ended. This Era of Darkness—where monsters rule and chaos reign—she is to blame!"

A flame ignited in the hearts of people, and the fire grew as the commander fuelled their hatred. Mara took a step back, shaking her head. How could he do this to her?

"Death to the Cursed Herald!" shouted one of the followers.

Mara grew afraid. If anyone in this crowd saw her face, for resembling the woman who awoke the Dark One, they would tear her apart.

"The Cursed Herald returns once again, seeking to destroy Kallisto and the Faith, and awaken the Dark One," Commander White boomed. "She already threatens the world by breaking four of the seven seals! I shall stop her!"

The crowd roared in agreement.

Realizing she could not stay any longer, Mara slipped away. So far, no one noticed her.

Walking down the streets, she witnessed two men in golden armour accosting a woman. They were Holy Blades, while the young woman was a middle-class citizen. She possessed tanned skin, brown eyes, and dark brown hair. The huntress hid behind a corner and watched. What were they doing?

"By order of the Faith, you are under arrest," said one of the Holy Blades. The other walked behind the woman to apprehend her.

The young woman looked frightened. "Why? What have I done?"

Instead of answering, they arrested her without hesitation.

"What are you doing to my daughter?" shouted an older man as he approached them. He shared the same skin, eye, and hair colour as the young woman.

Mara figured he was the father.

The man appeared unhappy at the treatment of his daughter. "Why are you arresting her? She committed no crime."

One of the Holy Blades responded by delivering a fist to the man's face, knocking him out cold. The father fell to the ground, where he remained unmoving. The daughter grew horrified.

"Father!" She tried to run to him, but the Holy Blade restraining her would not relent.

Mara watched as they took the woman away. She could not believe they were doing this. Those two Holy Blades acted like thugs. She glanced at the father, who remained on the frozen ground until someone else found him and called for help. When the coast was clear, she exited the shadows. After she took a few steps, another pair of Holy Blades came her way. With quick thinking, she dashed back into the alley. The Holy Blades did not notice and walked by.

Getting around would be difficult, but Mara refused to let anything get in her way. She needed to find her parents. As she emerged from the dark alley, she found herself in the lower quarters. The scent of smoke reached her nostrils. Mara spotted a plume of black smoke rising over the other buildings. A sense of dread washed over Mara as she decided to investigate.

She had hoped that Talon's shop would remain, only to be greeted by a smouldering building. An older man coughed as he emerged from the charred remains of his workshop. Mara recognized the muscular blacksmith by his long grey hair and beard. Ashes covered his entire body. Even his blacksmith's attire was dirty from the smoke and ashes.

"Talon?" Mara asked. "What happened?"

"What does it fucking look like?" Talon snapped. Rage filled his dark eyes.

She was speechless at first. Her eyes locked onto the blacksmith.

"How did this happen?"

Talon took some deep breaths to calm down, then scratched the back of his head. "It started with a rumour, claiming I was offering my services to an enemy of the Faith. The next thing I knew, the Holy Blades showed up and burned my workshop to the ground!"

She frowned. "I'm sorry. You didn't deserve this at all."

"Don't be," he responded, becoming calmer. "Edwin must have spread that rumour to get back at me. That old bastard was laughing as my workshop burned to the ground!"

His words did not alleviate some of the guilt building within Mara. "No, I'm the reason why you lost your workshop," she murmured.

"I assure you it's not your fault."

Talon kept his right hand behind his back. When he brought his arm around, she noticed a wrapped sword in his possession. The blade had a curve, like a katana.

He handed it to her. "Here, take this."

Mara eyed the sword. She had seen it before. After removing the black cover, her eyes widened upon seeing the blue gem mounted in the black and gold hilt.

"Lord Slayer Godstruck?" Mara gazed at Talon in bewilderment.

He shrugged. "Figured now's a good time to give you this, especially since you pissed off the Faith!"

Mara glanced back at the blade. She now possessed the sword capable of killing anything. "You had this?"

Talon nodded. "It was delivered by the former master three days ago. He requested this to be handed to you, if and when you escaped."

She stared back at Talon. "What day is it?"

"Today is December 7."

"It's been a week?" Then she recalled the last time she saw Harold, the former Silver Thorn master. "He sent me to kill the Marionette near Haranta. After I slew the undying, I ran into the Holy Blades. The commander's guardian was also there. He claimed Alena would help me." She shook her head. "But it was a trap."

"The old master knew this would happen and planned this," Talon said. "He said you were the rightful heir to Godstruck."

She looked back down at the sword. Seeing the blade reminded her of someone who once wielded this weapon. It had been a month and two days since she met Saskia before getting swept up in all those unfortunate events.

"You should leave," the old blacksmith told her. "The city is no longer safe."

Mara glanced up at him. "Why?"

"The Faith is hunting the Cursed Herald. They persuaded their followers to turn in possible suspects. And the Holy Blades are using lethal force on anyone who resists. Not too long ago, I saw a young lass slain before my eyes." He looked at the remains of his business. "Damn those Holy Blades. They make my stomach turn."

She sulked. "But they know what I look like."

"They could be doing this to lure you out. Guilt you into surrendering."

She gazed down at Godstruck. Despite obtaining a powerful weapon, she had not forgotten her objective. "I need to find Mom and Dad. They live in this city."

"Very well, but be careful," said the blacksmith. "I also intend to leave."

"Where will you go?" Mara asked, looking at him again.

"Neither Mirahyll or the Guardsmen did anything when my workshop burned to the ground," he revealed. "To make matters worse, they went back to using Edwin's services. I refuse to forge weapons for anyone from this city ever again." Then, "Now I'm looking for a new place. You mentioned an abandoned house near Haranta Village."

Her ears perked up when he mentioned the former herbalist's house.

"Yes, I killed the undying there." Mara nodded. "It should be safe, but you'll have to deal with the corpses."

Talon rubbed his chin. "Hmm, I see. I'll see you in a few days if we're lucky."

Before leaving, the blacksmith noticed her attire. Her Silver Thorn armour had seen better days. Both the black shirt with gold trimmings and the white tunic underneath appeared fine in the front, but the backside showed several small slices through the cape protecting them.

Talon's eyes remained on her back, figuring several assailants had attacked her. The black sleeves looked to be intact for the most part. But the open-bust leather corset—held together by two dark leather belts and golden buckles—had a notable slice. The long cloth going down the legs possessed a few worn-out spots. Her black pants appeared fine, though the pale fur and feathers lining the thigh-high stockings were matted. Mud caked her black knee-high boots. Her gloves appeared to be in the best shape, but that was due to her cleaning them earlier.

The belt on her hips remained intact as well, holding two pouches, a flask filled with moon water, and a sword.

He frowned at the sorry state of the attire. Mara reckoned he was either upset by the brutal attack she suffered a few days ago, or the armour, he had a hand in making, was damaged. It once belonged to Saskia, who brought it before Talon to modify.

Then his eyes fell onto her sword. "Where did you get this? What happened to the one I gave you?"

She unsheathed the Holy Blade long sword. "Lost my sword when I got captured. Had to steal this one during my escape."

Talon eyed the blade. "Give it here."

She handed the sword to him. The blacksmith studied the blade.

"These swords look nice at first glance," Talon explained before slamming it down onto the metal anvil. The sword shattered upon impact.

She gaped at him, wondering why he did that.

"But they have low durability," he continued. "This will never help you slay anything besides human foes. And Edwin is supposed to be a master blacksmith." He then handed her another weapon. "This is one of the few weapons I have left."

She drew the weapon from its black sheath, revealing a Silver Thorn long sword. It appeared similar to the previous one, yet with an elegant silver curved hilt. She could grasp the black grip with both hands. The width of the blade was thinner, though longer and weighed about the same. With God-struck in her possession, she would be walking around with a target on her back. She might as well use another sword to keep her enemies from being aware that she now owned the Lord Slayer.

"A reliable blade is the difference between life and death. Never forget that." Talon switched his attention back onto her attire. "Your armour could use some repair. I have a few tools left, but they should do the trick."

She accepted his services. Even with a few tools, he was able to restore her armour to its former glory; it was almost like new. She was about to pay him, but he shook his head.

"No, it's on me," Talon said. "After what you went through, I can't take your money."

"Oh," Mara replied, taking her gold back.

In a way, he was right. She only had five hundred gold to her name. Before being captured, she owned at least six times more. Thanks to Boyd, Mara was fortunate to get some of it back.

She watched while Talon made his preparations to leave. She also intended to leave Mirahyll for the time being. Mara wanted to compose her thoughts. She needed to figure out how she was going to explain her predicament to her parents.

While leaving, Mara spotted a posting on an information board. Her suspicions were confirmed about the Winter Festival not happening. The reason for it was because of the Dark One's possible awakening. With impending doom approaching, the Faith of Kallikratés had requested the Council Hall to cancel all festivities. And all of Terra complied. She was unsure if Hema did the same, but since the Faith finally gained a presence after a thousand years, it was likely the case. Mara frowned at the notice, then left the city.

Chapter Two

The First Truth

The moon peeked through the clouds as an aurora borealis shimmered across the sky. It was past midnight. Mara stared up at the night sky, unmindful of the snow falling around her. Her eyes then drifted to the sleeping city of Mirahyll. It was time to go home.

She hoped that Kallisto was lying, that her parents stayed the same, as well as Allen and James. Mara wanted to go home and live as a typical human. Though it might be impossible, for she became one of the undying. Still, she needed to see them.

Mara reached into her pocket to retrieve her only healing stone. No longer could she put this off. Holding the shimmering gem in her right hand, Mara pulled her mask down. Cracks began to form in the white gemstone. It shattered into fine dust, releasing the magic within. It spread over her arm, then her whole body. Every cell tingled with life as she transformed from a raggedy undead creature to a human woman. The colour of her flesh changed from a greyish tint to a healthy tan. Her face grew fuller while the colour returned to her full lips. The scleras in her doll-like eyes turned white, and her irises became a light brown hue. As soon as the scars on her face closed up, Mara turned her gaze onto Mirahyll and approached it.

* * *

She wandered the streets while the city slept. Mara stayed wary of her surroundings in case she encountered a Holy Blade or a guardsman. At least the cover of night concealed her presence. Everything seemed familiar, yet different at the same time. There were some places she had never seen before nor recalled. She never considered this before because of her amnesia.

At least the path to her home remained the same. She arrived at a two-floor wooden house—the Ashwood Residence. It appeared the same as in her dream. Mara hoped her parents remained here as well. She peeked through the window, only to find it much different. Her parents might have bought new furniture. She wandered around to gaze into another window. A couple slept in their bed, buried underneath the covers. Mara finally went to the window to her old room. It sat on the second floor at the back of the house. She scaled the wall as she did in her youth. Reaching the window, she opened it from the outside and crept into her old room.

Her room was no longer the same. The furniture was different compared to the last time she left it, including the frightened little thing in the corner. Mara was unaware of the small girl tucked away in bed. But the child was already aware of the stranger who entered her room. The little girl whimpered in fear. By the time she noticed the girl, it was too late.

"Mommy!" screamed the child. "Daddy!"

Mara dashed out the window before the parents came to their daughter's rescue. Upon landing, Mara ran away from her former home. To where she did not know. Tears flowed from Mara's eyes as she wondered what happened to her parents.

* * *

She hid in an abandoned home outside the city. The fallen snow-covered her tracks. Mara laid on the floor, staring up at the ceiling. It had been a couple of days since the blunder at her old home. She was a fool to believe that her parents remained alive. Perhaps she should have listened to Boyd, no matter how sick it was to entertain such an idea. But she wanted to find them, or at least know where they were.

Also, Mara wanted to do something about the hunt started by the Faith. So far, the Holy Blades had arrested forty women. All the accused came from the middle or lower class. Some resisted, only to suffer the consequences of avoiding arrest. Twenty women died. More than half had friends and families killed for trying to hide or defend them. At least in Terra, around fifty people lost their lives in this senselessly cruel act.

Why were they doing this? Was it to draw her out? She considered surrendering, but what would happen to her? What should she do? Mara glanced at Godstruck. A thought crossed her mind—the goddess was to blame for all her misfortunes.

Kallisto transformed Karl into the cold-hearted commander. He was never like this.

While Mara thought about her prince, she saw the commander's cold eyes as he hurt her. She instinctively reached for the spot where he stabbed her. Mara remembered pleading to her former fiancé, but none of her words reached him. Her whole body shook while tears formed in her eyes. She rolled onto her side and tried to sleep. Tears fell onto the cold floor, transforming into frozen crystals.

* * *

"Mara," called a female voice.

Mara opened her eyes to see a familiar face gazing down at her. The dark silver armour, with blue gems and golden trimmings, was familiar to her. The female creature wore a gold-hemmed red hood attached to a flowing cape. The same fabric adorned the sides of her legs. On her face was a visor with seven glowing blue eyes.

"Watcher," Mara called the creature while rising to her feet.

The morning sun rose. A new day had begun.

"I've been watching you," the creature began. "You, who have been lost and cursed for thirty years, have finally returned."

Mara sulked. "Did you watch as I broke into some family's home?" She glanced down at the floor. "I thought they would still be there, but... I don't know where they are."

"There is someone who may know," the Watcher said.

Mara looked back at her. "Who?"

"I will show you." The creature held out her hand.

As soon as Mara took the Watcher's hand, a bright flash of light blinded her, forcing her to shut her eyes. Upon opening them again, she found herself standing inside a well-known laboratory. She cast her eyes onto a desk with a microscope and a strange-looking black box on top. The examination table was near. She remembered laying on it during a procedure performed on her. Various test tubes and samples sat on a shelf.

"What's going on?" called a male voice from another room.

A middle-aged man wearing a white lab coat walked in. Dr. Moen appeared to own some additional grey strands in his blonde hair as opposed to her previous interaction with him. He also gained a few more wrinkles on his face. However, his blue eyes remained vibrant behind his glasses.

The doctor saw Mara and froze. He appeared stunned to see her here. He raised his hand and pointed at her.

"How did you get here?" He shook his head. "No, no, no! You have to leave. As much as I despise the Faith, I can't let you stay. They will burn this place to the ground!"

Mara watched as he rambled. The goddess was right. Thirty years had passed since Mara became cursed. It was like a bad dream in which she could not awaken. Many thoughts ran through her head as she tried to sort out the facts from the lies. The last three decades remained a mystery. She looked at the middle-aged doctor. After all this time, his personality had barely changed. Once, she thought he was the father of Allen and James, but then she remembered—when the twins were children, they lost their father and lived with other relatives.

The Watcher walked in front of the doctor and gazed at her.

He took notice. "What are you doing?" Dr. Moen questioned his creation. The creature ignored him. "Show him your face," the Watcher addressed her. Dr. Moen was baffled, but then he saw Mara removing her hood.

"Hello, Allen…" Mara pulled her mask down. "It's been a while."

Doctor Allen Moen froze while Mara gazed back at her old friend. While he became a brilliant scientist, inventor, and advisor to the chancellor, she did not change at all. Allen was now fifty-five while Mara looked not a day over twenty-five. The doctor broke down in tears. She approached him and wrapped her arms around him as he continued to sob. Watching him cry made her want to cry as well.

"I've been searching for answers all this time," he sobbed. "But you were right in front of me for the past month." He pulled away and wiped his tears before giving a questioning glance. "Why didn't you say anything?"

"I had amnesia," Mara replied, "and I didn't recognize you at first, given it's been thirty years." She glanced at him from head to toe.

Allen sat down on a chair and gawked at her. "You lost your memories?"

"Last month, I woke up in the Dark Labyrinth, not knowing anything. I ended up in Ozin and met Saskia, who took me in. That night, the White Lady returned. Saskia persuaded me to come with her to slay the monster." Mara paused. "That's when I found out. I'm one of the undying. Saskia knew what I was. She wanted me to meet Harold of the Silver Thorns. We were to leave the next day, but…"

"Someone murdered Saskia," Allen said.

She nodded. "And I was accused. After my secret was exposed, the village hanged me. Thanks to the curse, I returned to life and went to Greyward Hold to meet Harold. He offered to help me in exchange for finding Saskia's murderer. Then came all those events, like the deception leading to Heru's death, having to save the commander and his adopted father from Lady Isabella…"

"And having to save the commander yet again from Anna," Allen added.

"That is correct," Mara said. "I am also searching for a way to lift my curse. Harold had me hunt the undying and claim their souls. He said it would help me. So far, I slew the White Lady, the Siren, and the Marionette."

"It helps you?" Allen asked.

"Every time I claim an undying's soul, I regain my human appearance until the next death," Mara explained. "Healing stones also work, but they are rare. And there's also the blood of the Great Lord, though temporary."

The doctor exchanged glances with the Watcher before turning his gaze onto Mara. "Interesting," he said. "Do you remember anything from your human life?"

"I do," Mara replied, glancing at his creation.

Allen took notice and looked at the Watcher as well. "Yes, you had your humanity shut off, courtesy of Lady Isabella. The Watcher restored it by recovering your memories." He looked back at her. "So, you remember me, right? We went to college together."

"Yes, I remember you and James," Mara answered. "Mr. White was our history professor. He told me the last time I saw him." She frowned. "Karl was my fiancé."

Allen folded his arms and gave a sad smile. "Mr. White always apologized for his son's behaviour."

"Mom once introduced us," Mara said. "The first time I met him, I didn't exactly meet his expectations."

"You mean he was racist?" Allen questioned bluntly. "Karl was a jerk, albeit a very smart one. Claimed to have the best education and studied at some prestigious academy in Corlin. Everyone called him the smartest man in all of Ardana before he became the most powerful man in this land."

It was all coming back to Mara. Talking to an old friend brought back some aspects of her former life.

"He accused you of lowering the class average, even though you didn't have the lowest grade!" Allen exclaimed. "Created a petition to have you removed from class. James and I helped you raise your grades, but he accused you of cheating! He never wanted to admit you were…"

"More than a filthy savage?" Mara interrupted.

"You said it, not me!" He raised an eyebrow. "What did you see in him?"

"I don't know," Mara murmured. "I never wanted to attend Graduation, but Mom and Dad insisted I go." She then recalled her parents. "Where are my parents?"

Allen's face fell to a frown. He stood up and watched her. "Since you told me everything, you deserve to know," he said sombrely.

Taking notice of his tone, Mara grew concerned. Still, she wanted to know where they were since they no longer lived in their old home.

Allen took a deep breath. "Mara, your father is dead, and your mother is in a coma."

Mara froze. An intense feeling of dread washed over her as tears threatened to spill.

"How did he die?" Mara demanded while fighting back her tears.

Allen placed his hands in his lab coat pockets. "It happened thirty years ago. They went to confront the Faith in Golden Mountain after Mr. White said you died. Your mother now resides in Mirahyll Hospital, a few blocks from here. James is her current doctor. He's been watching for any progress, but she's been like that since you and your dad…" Allen stopped as soon as he saw her face.

Mara was silent for a while. "I want to see her."

Allen nodded. "Okay, but we should go with you." He gestured to the Watcher. "Considering what is now happening, you shouldn't be alone."

Chapter Three

Always Your Daughter

Allen and the Watcher accompanied Mara to Mirahyll Hospital, which was a few blocks away. Getting there was simple, with no one casting any suspicious gazes at her. The three arrived at a large brick building with several windows. At the main entrance were a few people standing around. They did not seem to mind the three as they walked inside.

Entering the hospital, Mara saw a large group of people. Many of the sick or injured were lying on hospital beds. Doctors and nurses were also present, taking care of the patients and assigning them to different places within the hospital. The doctors and nurses appeared understaffed. The number of patients was overwhelming. It reminded Mara of her last visit to this place. Once, she got critically ill. Mom brought her here, but none of the doctors could diagnose what was wrong. It was so long ago; she was only a toddler.

"James is the Chief of Staff," Allen explained, looking around. "Hmm, he's not around here. He must be somewhere else in the hospital."

Mara remained quiet while they searched for the closest staff member who did not appear too busy. They spotted a plump middle-aged nurse. She was replacing dirty linens and sheets with clean ones before noticing their approach.

"How can I help you?" asked the nurse.

The words became lodged in Mara's throat. Allen glanced over at her and realized she would not be in the mood for talking, so he spoke for her.

"We're here to see Mrs. Daniella Ashwood."

The smile faded from the nurse's face upon hearing that name. She gazed at Mara, noting the sadness and fear in her eyes, yet one strong emotion stood out the most—guilt.

The nurse gave a sympathetic look. "I am sorry, but I don't think Mrs. Ashwood is well enough to receive visitors today."

Mara's eyes narrowed. "Please, I want to see my mother," she whispered.

The nurse appeared surprised to know her relation to Mrs. Ashwood. "I'm sorry, but your mother is unwell. She may pass by the end of the day."

Mara fought back her tears. "She's that bad?"

She could no longer speak. It was then she felt a hand resting over her own. Mara looked back to see Allen's comforting gaze.

"Let's see your mother," he spoke. Dr. Moen then addressed the nurse. "Where is she?"

The nurse pointed to her left. "It's down this hall. Last room on the left."

Allen nodded. "Thank you."

On the way, Mara peered inside an open hospital room. An older man with a large bruise on his face was lying on one of the beds. She identified him as the father who tried to stop the Holy Blades from arresting his daughter. He appeared to remain unconscious. She wondered if there were others like him.

After walking past the room, a sense of dread swelled within her mind. Mara was going to meet one of her parents after thirty years, yet she did not know what to expect. Would her mother even recognize her? She struggled to keep her tears from flowing. She was afraid of what she would see, but Allen and the Watcher encouraged her to keep moving until they reached the end of the hall. The door to Mom's room was wide open.

When Mara saw her, she barely recognized her. The dark hair Mom maintained was now pure white. Many wrinkles adorned her face; she had to be at least in her eighties. The aged woman was lying in a hospital bed. The only sign of life was the slight rising and falling of her chest. Mom was a shell of her former self; all these years in the sanatorium took a toll. Now she was kept here to die alone. Mara did not know if she should be horrified or ashamed. The daughter pulled down her mask and lowered her hood, hoping her mother would recognize her face.

"Mom," Mara choked out.

Mom did not respond. She was still in her deathbed.

Coming closer, Mara grew horrified to see her mother's glazed eyes. Her wrinkled face was devoid of emotion.

Tears threatened to spill from Mara's eyes. "What happened, Mom?"

Mrs. Ashwood stared into space as if her daughter was not there. After approaching her mother's side, Mara fell to her knees.

"Mom, I'm here." Tears leaked from Mara's eyes. "I came back to see you. I am sorry. I'm so sorry I couldn't get back to you sooner." She broke down and cried.

Allen placed a hand on her shoulder. "It's not your fault."

She glared at him with bloodshot eyes. "I said yes to marrying Karl! I agreed to go to the temple without them knowing!" Mara cried. The daughter switched her attention back onto her mother and took her frail hand. The glare lightened up from her face.

"Mom," Mara called but got no response. She squeezed her hand gently.

Allen and the Watcher looked on while Mara pleaded with her mother.

"We can help her," Allen said. "We can break her out of this coma."

Mara glanced back at him. The Watcher turned her head to him as well.

He nodded and gazed back at his creation. "Yes, we can use the Watcher."

"What about Davis?" asked the Watcher.

Allen gave a sour expression. His creation stared back at him with glowing eyes.

"You intend to do this despite promising him you would not," she said, the glow fading from her eyes.

"I'm not one to do things behind the chancellor's back, but this is Mara we're talking about!" Allen declared.

"I see," the Watcher said, "but the decision should fall to her."

They both gazed at her. Mara looked at Allen, then the Watcher. She rose to her feet while keeping her eyes on the creature.

"Do it." Mara glanced back at Mom. "I want her to know I'm here."

Allen nodded to the Watcher, telling her to do her part. The Watcher stepped towards Daniella. She placed her right hand on the older woman's forehead. The creature's eyes glowed brightly. Mara and Allen watched in silence. After a few moments, the creature froze and began to shake. The two looked concerned.

Mara turned to look at Allen. "What's going on?"

She then noticed the worried expression on her friend's face.

Allen took a step forward. "Something is wrong."

Mara glanced back and noticed Mom convulsing. Whatever was happening, it could endanger her as well. She reached for the Watcher's hand, hoping to remove it from her mother's forehead. The doctor took notice and held out his hand.

"Mara, no!" Allen cried, but it was too late.

She grabbed the Watcher's hand, only to feel a powerful shock rushing through her body. A flurry of images assaulted her mind. She saw Dad, being kissed by the goddess, Kallisto. The next thing she saw was her father dead on the ground. She even saw herself in a distorted vision. A dark aura exuded from her as she glared at Dad's murderer with glowing eyes. Commander White and his father were also present, yet did nothing. They were on Kallisto's side. The undying attempted to lunge at the goddess but was held back by chains binding her wrists and ankles. She tried again and almost broke free. A Holy Blade approached to protect Kallisto. But Mara hit him in the face, tearing his bottom jaw off. It was the first time she had ever killed someone.

Mara blacked out, but not before hearing her mother screaming in anguish.

* * *

"Mara, can you hear me?"

Mara's eyes fluttered open upon hearing Allen's voice. She found herself lying on the ground beside Mom's bed. She looked up at the concerned face of her friend. The Watcher was also gazing at her.

"What happened?" Allen questioned.

Mara trembled while struggling to her feet. Not only was she shaken up by the disturbing vision of Dad's death, but the lingering volts also remained in her body. It took a while for the tingling sensation to fade.

The Watcher stared at her with glowing eyes. "You witnessed your father's murder." She then looked at Mrs. Ashwood. "Kallisto killed him before his wife and daughter. That moment always in her eyes, reliving the nightmare for three decades. Mrs. Ashwood blamed herself for both her husband and daughter's death."

Allen gawked at the Watcher before turning back to Mara. He gave a sorrowful look.

"I'm sorry," he said softly.

Mara stared off into space. "She murdered him," she hissed.

She remembered being dragged out of the dungeon in chains to watch Kallisto murder her father. Her captors said her parents came looking for her. Despite being struck down by Kallisto and torn apart by the Dark Dweller, Dad's death was the trigger. The intense feeling of anger grew within her.

Allen looked sympathetic. "If you don't mind me asking, how did she kill him?"

Mara had no desire to say anything.

"Kallisto kissed him," the Watcher answered for her.

His eyes grew wide. "So, the legends are true?" Allen questioned. "Kallisto is powerful, capable of killing a mortal man with a kiss!"

Mara looked away. She wanted to recede into her shell. After learning what the goddess did, the rage grew stronger. The truth became a harder pill to swallow. All she could think about was Dad's death and Mom's anguish. Her mother's screams echoed in her mind. Mara clenched her teeth while dark emotions overcame her. Not even the voices of her friends could calm her. She wanted revenge.

A loud gasp snapped Mara out of her anger. It sounded as if someone emerged from being underwater for a long time. She gazed at her friends. They were looking at the older woman lying in bed. Allen and the Watcher glanced back at Mara. They parted ways to reveal the older woman now awake and alert. Mom's eyes were no longer glazed; they were now the pale blue colour Mara knew.

"Mom!" Mara dashed to her bedside. The daughter fell to her knees so her mother could get a good look at her face.

Mrs. Ashwood glanced over at her. No smile was present on her face, but a look of horror. She released a weak cry of fear.

This confused Mara. Why was Mom terrified of her?

"Your face," Allen said.

Mara noticed a mirror hanging on a wall, reflecting her transformed visage. Mrs. Ashwood could not see her daughter beyond the glowing eyes, the dark blots on her face, or even the elongated canines. Gazing back at her mother's face brought Mara back to the time of Dad's death. Mom had also witnessed her daughter's transformation. Now the undying was sitting next to her. Mrs. Ashwood's breathing became raspier. Mara stood up and backed away, wondering if her appearance was causing Mom to have a heart attack.

Allen and the Watcher took notice.

"Mara?" Allen asked.

Mara placed her hood back on, then lifted the mask over her mouth and nose. She was ready to walk out the door.

"Hey, if we explain to her what's going—"

"No, it was a mistake coming here!" Mara snapped. She began to walk out the door. Neither Allen or the Watcher could stop her.

"Mara…" called a frail female voice.

Mara froze, then turned to look at the one who said her name. Her mother gazed at her with a raised arm. After hearing Allen call Mara's name, Mrs. Ashwood realized that the creature beside her bed was her daughter.

Tears filled her old eyes. "I'm sorry. Please come back."

Both Mara and Allen watched her.

"Mrs. Ashwood," Allen addressed the elderly woman. "Mara came to see you. She may have died thirty years ago, but she came back to tell you it's not your fault." He gazed at Mara. "Isn't that right?"

Mara looked at him, then her mother. She closed her eyes and revealed her face. As the hood and mask came off, her fangs had already shrunk, and her dark markings were almost faded. She opened her eyes to reveal their light brown colour.

"Yes, I forgive you," Mara said as tears filled her eyes again.

She approached her mother. The daughter reached out to hold Mom's hand, but the withered hand fell limp. The strength of its owner was no more. Mara stared at her mother with wide eyes. Mom exhaled and closed her eyes for the last time; she went with a smile on her face. The daughter stood frozen as she watched her mother die before her eyes.

Allen and the Watcher looked on in silence. After watching her mother's departure, Allen placed a hand on Mara's shoulder.

"I'm sorry," he said. "Your mother blamed herself for your death, but I believe seeing you and gaining your forgiveness allowed her to go in peace."

Mara grew silent. She looked at her friend, her eyes red from crying.

"Thank you," she said in a quiet voice.

The Watcher approached them. "We should leave. The doctors and nurses will arrive soon."

"You're right." He glanced at Mara. "We should go."

As the three left, Mara looked at her mother's body one last time.

"Goodbye, Mom…"

* * *

The walk home was quiet; the silence bothered Mara. She looked down at the ground as they returned to the laboratory.

"I hear the prophecy is about to pass," Allen began.

"Thanks to me," she muttered.

He sighed. "I am not one for religions, and prophecies don't strike a chord with me."

"Why bring it up?" Mara then sighed, "It no longer matters. The Faith painted me as this Cursed Herald. Quite fitting since I broke most of the seals."

"That was not your fault," Allen said. "You were just at the wrong place at the wrong time."

As they walked, Mara spotted an information board. A wanted poster, depicting a familiar face, was pinned on. She recognized the short black hair and the smug expression.

'WANTED: Boyd Masterson. Reasons: For the crime of desertion. If spotted, please report to the Holy Blades. Reward pending...'

She stopped and stared at the poster. The other two took notice and halted as well.

"What's wrong?" Allen asked.

Mara approached the poster and took it down. She studied it for a while before glancing up at him. "The Faith is looking for Boyd."

He gazed at the notice. "Yeah, the Holy Blades are questioning his whereabouts. If they find him, they will execute him. Desertion is punishable by death."

She recalled the last time she saw Boyd.

"I helped him escape," Mara revealed. "I ran into Boyd during my last escape from the Dark Labyrinth. He told me a bunch of things to save his own life."

Allen raised an eyebrow. "Really? Like what?"

Mara took a deep breath. "About Saskia... Commander White killed her and had him frame me," she revealed. "Boyd claimed it was to recapture me. The commander also tricked Heru into abducting me. I took the cure, but it angered Heru so much, he wanted to kill me. So I stabbed him in self-defence. Then Commander White took advantage of Lady Isabella's hatred of Kallikratés, anticipating her to abduct him and Mr. White. And he tampered with the seal on the Black Tower, putting himself in danger because he knew I would save him."

Allen's jaw dropped. "The Faith is behind the seals failing? Why didn't you say anything?"

She shrugged. "Boyd could have said those things to save himself."

"Okay, but these are some pretty significant details."

"You believe him?" Mara questioned. "The same man who exposed my secret and framed me in Saskia's murder—a murder he had a part in."

"After being expelled from the Guardsmen, the Holy Blades took him in," Allen reminded her. "He was declared by Commander White to be under Kallikratés' protection. As a result, he was untouchable. They might have known all along. Saskia and the others were known enemies of the Faith. I would not be surprised if they orchestrated the possessors' deaths, and used you to avoid suspicion."

"Why are they breaking the seals?" Mara asked. "Don't they realize it will awaken the Dark One? What about their prophecy?"

Allen's face fell. "Maybe there is no prophecy," he murmured. "It's all about power—to control and manipulate others for their benefit. Father was right." Allen then said, "My dad once told me that Kallikratés only benefits those who can fill their coffers. It's why most of their members are nobles. In the last few days, many disciples fled to Corlin."

Mara stared at him. "What about the rebirth of Lord Kratés? Karl is his reincarnation. Now he's with Kallisto, who was disguised as High Priestess Alena all along."

Allen looked surprised. "Are you sure?"

"I saw it with my own eyes." Mara frowned. She turned away, envisioning Karl before he became the commander. "And Kallisto changed him." She then discarded the wanted poster.

Allen gave a sombre look. He remained quiet while they returned to his home laboratory.

* * *

Upon approaching Allen's workplace, they found the door forced open.

"What the hell?" Dr. Moen cried.

Agitated, the doctor ran inside with Mara and the Watcher not too far behind. While running in, Mara saw three carriages outside the building. They appeared familiar, but by the time she figured who the transports belonged to, it was too late.

The Holy Blades surrounded them as soon as they entered. Mara unsheathed her Silver Thorn long sword. With Godstruck concealed under her cape, she had no intention of letting the enemy know she possessed the weapon.

"We are seeking the woman named Mara," announced one of the Holy Blades.

Mara glanced at the one who called her name.

"What do you want?" Mara demanded.

"Queen Kallisto demands your surrender. You are to return to Golden Mountain with us."

She frowned. "Why should I?"

"You don't have a choice," replied a familiar male voice.

The Holy Blades parted, and a single man stepped forward. The dark grey long coat fitted with armour and a red cape was familiar.

Commander White stood with his hands behind his back, giving his classic glare. "We have Doctor James Moen."

Allen gaped at him. "You took my brother?"

Commander White nodded. "Yes, we arrested him under the suspicion of conspiring against the Faith. However…" He glanced over at Mara. "If she surrenders, we may release him."

The doctor scowled at the commander. "You can't do this!"

"We already have." The commander glared at Mara. "The choice is yours."

Mara frowned at the commander, who stood his ground, not caring if an innocent life hung in the balance. But an epiphany struck her. A window of opportunity opened, and revenge was still on her mind. Glancing down at the long sword, Mara began to sheathe it. Then she took a step towards the Holy Blades.

Allen watched in horror. "Mara, no!"

The Watcher raised her right hand, summoning a wall of light between them and the enemy. The Holy Blades gasped in shock at the wall of transparent blue light. Mara stared at the wall, then looked back at the Watcher with glowing eyes.

"Let me go," she addressed the Watcher. Mara gazed at Allen. "You have to let me go."

"There has to be another way," Allen said. "You don't have to sacrifice yourself."

"I can save him."

"It's been thirty years!"

Mara gave a sympathetic look. "Yes, but your brother is still alive." She took Allen's right hand. "Many lives were lost because of me. If James dies, would you forgive me? I wouldn't live with myself, so please."

Allen stared at her and sighed. "Let her go," he ordered.

The Watcher obeyed and dispelled the barrier. Mara began to approach them. She looked back at Allen while their hands parted.

"It will be okay. I'll come back."

She put on her hood and left with the Holy Blades, hoping she was right.

Chapter Four

Now or Never

Mara sat in the carriage as it drew near Golden Mountain. The sun was setting, and the night would soon follow. She stared out the window, avoiding eye contact with the commander, who was also in the coach. But she could see his reflection in the glass. Commander White glared at her before turning away to gaze out the window on his side. She took a brief glimpse of him. The commander had not aged a day despite thirty years passing. Mara could also smell a faint scent of alcohol in his direction. After a moment, she switched her attention to the snowy scenery.

"Was it worth it?" Mara began.

"What are you talking about?"

"What did she offer you?"

"None of your business," came his cold response.

She frowned. "How could you say that? Does our past mean nothing to you?"

"Kallisto is my everything," he claimed.

She shook her head, for this was not the man who asked her to marry him.

"Why is the Faith hunting me?" Mara inquired.

"You already know, Cursed Herald."

Mara kept her frown while looking out the window. "That's not what Boyd told me." She saw his reflection glaring back at her. She now got his attention. "Ran into him before I escaped. We had an interesting conversation."

The commander kept his fiery gaze on her.

"What did he say?" Commander White demanded.

Mara realized she had obtained some information confidential to the Faith; no one else was supposed to know. Returning her gaze to him, she remained unfazed by his look of contempt.

"You murdered Saskia and had me framed. And you used me to kill Heru, Lady Isabella, and Anna."

He kept staring at her. The hatred still radiating from his face. Then the commander turned away. She watched him pull a flask out of his pocket. He undid the cap and took a swig. Mara kept frowning. Her former fiancé was never a heavy drinker. What happened to him?

* * *

When they reached the temple, the carriage stopped. The commander was the first to exit, but not before barking at her.

"We're here. Get out!"

The alcohol seemed to have made him more hostile.

She sighed and left the coach. The Holy Blades surrounded Mara while escorting her up the mountain path. Commander White walked ahead, leading them into the temple. She could not believe she was back here again. In all honesty, this was the last place she wanted to be.

Mara entered the temple, ignoring the stares of priests and followers. Upon entering the ivory throne room, the undying's gaze fell onto the one atop the stairs. Just like in her dream, Mara's murderer wore a white and gold dress with jewels. Despite the veil, Kallisto's face remained visible. Even her golden eyes pierced through the gauzy fabric.

Kallisto sat on her golden throne, looking down at Mara as the commander joined his goddess. Dark red drapes cascaded behind the throne.

Mara glanced at Mr. White, who happened to be near. Unlike her dream, the older man's hair was pure white. A few more wrinkles were present on his face. She recalled the man being in his sixties. Mr. White possessed a look of guilt, but he would find no sympathy from Mara. He played a role and lured her into a trap not too long ago. He also drove her parents to confront the Faith, thus putting them in danger.

Mara turned her gaze to Kallisto.

"I see you've made the right decision and surrendered," Kallisto began.

"You gave me no choice," Mara spoke, revealing her face. "I demand you release James!"

Kallisto gave an angry stare before nodding to one of her servants. A Holy Blade approached a door on the left side of the stairs and opened it.

A man, resembling Allen, stumbled through with a bruise on his left cheek. The Holy Blade pushed him out, making him fall forward. He was James Moen, the younger twin brother of Allen. Mara wanted to help him, only to be stopped by the Holy Blades. James groaned as he stood up and walked past her. Upon noticing Mara, his eyes widened as his jaw dropped.

"Mara!" James exclaimed. He stood frozen in his tracks.

Mara gave a sad smile.

He continued to gawk at her. "I can't believe it! You're alive!"

"James," Mara spoke.

"I'm sorry. I never meant—"

"It's okay. Go home. Allen is worried about you."

"Okay…" James left the throne room.

Mara watched while he stumbled away, noting that he had a rough time. When she glanced back at Kallisto, she noticed Commander White leaning over and whispering into her ear. The goddess gazed at him, appearing to be surprised. She then glared back at Mara.

"I hear you met the deserter," Kallisto said with a hint of disdain.

"I have," Mara replied, folding her arms. "I know the Faith is planning to awaken the Dark One. You used me to avoid suspicion."

The goddess sneered at her. "And who would believe you?" Kallisto asked in a cruel tone. "If you continue to seek the truth, you will find nothing but tragedy."

Mara gaped at the goddess, aware that Kallisto did not deny her claim. She then took a deep breath.

"So, why capture me again?" Mara questioned. She noticed the space around her. "By now, I would've been killed and thrown back into the Dark Labyrinth."

Kallisto's eyes narrowed. "There is another reincarnation."

Commander White gave a dismissive look while holding his hands behind his back. "We have reason to believe you know where she is, and have been in contact with her."

Mara gave a strange look. "This is my first time hearing about it."

"Is that so?" Commander White questioned. "All the undying are drawn to each other."

The undying shrugged. "If that were the case, then I wouldn't need Harold's help."

The commander sulked at her. "When you first escaped, we sought to recapture you," he admitted. "Saskia discovered your true nature and plotted to keep you out of our reach."

"Is that why you killed her?" Mara questioned, glaring at him.

"She and the others have outlived their usefulness," the commander said nonchalantly. "For our plans, it would have been convenient." He kept frowning at her. "But you escaped, and reached Harold."

"What do you mean?"

"We knew what that old geriatric was planning," Commander White claimed, "setting you on a quest to claim the souls of the undying. We never deemed you could do it since none have done it before. That's why we were in Har' Yhan. We knew you were going to slay the Siren. And after you killed the Marionette, we concluded that you are too dangerous!"

Mara was mystified. Was this why they captured her?

Kallisto sneered at her. "If you want your friends alive, you will find her."

It was one thing to know a reincarnation was out there. It was another to know Kallisto wanted her dead. Mara began to remember why she became cursed. According to the goddess, Mara's predecessor went after her throne and husband. Yet Kallisto never bothered to explain everything, like the so-called usurper's name. Although Mara knew her name, recalling Khan's words. His daughter, Amara, was taken away from him after refusing Kratés' offer to buy her.

Mara glanced at the two men beside the goddess. For some reason, she had an idea they could help but was foolish to think this way. Commander White was belligerent, and his father was useless. She gazed back at Kallisto. The goddess looked arrogant, showing no remorse for her actions.

Glancing around the room, Mara remembered this place; Dad died in this throne room. She knew the exact area where he fell to the cold hard floor. For a brief moment, she thought she could see his corpse. The memory of seeing Dad die replayed in her mind. Mara lifted her gaze to the murderess and came to one conclusion. So far, no one noticed her possession of Godstruck.

Mara glared at the goddess. "No…"

One word drew the fury of the goddess.

Kallisto looked daggers at her. "What did you say?"

Commander White frowned while folding his arms.

"I made myself clear," Mara replied. "I don't know why you need my help." She gestured to the Holy Blades. "They are doing such a fantastic job."

Everyone caught onto her sarcasm.

"How dare you talk to the Goddess like this?" Commander White scowled at her.

Mara ignored him and kept gazing at Kallisto. She reached behind her back and retrieved the second blade. The disciples gasped upon recognizing the black and gold sheath. The Holy Blades watched with apprehension while unsheathing their swords. Even Kallisto and her commander were stunned to see the one weapon capable of slaying a god.

"How dare you threaten me with that sword?" Kallisto raged.

The huntress glowered at the goddess while unsheathing Godstruck. The silver and steel sword gleamed in the light. Mara could have asked herself what she was thinking, producing a blade upon a deity, but this was her one chance. With the sword capable of defeating a god, Mara decided that Kallisto needed to die. The consequences were irrelevant. She gripped the hilt with both hands as a dark aura exuded from her body.

"You murdered my father and hurt my mother," Mara hissed, glaring at Kallisto with glowing eyes. "How about I return the favour?"

The commander stepped forward and gave a hateful look at Mara.

"Blades, defend your Goddess!" Commander White ordered.

The men let out a battle cry and ran at her. When the first one approached her, Mara gripped Godstruck and swung. In a flash of silver, the sword slashed through his neck, making his head fly off with ease. The others froze, for she slew a Holy Blade in one hit. They regathered their courage and attacked, but Mara was not about to let her guard down. A vertical slice cut one in half. She decapitated another, like the first fool who tried to challenge her. One of the Blades bled to death after losing both of his legs. Another Holy Blade ran at her. Mara sidestepped. With his back to her, she gave a quick punch and stunned him. She drove the sword through his back. He fell to his knees, blood seeping from his mouth. She kicked him off of her sword. One remained, shaking in his boots. She could sense that he did not want to die.

"If you value your life, the door is over there," Mara addressed him.

The Holy Blade dropped his weapons and ran out the door.

Mara turned her attention onto Kallisto. The goddess showed no fear, only anger. She might have been scared of the sword but did not show it. After all, the greatest enemy of the Faith owned a weapon capable of slaying their goddess. With her target within sight, Mara dashed towards her. None dared to stop the undying. If they tried, she would cut them down without a second thought. Kallisto remained on her throne. It seemed too easy rushing a vulnerable target, but Mara did not care. Killing Kallisto was important above all else. She thrust Godstruck forward, driving it into her intended target.

Gasps and cries of distress filled the room. Mara looked down, gripping the hilt. Blood dripped onto the marble floor; Godstruck had found its target. Mara lifted her gaze to see the dark grey long coat turning red. Looking up further, she discovered the pained and enraged face of Commander White, who stepped before his goddess and took the hit. The sword went through his chest but missed his heart. The commander stood frozen like a statue.

Mara's eyes widened as she began to tremble. She just stabbed him! He was never the intended target. The undying believed killing Kallisto would not only avenge her and her family, but it would also save Karl. She wanted to apologize but got punched in the face. Mara was stunned as she hit the ground. The force of the fist made her skid a few feet away. Black blood poured from her nostrils. She managed to recover and wiped the blood from her injured nose.

The commander remained standing as he pulled Godstruck out of his torso. He winced in pain and breathed heavily while holding his wound. Through his fingers, Mara saw the gash closing up. He turned his attention to the blade and lifted it. Commander White furrowed his eyebrows as he studied the sword.

"The sword is fake," he announced.

Mara gawked at the sword. How could it be fake? It was delivered to her by Harold! The commander then glared at her and dropped the sword. The fake Godstruck fell to the floor with a loud clang. Raising his foot, Commander White slammed his boot onto the blade. The impact caused the sword to break at the centre, shattering it into two pieces. Unsheathing the Hand of Kratés, he gave a menacing look at Mara.

"I will defend my Goddess from vermin like you!" Commander White spoke, pointing his sword at her.

Mara did not want to fight him but had no choice. Rising to her feet, she glanced at her Silver Thorn long sword. Mara placed her hand on the grip and drew her blade. The commander raised his sword and dashed at her. His speed caught her off guard.

Once, she believed he was a weak coward who hid behind his Holy Blades. His lack of experience was the reason why she always rescued him. Right now, the commander was proving her wrong. Not only did his first strike break her guard, but he chose to reveal his real power. His attack inflicted a terrible cut on her left arm. Mara recovered but had to fight for her life. She gripped the hilt of her sword with both hands. She tried to counter, but he shrugged it off like it was nothing.

Of all the opponents Mara fought, Commander White was the most difficult other than Kallisto. His fighting style was elegant, fluidly combining hard strikes with fast stabs. He used one hand for all of his attacks. His footwork was very unpredictable; Mara could not anticipate his moves. He put her on the defensive. She could only evade and block his attacks for so long. He wore her down with each blow.

It was a matter of time before Commander White knocked her down and defeated her. Mara never planned for this. She wanted Kallisto to pay, but it turned disastrous. The commander towered over her. He raised his blade above his head, ready to give the final blow.

"This will end it!" Commander White declared.

Mara squeezed her eyes shut, waiting for the fatal strike. After a few seconds, nothing happened. She opened her eyes. The commander was frozen. He remained this way until his face softened and lowered his weapon. He stared at her for a while, then his eyes filled with horror. His body trembled. The Hand of Kratés fell to the floor. He dropped to his knees and clutched his head.

"No!" Commander White roared.

She was stunned by his outburst. Before Mara could do anything, the ground began to shake. A massive earthquake shook the mountain. Chaos and confusion ensued.

"Mara," the Watcher called. "You must leave this place. I am outside."

Mara scrambled to her feet and dashed to the exit. No one stood in her way as the earthquake caused chaos. She ran outside to see a flash of blue. In the light, the Watcher appeared and offered her hand. Mara took the Watcher's hand, and the two teleported to safety.

Chapter Five

Hidden in Plain Sight

Mara awoke on the morning of December 12. Opening her eyes, she found herself lying on an examination table. She was back in the safety of Allen's home laboratory. Someone had removed her mask. While sitting up, Mara discovered a bandage through the slice in her left sleeve. Someone had dressed her wound, even though it might have already healed; regeneration was one of her abilities. Most of the scars she received as a human had long since faded away except for the deformation on her lower abdomen. Mara hoped she would never have to explain to the brothers why she had such a scar.

After getting off the examination table, she saw her friends on the other side of the room. Allen was looking over his brother's injuries.

"Are you sure you don't need to see a doctor?" Allen asked.

"I'm fine," James said, rising to his feet. "I was just roughened up by the Holy Blades." Then he took notice of Mara and stared at her.

Allen also noticed and turned around. "Are you okay? You sustained many injuries." He gestured to her arm. "We saw the wound you got there. James patched you up."

Knowing Allen was addressing her, Mara gazed in his direction. All three were watching her.

"Yeah, I'm fine," she murmured, looking at her arm.

Allen gave a serious look as he approached her. James joined him as well.

"Mara," James murmured. The younger twin remained mystified to see her still appearing in her mid-twenties when she should have been in her fifties.

Allen gazed at his brother before folding his arms. "I just filled him in on what you went through," said the older twin.

James kept watching her. "I'm sorry this happened to you. I can't believe anyone would ever wish this on someone."

"The Watcher told us what happened," Allen also mentioned, keeping his serious gaze on her.

Mara glanced back at him, then to the Watcher. "I guess she also told you how disastrous it went," she grumbled.

The twins exchanged glances before looking back at her.

Allen stormed past her. "Damn right, it didn't go well! Come here, take a look at this…"

He led her to a window. Outside was a town crier making a public announcement. Several people surrounded him.

"Hear ye! Hear ye! The Cursed Herald tried to murder Queen Kallisto and the reincarnation of Lord Kratés!"

Mara stared at the town crier while he made his announcement. Then a piece of paper was shoved in her face. It was a wanted poster depicting her visage. The description read:

'WANTED: If this woman is spotted, please notify the Holy Blades. Very dangerous, do not approach.'

Mara studied the poster held by Allen. Now she could not take off her hood in public.

"That was fast," she muttered.

"The mass arrests have stopped," James mentioned.

"Because I got their attention," Mara sighed. "So much for trying to kill Kallisto."

Allen took the paper away and led her from the window. "I sent the Watcher to help, but some sort of interference prevented her from teleporting into the temple. At least she was able to instruct you to leave." Then he asked, "What happened?"

"You mentioned trying to kill Kallisto," James added.

Mara nodded. "I wanted revenge for what she did to me, my family, and Karl. I thought killing her would free him. Could have succeeded had Karl not got in the way."

Allen looked surprised. "Is he…?"

"He's still alive," she answered. "I had Godstruck, or at least I thought I did. Harold had it delivered to Talon in secret, to hold onto until I met him. Thought I could kill Kallisto with it, but Commander White took the hit. His wound healed quickly. The sword was fake."

The brothers glanced at each other before looking back at her. They appeared surprised that she possessed the sword or a fake version of it.

"So, he's not some snobby noble who was given his title on a silver plate." Allen folded his arms. "Not only is he pretty damn good with a sword, but he looks great for a guy who should be in his fifties."

Everyone stared at him.

"Do you think he's…" James spoke but stopped mid-sentence.

Mara's mouth dropped open. She recalled looking at the commander earlier, noticing how he did not change despite thirty years passing. Fake sword or not, he should have been dead, and she underestimated his swordsmanship.

"Kallisto must have made him immortal," Mara said.

Allen and James appeared stunned by her suspicion.

"You think so?" Allen asked.

The Watcher stepped forward. "It is possible she offered him a piece of the Flame of Life."

The three looked at her.

"The Flame of Life?" Mara questioned.

James nodded. "According to legend, the Flame is the very essence of the gods. Long ago, they planted it upon the earth to prove their existence. It birthed their flesh, and they united the world in the Golden Age. Stories claim that it is located deep below Golden Mountain."

Mara stared at the ground while taking in the tale. "I'm now dealing with two gods?"

"And the prophecy," the Watcher reminded her. "If all the seals fail, the Dark One will awaken and destroy this world."

"I know," Mara said. "That earthquake was no doubt the Dark One."

"It even reached Mirahyll," Allen revealed. "It had everyone up in arms."

"Can't believe Kallikratés is behind this," James said. "Why would they want to awaken it?"

"I believe the answer lies with the remaining seals," the Watcher replied. "Harold, the former master of the Silver Thorns; and Morgan of Désir."

"What about Khan, the wandering monk?" Allen asked.

Mara recalled her last interaction with the elusive monk. "I met him after I…" Then she noticed the questioning gazes of the three. Mara grew flustered. "It was an accident! He was a monster who tried to kill me. I didn't know who he was." She then revealed, "Before he died, he told me about his daughter. Amara was one of the reincarnations the gods captured. She awoke the Dark One, causing the cataclysm a thousand years ago. Khan went to confront the gods. Kallisto tried to persuade him into thinking his daughter was evil, but he saw through her lies. She turned him into the Dark Dweller, then imprisoned him for the past millennia."

The Moen twins gave a sympathetic look. They appeared to believe her.

Mara changed the topic. "I've intentions to see Harold. I have some questions for him."

The Watcher gazed at her with glowing eyes. "You wish to know why he gave you a fake sword."

"He must have the real one," Mara said. "If I had it, I could have defeated Kallisto."

"And draw the ire of her followers, hunting you down to the ends of the earth," the Watcher said, "or you can use the sword to kill the Dark One."

Mara and the twin brothers watched her. Realization began to set in.

"She's right," Allen said, gazing at Mara. "All we need is someone who is both capable and willing to go inside and destroy the core."

Mara placed her hands on her hips. "I offered to do it, but Harold refused."

"Maybe he thought you were not strong enough," James suggested.

"She should be able to do it now," Allen said. "She killed three undying and absorbed their souls. That has to count for something unless there's more out there."

An epiphany struck Mara, recalling her conversation with Kallisto. "There is."

The twins gaped at her.

"What are you talking about?" Allen questioned.

"You're saying there's a reincarnation out there?" James also inquired.

She looked back at the two and nodded.

"Who told you this?" Allen asked with a hint of apprehension in his voice.

Mara found it odd with all the questions, but since they were friends, she decided to tell them. "The Faith is looking for her."

"And they're unable to find her?" Allen questioned.

"As far as I'm concerned, yes." Mara shrugged. "It's the reason behind the mass arrests and capturing me. For some reason, they think I know where she is. Kallisto demanded that I bring her to them if I care about your safety."

The twins were astonished.

"You didn't make a deal with her, did you?" James asked.

"Not after the stunt I pulled at the temple," Mara replied.

Allen kept his serious look. "Good," he said, turning around. The older twin placed his hands on his hips. "You don't need to worry about us or this reincarnation."

Mara grew confused. "What do you mean? If they find her, the same thing will happen."

"If they find her," Allen interjected. "If they haven't found the reincarnation by now, I doubt they ever will."

"How do you know?" Mara asked.

James looked at Allen. "I think she should know," he told him. "She's our friend."

Mara watched James with a curious expression. "Know what?"

The older twin remained silent. After a few seconds, he turned around and gazed at her.

"Watcher," Allen called.

The Watcher approached Mara and stopped before her. She removed her visor, revealing glowing blue gems in her eye sockets. A small vertical slit sat on her forehead. A mask, similar to Mara's, covered much of her face. The Watcher pulled it down to reveal a face almost identical to Mara's visage, except for the two pairs of horizontal slits below her eyes. Her red hood hid most of her hair. Her skin was a little pale with a blue tinge on the sides of her face and forehead.

Mara gawked at her. It was almost like looking in a mirror, except the Watcher's face appeared younger in comparison.

The Watcher looked back with a neutral expression. "My name is Aspen Williams. I was born thirty years ago after you died." Her voice sounded much more human.

Mara gaped at her, trying to register this information. "How is this possible?"

Allen smirked at her. "The same thing could be asked about you and your curse."

James also smiled. "I was just as surprised when Allen brought her home. Her resemblance to you was unmistakable as if you returned to us."

Mara kept studying her look-alike. "Why is her face…?" She trailed off upon seeing the frowns forming on the faces of her friends.

Allen took a deep breath. "Remember the story I told you about the research hall?"

She glanced back at him. "Yes, it happened in Thoron."

Allen nodded. "The Seekers once created an entity called the Prodigy, a genius whose intelligence was further augmented, gaining psychic powers." He turned away. "But the Seekers weren't satisfied and wanted to experiment on the average brain of an individual."

Mara looked back at Aspen and saw the odd slits on her face opening to reveal extra eyes.

"I was the test subject who destroyed their research hall. I once attended the Academy of Thoron at the age of eighteen," Aspen revealed. "The headmaster claimed I had a gift, encouraging me to apply. In truth, I had no business attending the college, let alone mingle with those of greater intelligence."

Mara gaped at her, not expecting Aspen to spill her heart out and tell her life story. Nevertheless, it was interesting to hear about her past.

"So, you're from Thoron?" Mara asked. "At least you were out of Kallikratés' reach."

Aspen shook her head. "I was targeted by the Seekers, who wished to experiment on my plain and simple mind. All in the name of human evolution."

"I believe they also knew about Aspen being a reincarnation," Allen said. "They subjected her to a variety of experiments for two years. It changed her on a biological level. She's half-darkling."

Mara gazed at Aspen in awe.

"What about the other half?" Mara wondered out loud.

Allen's face fell sombre as he became silent. Mara took notice of his facial expression.

"I am also cursed," Aspen answered her question.

Mara looked back at her with her mouth open.

"She was twenty at the time of the experiments," the older twin explained. "After destroying the research hall, she ran away unbeknownst to her parents. With her newfound powers, she learned many things from everyone around her. She was homeless for three years before meeting me. I was skeptical about her powers until she mentioned your name. She also knew about my hatred of Kallikratés and persuaded me to take her to Ardana. In exchange, she would help me defeat Kallikratés for what they did to my father and you. For many of my inventions, she played a role in their creation."

"We hid her for the last five years, knowing the Faith would come after her," James said.

"And I came up with the design for her armour, allowing her to hide in plain sight," Allen added. "Even the commander, who often visits the Council Hall, was oblivious to her identity."

Mara stood there in silence. She then turned her gaze to Aspen.

"So, you're not Allen's creation?"

"No," Aspen replied, "but they did so much for me. If not for them, I would not be able to guide you."

Allen and James gazed back at Aspen.

"What are you talking about?" Allen asked.

"I knew about Mara all along," the Watcher confessed. "I guided her out of the Dark Labyrinth. After Ozin Village hanged her, I was there when she returned to life. I cut her down from the tree and instructed her to find Harold."

"You couldn't tell me this?" Allen looked cross.

"It's okay," Mara said. "I understand why she never told you."

Allen sulked. "Mara…"

Mara shook her head. "They targeted my family. What if they came after you as well?"

Allen sighed. There was some truth to her words.

Thoughts of the former Silver Thorn master returned to Mara's mind. "I should see Harold. See if he has the real Godstruck."

"Then you should go as soon as possible," the Watcher advised. "Kallikratés is planning an attack at Greyward Hold."

Mara gawked at her.

Allen placed his hands in his pockets. "She got this information from one of the higher-ups last night. They were just outside our door, and Aspen picked it up." He shrugged. "Since the Faith was responsible for the possessors' deaths, we have reason to believe Harold is next."

"Why didn't they attack after the Silver Thorns disbanded?" Mara questioned.

"Probably thought it was too much trouble to deal with a lich and an undying, so they decided to capture you," Allen speculated. "Not just because you're dangerous to them, but to draw you away from Harold."

The huntress looked back at him. "If he's in danger, I must help him."

Allen nodded. "Okay, don't die again. We can send you through the Gateway. We've set up a marker at Greyward Hold. Aspen will be watching you. Once you get the sword, we'll send her to get you."

He led her to the Gateway, the familiar elegant, golden construct. Mara used this during a rescue mission at the Black Tower. According to Allen, it was a modified version of an ancient device he saw while visiting Thoron. The original was a time-travel machine, in which the Thoron Sages forbade its use due to the dangers. Mara gazed at the giant clock face with a hollow centre, where runes adorned the outer ring. Sitting near the device were some staves or markers. Each marker had a blue gem on top, though they were inactive.

Allen approached a lever and pulled on it, activating the instrument. The lights flickered as the Gateway drew power. A light hum came from the machine. The runes on the outer ring glowed bright blue. Allen went to the pedestal and pushed some tiles on the dial, setting the coordinates for Greyward Hold. An image appeared in the hollow centre, showing the frozen fort on Grey Mountain.

Mara took a step forward, then stopped. She looked back at the three who were anticipating her departure. It was clear they were concerned for her safety. But if she could get the real Godstruck from Harold, everything would be fine, and they would have a weapon capable of defeating Kallisto. The brothers nodded to her to wish her luck. She then looked at the Watcher. Aspen also nodded, equipping her visor back onto her face.

Mara placed her hood back on, then lifted the mask over her nose and mouth. She turned around and entered the portal.

Chapter Six

The Second Truth

Mara arrived at Greyward Hold with the help of the Gateway. It seemed quiet while she exited the portal. She never thought she would ever see the frozen fort again. Approaching the entrance, Mara noticed several footprints before the iron doors. They looked fresh. She furrowed her eyebrows. As far as she was concerned, only she and the former guild master inhabited this place after the Silver Thorns' dismantling.

Opening the doors, she froze at the sight of several bodies before her. They were Holy Blades, judging by their golden armour. The dark residue covering the rotting corpses made them appear black. It was a lich's miasma. Mara had seen what it was capable of, recalling the previous incident with a snow beast. Harold probably filled the entire fortress with it, killing the Holy Blades as soon as they entered. It appeared the former master did not need her help. The silence, however, was unsettling. There was no roaring fire in the grand hall. Everything was cold and dead. Yet Mara knew where to find the former master.

Approaching his quarters, Mara noticed her surroundings growing darker. It could be the lich's haze, but it would have affected her by now. She reached the doors, knowing he had to be on the other side. Mara opened them and entered his chambers.

She identified the former master by his dark grey robes decorated with dull-gold trimmings. As far as Mara could tell, he remained the same from her last encounter with him. He still wore his black gloves and boots. The hood covered his head. It was hard to see his dark silver mask, for he was facing down. The wooden staff with two silver stones sat in his hands.

Harold sat in his chair atop the stairs as Mara approached him cautiously. The haze seemed to grow stronger. Mara stopped, not daring to go any further. He was as still as a statue.

"Ah, you have returned," he greeted.

Mara gazed at him. "I was told you were in danger. Kallikratés planned to kill you, but I can see they had already arrived."

"And you had quite the adventure yourself," Harold said. "I knew they captured you."

"How did you know?"

"Through Khan," he answered. "All who possess a seal can sense each other. Khan's seal remained unbroken until several days ago, and we have you to thank. But I do not bear ill will towards you. It is almost a relief to know his suffering has ended."

"He thought I was his daughter." Mara glanced down at her abdomen. "He mutilated me as the Dark Dweller."

"Oh, so you know about Amara?" Harold asked.

She nodded. "She was one of the reincarnations the Faith hunted."

"She was," the former master spoke. "Khan raised her alone since her mother died. One fateful day, the father and daughter were approached by an envoy, inviting them to the palace for three days. Khan thought the invitation was strange until he discovered the reason behind it."

"The Great Lord wanted to buy Amara," Mara said.

"Yes," he responded, "but Khan refused his gold. Kratés threw him out and kept his daughter, separating them for a year."

"What happened to Amara?" Mara asked.

"None of us knew until that day," he said. "After defeating the creature, we entered the Dark One and discovered the source of her awakening. We found Amara fused to the beast's core; she was barely recognizable. It was then we learned about the immense power of the undying. The Dark One tapped into the magical energy fuelling her curse and used her as a source of power. We were unable to remove Amara at the time. In anger, Khan went to confront the gods and their followers. It was the last time we ever saw him."

She folded her arms. "So, Kallisto was right. Amara did awaken the Dark One."

"Yes, but none of us believed she did so on purpose," he said. "If I were you, I would do my best to ignore any dreadful words used to describe Amara, especially if they come from Kallisto." Harold then claimed, "I have known Amara personally, and a depraved slave girl is not something I would describe her as. I remain disheartened to know the depths of Kallisto's hatred for her rival, even going as far as hunting her reincarnations."

His words caught her attention, making her think about the White Lady, the Siren, and the Marionette.

"So, Kallisto was responsible for those undying?" Mara asked. "Why is the Faith hunting us?"

"I shall answer, but you must answer my question." The former master looked at her. "Do you still have the resolve to stop the Dark One?"

Mara never expected such a question. Once, he rejected her offer to slay the great beast. But after learning about the undying fused to the creature's core, the answer became clear.

"I do," she replied.

He looked down. "Very well. I wish to test your resolve."

She noticed a change in the air. Not only did it grow darker, but it also became poisonous. The toxic air made her cough. She lifted her hand to cover her mouth. Pulling away, she discovered her hand withering. Mara looked up at Harold and noticed the black mist billowing from the eyeholes, nostrils, and the thin mouth on his mask. She recognized the miasma.

"Show me your resolve!" Harold called. He stood up and descended the stairs.

Growing weaker, Mara fell to her knees. It became harder to breathe. She felt as if acid splashed onto her skin. It was destroying every cell in her body.

"You know what my miasma is capable of," he warned as he approached her. "It is unfortunate the Holy Blades were unaware."

Needing to get away, Mara struggled to her feet and ran. The former master watched as he followed. She entered a room. There was nothing here, so she fled through another door. She had some time to recover while her flesh regenerated.

"I fail to see your designs," Harold called from beyond the door. "Do you hope to kill me this way?"

Glancing around, Mara spotted a katana with a blue gem in its black and gold hilt. The blade gleamed in the darkness. It was the real Godstruck!

The black haze began to billow from under the door. Harold stood on the other side. Mara needed to act now or face defeat. After grabbing the sword from its pedestal, she dashed towards the door. She swung it open, knocking the former master to the ground.

She went into the grand hall. He recovered and followed her.

He stopped upon seeing the sword in her hands. "Ah, you found Godstruck?"

Mara unsheathed the sword. She gazed at the blade before looking back at him.

"Why did you give me a fake sword?"

The former master went silent for a moment, then chuckled. She watched him in confusion.

"Did I give you a fake sword?" He chuckled some more.

Mara frowned. "I was going to use this on Kallisto, but was almost made prisoner again."

"You attempted to slay the goddess..." said the former master. "Very well, though I wish to clarify one thing: the fake was forged the same way as the real one, with the same materials." Then, "I wanted to see if you were the one. When you offered to stop the Dark One, I refused because your destiny lies elsewhere. You play a much larger role than you realize."

She was perplexed. If true, Karl would be dead. Shaking her head, she ran at him. But he caught her by the throat, then lifted her. Mara struggled, but he had a firm grip.

"What is it like to die?" Harold reached for his mask and pulled it off. Underneath was a skull with leathery skin stretched over it. He had sunken eyes. His lips had rotted away, revealing decaying teeth.

For the first time, Mara came face to face with a real lich. There was nothing but bone underneath the skin.

"I have never died since that fateful day," Harold spoke. "All thanks to Kallisto."

Then he breathed on her face.

Mara's hair fell out. Her skin rotted away as her eyeballs melted from her sockets. She tried to scream, but the dark mist filled her throat, burning away her vocal cords. Her grasp on Godstruck loosened.

It appeared to be over, but something washed over her. A blue ember flickered in the dark, growing more powerful. Her hand began to tighten around the grip of the sword.

The tiny spark burst into flames and surged throughout her being. Her body unleashed a powerful force, dispelling the miasma. Mara's regenerative powers began to activate, restoring her muscles and skin within seconds. Even her hair grew back. It was as if she was never affected by the haze.

Harold looked as if he were staring into the face of a ghost. Her body exuded powerful magic, appearing like blue flames. He gazed back at her face, seeing her glowing blue eyes.

"Thalia," he whispered.

Mara tore his arm away from her neck, then plunged the sword into his chest. He froze while the blade began to rob him of his life. His staff fell to the floor. After a moment, she pulled the sword out of him. Mara kept staring at the lich until the blue glow faded from her eyes.

Another strange sensation overcame her, almost throwing her off balance. She lifted her hand to her face and rubbed her eyes. The dizziness went away, and her mind became clear. Mara lowered her hand. When she looked at the former master, a sense of shock washed over her. Not only did she fatally stab the one who was helping her, but she also broke another seal.

As Harold fell to his knees, his face began to change. The skin softened, growing loose and wrinkled. His nose and lips regenerated, making him more human. Pale blue eyes filled his sockets as thinning grey hair sprouted on his head.

He lifted his gaze to her. "She would never let you die."

She looked confused. "Who?"

"Thalia…"

She was surprised to hear him say that name. "You know her?"

"We belonged to the Order of Aazalith." Then he asked, "Remember when I told you about the defeat of Aazalith?"

Mara nodded.

"Aazalith could not be reasoned with, so the ancient Thoron Sages removed her soul as a last resort," he revealed. "While her body was sealed deep below Ghost Mountain, her soul went to Golden Mountain, where it remained for thousands of years. The Thoron Sages sought her soul so they could purify it and have the divine reborn without any malice. However, Ardana refused to return the soul and betrayed Thoron. Little did they know, the slumbering dragon and her soul was the source of the magic blight."

Mara gawked at him.

"Magic is dangerous," he continued. "Not only does it create monsters, but it can corrupt the hearts and minds of the living. Even the purest hearts could become wicked. The Order of Aazalith existed for that reason."

"Like the Silver Thorns?"

"Yes, but the covenant consisted of guardians, purifiers, and keepers," said the former master. "Purifiers neutralized the land of magic while the guardians protected them, slaying monsters created from the magic blight. Most purifiers were female, while most of the guardians were male. Eventually, they are interred together in the Dark Labyrinth, to continue their duties as they did in life. And the keepers were tasked with guarding the soul of Aazalith, protecting it from humans with ill intentions. They were the only living beings allowed in the labyrinth." Harold then revealed, "I was the last keeper, while your progenitor was a purifier. We protected humanity until that fateful day, two thousand years ago."

Mara looked on in curiosity. "What happened?"

"Another purifier stole the soul and used it to become the goddess, Kallisto," according to Harold. "Aazalith was renamed the Dark One while her soul was called the Flame of Life to hide the truth."

Her jaw dropped. "Kallisto and Kratés are not gods?"

"We tried to stop her, but it was a massacre," he said solemnly. "Most fell under her thrall and defected, slaying those who resisted. I tried to stop her with a Keeper's Dagger, the one thing capable of defeating her at the time. She struck me down and turned me into a lich." Then, "Thalia was stabbed by her guardian. For his betrayal, Kallisto eventually made Kratés into a god and took him as her husband. Thus, the Faith of Kallikratés was born."

She watched him. It was a huge story to take in, but she noticed one detail.

"It's just like Karl," Mara murmured.

Harold noted her response. "You intend to save him?"

She blushed while nodding. "We were to marry," Mara replied. "Thirty years ago, Karl and his father invited me to the temple. They claimed it was a ceremony before the wedding. Kallisto appeared before us and bewitched him. I tried to save Karl, but she killed me. She made him immortal. And Kallisto murdered my father and hurt my mother. I want to kill her and save Karl."

"Very well," he said, "but it may be too late to save him."

She looked discouraged. "Why do you say this?"

"The power has corrupted him as it did to Kallisto."

Mara decided to switch the subject. "Why is Kallisto after the reincarnations?"

"To prevent Thalia's return," he answered. "The Prophecy of Kallikratés and the arrival of the Cursed Herald is a lie." Then, "Upon discovering Thalia's secret as an undying, and my transformation into a lich, the gods captured us. We were prisoners for a few centuries until our escape. I fled to Grey Mountain while Thalia went east. I never saw her since then. But I do recall an incident following our escape. A magical explosion destroyed a large portion of the forest at Ghost Mountain and wiped out a nearby village. I believe Thalia was responsible. The gods saw her true power and sought to recapture her. And I founded the Silver Thorns, taking in those who opposed the false gods' ideologies and oppression."

"Does Thalia still exist?" Mara asked.

"She exists in fragments," he replied. "She created the reincarnations, splitting her soul and power among them. The Faith knew about this and hunted them since Amara." He looked at Mara. "I have not been honest with you. This quest I sent you on—its purpose was never to remove your curse."

Mara's eyebrows furrowed. "What do you mean?"

"When the souls of the undying are united, you shall gain the strength to stop Kallisto." He glanced at Godstruck. "The powerful weapon in your possession is not enough. You must seek the Succubus and the Forlorn. The Succubus lives near Désir." He lifted his gaze to her. "I believe you already met her."

She began to realize who he mentioned. "Morgan? She's one of the undying?"

Harold nodded in response.

"And the Forlorn?" Mara asked.

"Amara, who is protected by the vessel of the divine, and possibly your greatest foe yet. And I am also aware of the Watcher."

"How did you know?"

"She has the same power once held by Thalia."

"Are there any others?" Mara inquired.

"Yes, but I do not know where they are. It shall be a task you must do on your own. I'm afraid I won't be much help for long."

Mara changed the topic. Since Harold did not have long to live, she believed now was the time to tell him. "The Faith was responsible for the seals failing. Commander White murdered Saskia, then used me to kill Heru, Lady Isabella, and Anna. Boyd told me everything."

Harold studied Mara while taking in her words. "Is that so?" He frowned, although he did not seem angry by the revelation. "I guess I am not surprised. Deep down, I knew the Faith was responsible all along. After Lady Isabella died, I chose to pin the murders of Saskia and Heru on her. It would have been difficult to implicate Kallikratés at the time." He gazed down. "I am glad that you were able to find the young man and get the truth."

Mara folded her arms. "But I don't understand one thing—why does Kallisto want to awaken Aazalith?"

"To be frank, I would have expected her to be the last person to awaken the divine," he answered, looking up at her.

She gave a curious expression. "Why?"

"After Amara awoke the divine, Aazalith targeted the gods' kingdom," the former master replied. "The divine was seeking her soul and knew where it was. Even though Kallisto and Kratés were gods, they were no match for her."

She gaped at him. "The Legend of Kratés is a lie?"

He nodded. "They fled to Corlin, leaving many behind to die. We, the possessors of the seven seals, were the ones who defeated Aazalith after she razed most of Ardana and slaughtered millions. We defeated the divine with the assistance of the Stone Mages, the Silver Thorns, and the Aristocracy. We became the seven seals that suppressed access to Amara's soul, forcing the divine back into a dormant state. The gods later returned to reclaim control over Ardana, or what remained."

"Can't imagine anyone being pleased to see them back," Mara murmured.

"No," Harold said. "By now, you realize this "Faith" does not care for Ardana, and you are not alone. Over the years, Kallikratés' power has waned in this land. The past will always remain. On many occasions, people have sought Ardana's freedom. Perhaps Lady Isabella was right to banish Kallikratés in Hema." He sighed. "The stolen power has driven Kallisto insane and corrupted her followers. They stand over a source of the magic blight, and many of their hearts have grown wicked. I've heard many have fled to Corlin while the rest shall perish."

Mara frowned. "They don't care about Ardana. It's insane."

"Yes," the former master said. "It is insanity. Before long, the power they have coddled will destroy them." Then he crumbled away into dust.

She took a step forward. "Wait! What about Amara and Aazalith?"

"When the seals began to fail, we never feared the divine's return," Harold told her. "Only an undying can kill an undying."

He closed his eyes and faded away. Mara watched while he dissipated into the air.

Chapter Seven

A Small Victory

Mara watched in silence as the last of Harold's body crumbled away. Only his staff remained. In his place, a shining stone caught her eye. It was a healing stone. She reached over to claim her prize. Rising to her feet, she turned her gaze onto Godstruck. This time it was the real sword and not a fake, or at least she hoped. She gained an advantage while giving her enemies more reason to target her. Kallikratés sent a group of Holy Blades, only to die at the hands of the former Silver Thorn master. Mara refused to stick around and see if they would send more. After sheathing the sword, she headed for the exit.

"Mara…"

Mara heard Aspen's voice. She searched her surroundings, but Greyward Hold remained empty. "Aspen? Where are you?"

"The Holy Blades are outside the fortress," Aspen said. "They have a device blocking most of my powers. I am unable to teleport to your location."

Mara sighed. "This doesn't look good, does it?"

"Escape is impossible," Aspen replied. "I also detect Commander White among them."

Mara shook her head. There was no easy way out.

"Hey, Mara!"

Mara heard Allen's voice and furrowed her eyebrows. "Allen?"

"I'm using Aspen to speak to you. Isn't it amazing?"

Mara raised an eyebrow.

After a brief silence, Allen cleared his throat. "Anyway, I believe they're using one of my anti-magic field generators, which blocks all magic use. If you're able to hear us, they likely stole a defective one. You can use it to your advantage. Since it will block most magic, the commander won't be at full power."

Mara contemplated his words. Despite knowing that one of her greatest adversaries was weaker, she remained outnumbered. She walked to the front door. Despite the arrival of reinforcements, Greyward Hold remained silent.

"Why haven't they stormed the place?"

"They expect you to walk into a trap," Aspen told her. "I can help, but you must destroy the device. One of the Holy Blades possesses it."

Mara nodded. "Fine," she said, approaching the main entrance.

Opening the door, Mara saw ten Holy Blades outside. At least she still had some daylight. As soon as she walked out, they formed a circle to prevent her escape. Commander White walked through. With his hands behind his back, he approached her with a dismissive air.

"Quite a convenience to find you here," he said condescendingly, "seeing how you escaped again."

As he came closer, Mara could smell the familiar scent of alcohol. He had been drinking again. She wondered when he began to drink excessively, though her mind was on other things.

"If you're looking for Harold, I'm afraid you missed him," she responded, glaring back at him. "He's dead."

The commander froze before sneering at her. "Is that so? How did he die?"

"He wished to test my resolve," she replied. "I'm going to kill the Dark One."

The Holy Blades murmured to each other, seemingly surprised by her plan.

The commander gave a mocking smirk. "How do you intend to slay the Dark One? My progenitor sacrificed himself to stop the creature. What makes you think you can defeat it?"

"I'm the only one who can," she said. "I know about the undying fused to her core, thanks to those so-called gods."

Commander White sulked at her. "So, it is true. A depraved slave girl awoke the Dark One." He looked to his subordinates. "The Goddess was right. The wicked girl sought Kallisto's throne and husband."

Mara frowned at him. "I see Kallisto failed to mention how her husband tried to buy Amara from her father." She saw the commander glaring at her, though he looked surprised. "I spoke with her father, Khan, who the Faith imprisoned for a millennium."

The commander's face darkened. "And I assume you killed him, like all the others? How many seals have you broken so far, Cursed Herald?"

"Aside from the one you murdered, five," she admitted. "Although you're the reason why most of them failed."

"Excuses," the commander kept deflecting. "The prophecy is coming to pass, thanks to you."

"You mean the one the Faith made up?" Mara inquired. "I know the real reason why Kallikratés hunted us."

The Holy Blades murmured to each other, appearing puzzled. The commander kept scowling at her in silence, but the look on his face confirmed Harold's claims.

"Harold told me everything," Mara said. "And I'll honour his wish."

"Did he?" Commander White asked, raising an eyebrow. "Did he also tell you what will happen when you collect all the souls of the undying?"

Mara grew confused.

The commander took notice as he studied her face. "Oh, he didn't? Otherwise, you would never agree to his plan to overthrow the Goddess."

"What are you talking about?"

"Once the soul of Thalia is complete, you will cease to exist," he answered.

Mara's eyes widened while her mouth dropped open. Not only did his words confuse her, but they instilled a sense of dread. She thought back to the moment she defeated Harold, recalling a strange but brief sensation overcoming her. Harold told her that Thalia would never let any harm come to her. She never understood what he meant, but it began to dawn on her.

"I see he left some details out," Commander White said, snapping her out of her thoughts. "After all, you're nothing but a fragment. An incomplete copy. He never cared about you."

She shook her head. "No, you're lying! He would never do that to me."

"You are more pathetic than I thought," he continued. "This is why we captured you. You should be thanking us." Commander White gestured to his men. "Holy Blades, arrest the Cursed Herald." He then glared at her. "We knew you would be here and made sure your friends won't interfere."

The Holy Blades approached her with swords drawn. She saw them coming closer.

"Wait!" Mara shouted. "I know the truth about your gods. Harold told me how the Faith came to be."

The men sported perplexed expressions and stopped. The commander opened his mouth, but no words came out. He regained his composure, then stormed over to her.

"What else did he say?" Commander White demanded.

"I know Kallisto and Kratés are not gods! They stole the soul of—"

The commander grabbed her face, clamping her mouth shut before she could finish her sentence.

"You will speak no more," he said in a low tone. "Such slander warrants an arrest." He kept his index finger over her full lips. Commander White gave a peculiar look while pressing it firmly against her mouth.

Mara could smell the alcohol on his hand. She glowered at him as he released her face.

"Speak another word, and I shall present you to the Goddess without your tongue," said the commander. He took a few steps back and drew his sword.

His subordinates followed suit.

Knowing she needed to fight, Mara unsheathed the sword obtained from Greyward Hold. The katana gleamed in the sunlight.

Commander White stared at the blade. His eyes grew wide with horror. His men also watched the sword with caution.

One of the Holy Blades asked, "Isn't that…?"

"Godstruck," the commander spoke just above a whisper.

Mara held the blade in front of her.

"Hope this is real," she muttered underneath her breath.

Commander White dashed at her, his sword ready to strike. Mara raised her weapon to block the hit. She parried his attack and countered. He tried to evade, only to receive a gash across the chest. The commander staggered backwards, holding his wound. He winced as he tried to stop the bleeding. However, the dark grey coat turned red again.

Mara glanced down at Godstruck. The blue gem glowed as the magical essence flowed into it. She looked up to see the commander glaring at her. A small cut from the blade brought him to his knees.

The Holy Blades saw this and dashed at her. With a powerful weapon, the first three men died swiftly. The fourth possessed a small, one-handed crossbow that caught her eye. The little crossbow reminded Mara of the ones Dad used to make. And a ranged weapon would be valuable. She took no time to kill the Holy Blade wielding it. Taking the crossbow, Mara noticed another holding an opened black box with a glowing blue gem inside. She reckoned this to be the anti-magic field generator. She aimed and fired. When the bolt embedded itself into the black box, sparks began to fly while smoke billowed out. The gem shattered as the device burst into flames. The Holy Blade dropped it and ran at her.

While dealing with him, Mara was unaware of another approaching her from behind. He was about to attack but went flying. He was smashed into another by an unseen force. In a flash of blue light, Aspen emerged.

With the device destroyed, the Watcher was able to help. Aspen glanced at Mara before turning her attention on three Holy Blades. Her seven eyes glowed as she levitated into the air. She looked at one of the men and held out her hand. The Holy Blades were shocked while Aspen lifted one of them off the ground. He was helpless as she threw him against the other two.

Mara glanced at the commander, seeing how displeased he looked. Thanks to the chaos created by the two women, the situation spiralled out of his control. Despite the generator's destruction, he remained vulnerable from the injury received from Godstruck. There was only one thing he could do.

"Holy Blades! Retreat!" Commander White ordered.

The Holy Blades gazed at him, yet obeyed his orders nonetheless. Those who remained alive got up and ran away. The commander frowned at Mara and Aspen.

"This isn't over!" he growled as he rose to his feet. Then he stormed away.

Mara watched them flee into some carriages and leave. The Watcher descended to the ground.

Mara looked at her and said, "We make a good team."

"The device is no more," Aspen said, holding out her hand. "I can take us home."

"Hope they didn't take anything else," Mara muttered as she reached for it.

The two women teleported back to Allen's lab.

* * *

The first thing Mara saw was Allen running up to them, then wrapping his arms around the two women. He pulled them into a hug. Mara was quite surprised but appreciated the gesture.

Allen gazed at her with a sad smile. "I had a horrible feeling you weren't coming back."

Mara watched him in silence.

James approached them. "Is Harold gone?"

She looked at James and nodded.

"Did you find out anything?" Allen inquired.

Mara took a deep breath. "There is no prophecy," she said. "According to Harold, Thalia is the only one who can defeat Kallisto, so the Faith hunted her reincarnations to prevent her return." Then, "He planned Kallisto's fall by having me collect the souls of the undying. Each fragment contained Thalia's power."

"So, he used you?" Allen questioned.

James remained quiet but looked concerned.

"He did," Mara replied, "but it might be the key to stopping Kallisto and the Faith. They seek to awaken the Dark One."

"Why?" James asked.

"They stand over a source of the magic blight," she said. "They're corrupted and insane. The Faith is losing power, so they'd rather see this land destroyed."

The Moen twins exchanged glances before looking back at her.

"I think we both agree," Allen said. "After what they've done, Ardana's grudge against Kallikratés is growing."

"Lady Isabella once mentioned Kallisto being power-hungry and wanting no opposition," Mara added. "Is awakening the Dark One her answer to the uprising?"

"Rather than destroy the nation herself, she will have another do it," Aspen added. "Someone else will take the blame, and that is Amara, fused to the Dark One's core."

"And I, who broke most of the seals," Mara said.

"What else did you find out?" Allen asked.

Mara recalled an essential piece of her conversation with Harold. "Kallisto and Kratés stole the soul of the Dark One, also known as Aazalith."

The twin brothers gave mystified looks.

"Aazalith?" James questioned.

"The Dragon Goddess, and one of the Seven Divines of Thoron," Aspen explained. "She was known as the firstborn of Nymera, the Mother of Gods.

Aazalith has been missing for thousands of years. The Thoron Sages still patiently await her return."

The three watched Aspen. It was no surprise the Watcher knew since she hailed from Thoron. Then the brothers turned to Mara.

"Then Kallisto and Kratés are not gods?" Allen asked.

"They never were," Mara revealed. "They were once members of the Order of Aazalith, a covenant sworn to protect humanity from the magic blight. Both Aazalith's body and soul is the source of the magic infecting this land. They betrayed the covenant and stole the soul."

"The Order of Aazalith?" James asked. "Never heard of any of this before."

Allen folded his arms. "I assume they destroyed the covenant and over-wrote it with their religion, given Kallikratés' intolerance for other religions."

"Only four knew about it," Mara said. "Harold, Kallisto, Kratés, and Thalia. Harold might have shared the knowledge with the other possessors, but one now remains. Then there's me, who shared it with you three."

"What else did you find out?" James inquired.

"He confirmed the locations of two powerful undying," Mara said. "The Succubus and the Forlorn. The Succubus is Morgan."

"Morgan?" Allen asked. "Doesn't she possess the last seal?"

"And I encountered her a few times," Mara murmured. "Who would have thought?"

"What about the other one?" Allen continued to inquire. "The Forlorn?"

Mara sighed. "Amara, and it's not going to be easy. Harold told me there were more, but he didn't know their locations." She gestured to Aspen. "He also knew about her."

Aspen stared at her. Mara gazed back, wondering if the Watcher had read her mind. Was she already aware of the consequences of collecting those souls? Though it wasn't like she believed it. The commander could have said those things to scare her from completing her quest. However, she could not shake off the uneasy feeling. Mara was unable to explain what happened when she defeated Harold.

Allen noticed the sword. "Where did you get this?"

Mara snapped out of her thoughts. Glancing at the sword strapped to her belt, she unsheathed it to show everyone.

James' eyes went wide. "Is that what I think it is?"

The Watcher approached her. "Lord Slayer Godstruck. It appears you obtained the real one."

The older twin gawked at Aspen before glancing back at the sword. "Wait, we have a weapon that can defeat them?"

"Tried it on Commander White," Mara said. "It's the real thing."

Allen looked stunned. "Did you...?"

"He's still alive, but far from pleased with me." Mara stared back at the blade.

"The Faith sought this blade's destruction for it is the one thing capable of killing their gods," Aspen said. "So, Harold had a spell cast to hide God-struck. He bound the spell to the life force of one of the most experienced Silver Thorns he knew."

"Saskia…" Mara looked back at the blade. "If she had this, things would have turned out different."

Allen gave a sad smile. "Now, you have it. I can't think of a better person to inherit it. Better not lose it."

Mara looked back at Allen and thought about her next plan. One of the known undying was out of reach, so this left the other one.

"You are going to look for Morgan," the Watcher announced, her eyes were glowing.

Mara stared at her, realizing Aspen had read her mind.

Allen's eyes widened. "Are you going to—?"

"I don't know," Mara interrupted.

The Watcher approached her. "I wish to help, but I need to at least recharge."

"She's right," Allen said. "If Morgan tries anything, she can get you out in an instant."

"And you can stay with us," James added. "We can offer you a room."

"Okay," Mara replied. She might as well take their offer since she had nowhere else to go.

* * *

The brothers hosted a dinner for the four of them. Allen was a terrible cook, which explained why James still lived with him. It was an agreement between the brothers—Allen paid most of their taxes while James did all the cooking and cleaning. Then again, they only had each other.

Chicken and some boiled vegetables were on the menu tonight. Mara watched while James placed a plate before her. The dinner looked very delicious, much better than the rabbit. It had been a while since she had a decent meal. She pulled down her mask. Her eyes were transfixed onto the chicken until she heard Allen clearing his throat. Looking up at everyone, Mara noticed their gazes on her. They appeared stunned by her appearance. Then she realized that she had transformed. Her eyes were glowing yellow. Her parted lips revealed elongated canines. The blotches around her eyes grew dark. Feeling embarrassed, Mara willed herself to change back.

"Sorry," she murmured. "I haven't had a decent meal in a while."

The three just gawked at her. James was the first to smile.

"That's okay," he said softly. "It just means you like it." James gestured to Allen. "He also tends to get like this whenever I cook."

The older twin snapped his gaze on him and sulked. "Hey!"

Aspen removed her visor and pulled down her mask. Mara saw her face as the latter gazed back at her.

"You're not alone," the Watcher said.

Mara gawked at her, then smiled. It felt good to have a little bit of normalcy, even though she was no longer human.

After eating their dinner, the brothers took Mara to her room.

"It's not much," Allen said while opening the door, "but make yourself at home."

Mara took a step inside to inspect her new living quarters. The plain-looking room had a bed, a side table, and a dresser. In the corner sat a chair. Despite being given a small room, it appeared to be an improvement over her accommodations at Greyward Hold. It reminded Mara of her old family home.

She looked back at the Moen twins. "Thank you."

The brothers left her alone and closed the door. Mara made herself comfortable. She approached the dresser, then placed her sword on top of it. The huntress discarded her hood and cape on the chair. She removed her Silver Thorn armour, leaving it on the floor. With only the white tunic and underwear on, Mara climbed into bed and went to sleep.

Chapter Eight

The Consequence

On the morning of December 13, the two women reached the town of Désir, sitting at the foot of Ghost Mountain. They reached it with the help of the Gateway, which teleported them to the marker outside the town. Désir reminded Mara of Har' Yhan, though much smaller and surrounded by a thick forest. The mountain was visible over the trees. The sunrise darkened its features, leaving only a silhouette. As soon as they entered the townsite, Mara noticed the lack of Kallikratés' presence. Almost every place had some form of cathedral or church for its worshippers. None of those were present here. More interesting was the lack of Holy Blades. It appeared the Faith had no presence in Désir. The townsfolk, however, did not seem to mind. If she knew this while on the run, Mara would have thought to come here.

The two women approached an older man on the streets. He owned white hair and several wrinkles on his face. His posture was crooked while one of his blue eyes was cloudy.

"Excuse me," Mara called. "We're looking for Morgan. Do you know where she is?"

The older man stared at them. "Oh, you are searching for Lady Morgan? Have you come to slay her?"

Mara froze briefly. "No, we're just looking for her."

He studied their appearance. "Hmm, you're not from the Faith."

"No, we are not," Aspen said. "The Holy Blades do not allow women to join."

"Oh, that's right," said the older man, "and the Holy Blades don't come here."

"Why?" Mara asked. "Is it because of the Succubus?"

He gave a weird look. "The Succubus? How rude! Lady Morgan is an upstanding member of our community. She is kind and generous, offering protection for our town. In exchange, she asks for a few lads."

Mara looked at him with a questioning glance. "For what?"

The man shrugged. "To help around the manor. It's not easy to run the place alone. Sometimes you need a little help. We offer whatever we can, and she pays well. I've helped a few times in my youth. I'd do it again if I weren't so old."

"Okay," Mara responded. "So, where is she?"

The older man gave a blank stare. "Who?"

Mara's jaw dropped. Did he just ask her such a question? She picked up her jaw and shook her head.

"Morgan... We're looking for Morgan," she said, feeling a little flustered.

"Oh, Morgan," he said. "Why are you looking for her?"

The older man might have dementia. Mara began to regret asking him. She glanced at Aspen, wondering if she could read his mind. The Watcher shrugged; even Aspen's mind-reading powers were ineffective. The Watcher turned her gaze elsewhere, leaving Mara to get her answer from the dithering man.

"Look, we need to talk to her," Mara said. "Please, can you tell us where—"

"She's in the forest, east to the town," Aspen interrupted.

Mara looked back at her, noticing the Watcher's gaze on an unassuming male on the other side of the street. Her glowing eyes indicated that she had obtained information from the younger man's mind. As soon as she finished, the glow in her eyes faded.

Aspen walked away. "I know where her manor is."

Mara frowned at her while following. "He might have given us her location."

"He was too old," Aspen argued. "With his dementia, we would have waited another hour for simple directions."

"So, you decided to read the mind of another who knew? Without his consent?"

"Last I looked, you never told Allen and James of your predicament."

Mara stopped and looked at her. "What are you talking about?"

"I know what Commander White told you." Then Aspen switched her gaze onto Mara. "If you collect all the souls of the undying, Thalia will take over. You will cease to exist."

Mara froze as she gaped at the Watcher.

"Do you believe it?" Aspen asked.

She kept her eyes on Aspen before passing her.

"I don't know," Mara muttered.

The Watcher gazed at her. She remained still for a brief moment before following Mara. The two women walked through the town, reaching the edge of the woods.

* * *

After a while, the two women approached a manor. The lights were on; someone was living here. Mara walked up to the door and knocked three times. She was unsure about seeing Morgan. The last time she saw her was in Har' Yhan. Much had happened since then, but it still felt awkward to come before her. The door opened to reveal a young man dressed in a black suit. He possessed pale blue eyes and short black hair. His skin was pale. The most notable feature was the goatee on his chin.

"Mara Ashwood, I presume," he greeted.

Mara was baffled. "You know my name?"

"Yes, Lady Morgan knew you would arrive." He bowed to them. "My name is Kai. Please, come inside."

She looked at Aspen in confusion, yet the latter did not seem too concerned. While being led into the living room, Mara took note of the fancy interior. Expensive paintings adorned pristine white walls, and the elegant furniture showed the owner's affluent state. Soon, Mara and Aspen stood before a woman dressed in a dark purple bustle dress. The dark shadow cast by her black hood and veil obscured much of her face as if she were in mourning. All Mara could see were her full lips.

"Welcome to my home," Morgan began. She watched Mara while rising from her seat. "I have not seen you since Har' Yhan."

Mara was unsure if Morgan said those words as a matter of fact or to rub it in. She decided to ignore the comment and said, "I guess you know Harold is dead."

Morgan smiled. "I'm aware, and have you to thank." She walked away. "I know why you are here."

Before entering another room, Morgan gazed at them as if to beckon them. Mara and Aspen followed her. They entered a large dining hall. All sorts of fruit, bread, and cheese sat on top of a long dining table. The butler Mara saw earlier was present, placing food on the table. He turned his head to gaze at her.

Morgan looked amused. "He is attractive, yes? Kai has been very good to me." She sat down at one end of the table. "Come, sit and eat. You must be hungry."

Mara gave Morgan a questioning glance. "What are you doing?"

The hostess frowned. "I am showing my hospitality. Is that a crime?"

The two stared at her.

"You realize what's going on?" Mara questioned. "Kallikratés is trying to break all the seals. Are you not worried they're coming after you?"

Morgan sighed. "The Faith has no power here. Besides, didn't you come here to kill me?"

The huntress froze. "Well, I... I..."

"I know Harold sent you," Morgan said. "You intend to honour his wish, but he never told you what will happen if you complete this quest. And I can still sense your resentment towards me over what happened in Har' Yhan." She frowned at her. "While you watched, you asked yourself why it couldn't be you."

Mara's hand tightened into a fist. Was it so obvious?

"No, I did not," Mara lied.

Aspen gazed at Mara. She seemed to be aware of her lie but said nothing.

Morgan smiled underneath her veil. "If it makes you feel better, Commander White thought I was someone else."

Mara gave a questioning glance. "What?"

"We were drunk," Morgan admitted. "He thought I was his late wife. And I mistook him for a long lost lover. One thing led to another."

Aspen gazed at Morgan with glowing eyes. "She is telling the truth."

Mara gawked at Aspen. It was true, for the commander had polished off one of the absinthe bottles before ruining her dinner. She recalled retiring to her room earlier while the rest stayed behind and continued to drink. It explained the commander's drunken tirade, and Lady Lorelei and Morgan pressuring her to join them as they watched him bathe.

Mara looked at Morgan and sat down.

"So, that's what happened?" Mara felt very guilty for getting upset. It was stupid to hold this grudge against Morgan when she did nothing wrong. "I'm sorry."

The older woman smiled. "There is no need to apologize. Yet the question remains—are you going to kill me?"

The huntress shrugged. "I don't know."

"If you wish to defeat Kallisto, you must collect all the souls of the undying. And I am no exception."

"What will happen when I obtain all of them?" Mara asked. "Commander White claimed that I will cease to exist, that I'm an incomplete fragment."

"You believe him?" Morgan asked. "A man who is under a vainglorious liar's thrall, believing anything she'll tell him. He only thinks what she wants him to think." Then the older woman said, "I know Kallisto has been trying to prevent the return of the one who can stop her." Morgan paused. "If you plan to kill me, then please hear my tale."

Morgan reached for her veil and loosened one end, letting it fall to one side. She reached for her hood and pulled it off. Mara got to see her face for the first time but was unprepared by what she would see. Morgan possessed tanned skin like Mara. Long dark hair flowed down to her back and past her breasts. The hairstyle was similar except for the lack of a braid and being more smooth. Her eyes were golden-blue. Overall, her face was identical, but her lips were a little more fuller on a slightly thinner face. Morgan appeared more matured in comparison, with a curvier body.

Mara stared at her face. It was the first time seeing another undying appear so human. Morgan watched her in silence before beginning her tale.

"I came to Ardana thousands of years ago. I joined the Order of Aazalith and became a purifier."

Rising from her seat, Mara pulled down her mask while gawking at the older woman. She also removed her hood. Unlike Morgan's smooth locks, the huntress' hair was in a messy braid with a few loose clumps in the front.

Compared to Morgan, Mara's face was not as thin. Her nose was a little bit wider. Her light brown eyes were more doll-like than the older undying. She still owned the faded markings around her eyes and down the sides of her face. Mara looked younger in comparison. Mara's body was more on the average side with some muscle tone. Although the commander once commented on how big her bottom was, and her legs belonged on a horse.

"Wait, you're—?"

Morgan nodded. "Yes, I am Thalia, or I was…"

Mara gawked at her, then glanced at Aspen. The Watcher nodded, confirming Morgan's claim. Aspen reached for her visor and removed it. She then pulled down her mask to reveal her inhuman face.

Morgan looked at the two. "We finally meet." The original undying gazed at Aspen. "I assume you are half-darkling. Unlike Anna, who was a gorgon-type, you appear to be a fairy. I've seen the kind back in Thoron. If you absorb an undying's soul or use a healing stone, I'm sure you can regain your human form."

Aspen remained silent.

Morgan switched her gaze onto Mara. "And you appear to be a little witch, but partially transformed. Lorelei told me about you. She had seen your true form." Morgan kept studying her face. "Though it is strange. With the travel ban placed upon Thoron, there is no way you could have met Wolf Goddess Ulrika or the Thoron Witches."

Mara looked back at the older woman. Morgan's words made her think about the ritual performed by Dad's village.

The original undying returned to her tale. "Like the two of you, I kept my curse hidden behind a veil. I had no guardians until one fateful night. It was the first time I met Kratés, who was one of Kallisto's guardians." Morgan then said, "Kallisto, who was born in Ardana, claimed to be the most beautiful woman in the world. According to rumour, her mother took her own life in fear that her next child would be less attractive. Many men sought her hand in marriage, but her pride made her refuse them all. Her father made her join the covenant at the age of eighteen after realizing she had no intention of marrying or bearing children."

"Sounds like a punishment," Mara remarked.

Morgan smiled. "Kallisto was unwilling to become a purifier, even though she had the most guardians. She was very vain and selfish. Within four decades, I watched her grow into a bitter crone who became jealous of those younger than her. Even as a goddess, she never changed."

"What about Kratés?" Mara inquired.

"Kratés of Thoron was a strong and beautiful man. But he was not without flaws."

Mara watched her in curiosity. "What flaws?"

"He was addicted to sex," according to Morgan. "For this very reason, his family disowned him after he entered adulthood. He became a drifter, taking on various occupations. Once, he was a bodyguard of a king with a mistress, who no man was allowed to touch. Yet she was attracted to Kratés and made advances onto him. He could not resist. After breaking his oath, Kratés fled to Ardana and joined the covenant to repent for his sins. By twenty, he became one of Kallisto's guardians but was unaware of her envious nature. She had him beaten into ugliness, his head shaved, and considered castrating him to control his urges."

Mara gave a strange look. She had speculated what Kallisto might have been like as a human, but not Kratés. It gave the impression that he was very careless and impulsive. He had no regard for his actions.

"It was during a gathering when I met them," Morgan continued. "That night, Kallisto plotted to castrate him. I saw this and intervened. Not only did we purifiers have an obligation to protect humanity, but we must care for our guardians since they protected us. Kallisto was incapable of upholding these obligations. I suggested her banishment from the covenant."

Mara looked at Morgan while taking in the story, then sat down. "Can't imagine she was pleased with you," came her response.

"Kallisto took to mocking me. She assumed I was an ugly old hag because I was veiled and had no guardians. She removed my veil, hoping to humiliate me before everyone, but they saw this." Morgan gestured to her face. "The others believed my youth and beauty was the reason behind the veil. Kallisto loathed me even more, while Kratés threw himself at my feet, vowing to become my guardian. I offered to nurse him back to his old self, nothing more. He kept insisting. In time, he became my guardian for ten years."

"You let him become your guardian?" Mara asked. "What about his philandering ways?"

"We managed," Morgan simply said.

Mara studied her face and began to realize what she meant. "You two were lovers?"

The older woman nodded. "He wanted to be more than just a guardian." She paused. "But we could never be together for he was human, and I was cursed. Unless…"

"Unless what?" Mara asked.

Morgan never answered her question. Instead, she continued her tale.

"He was my guardian until Kallisto betrayed the Order by stealing the divine's soul. I believe she did it out of jealousy and hatred towards me. It turned her into the goddess we all know. Upon seeing her, Kratés fell under Kallisto's thrall. On her command, he fatally stabbed me. I returned to life, resolved to reclaim Aazalith's soul, but she discovered my secret and captured both Harold and me."

Mara gazed at her in silence. Morgan appeared to be still hurting from the betrayal.

"While Harold rotted in a cell, Kallisto had me starved and beaten into ugliness. Though no matter how severe the beatings, I always recovered. So she sought to destroy me in other ways. She took Kratés as her husband and made him immortal using Aazalith's soul. Then she allowed her depraved guards to rape me every day. Sometimes, they dragged me out for public humiliation—all for their sick satisfaction. Kratés was always present. I begged him to help me, hoping he would stop the torture, but he never did. For a few centuries, I endured horrific abuse until we escaped."

"How did you escape?" Mara inquired.

Morgan closed her eyes and hummed an unknown tune. The notes reached Mara's ears, making her feel somewhat relaxed. While it sounded pleasant, she did not know why Morgan began humming. Then it dawned on her. She heard it before discovering Morgan with Commander White in Har' Yhan. Morgan began to transform. Shimmering scales of blue and green decorated the sides of her face and around her eyes. Morgan opened her eyes, revealing glowing blue gemstones with darkened scleras. The older woman removed her right glove to reveal scales decorating her arm as webbing formed between each finger. Her fingernails grew into sharp claws, like the Siren.

Mara gawked at Morgan's inhuman form. "That's—"

"A mermaid," Aspen interrupted.

Mara looked at her before turning her bewildered gaze back onto Morgan.

The older undying kept gazing at them with glowing eyes.

"Mermaids were beautiful creatures before being hunted to extinction," according to Morgan. "Eating their flesh granted eternal youth and beauty, but made the consumer inhuman. I did this to hide my undying form, but it made me into this." She gazed at her hand. "One day, I witnessed my transformation while being tortured. None seemed to notice, so I waited for the right moment to stage our escape. I used my voice to bind a guard to my will and had him free us." She glanced back at Mara. "Harold fled to Grey Mountain. And I fled to the woods at the foot of Ghost Mountain and changed my name. Kallisto slapped the title, Succubus, on me to make me look worse than I am."

Mara gaped at Morgan. At first, she was rendered speechless after hearing such a horrific tale. Based on the words she heard, it seemed Amara suffered a similar fate.

"I'm sorry." Mara glanced down at her hands. "So, what should I call you? Morgan or Thalia?"

"You are also Thalia."

Mara lifted her gaze to her. "What do you mean?"

"After my escape, a village took me in," Morgan revealed. "However, word of my escape had spread. Devoted to the Faith, the villagers captured me with intentions to send me back. It was my darkest moment. I used Banish to free my soul from my body. It is a spell often used by witches to send wayward spirits to the underworld. I hoped Death would send me to my final resting place; I had nothing to lose. As a result, my soul split in two. One half remained within me, while the other half took on a new life. Born to a young family, in which the mother died in childbirth, and the father raised her alone."

"Amara," Mara murmured.

Morgan nodded. "At the time, I never realized the consequences of using Banish on myself. All the reincarnations inherited the Curse of the Undying. Every time a reincarnation died, her soul split in two. And the gods still sought my recapture."

"Until they spotted Amara," Aspen said.

"Yes," Morgan responded. "It was heartbreaking. She did not deserve any of this."

"What happened?" Mara questioned.

Morgan gave a sombre look. "Sometimes, the truth is undesirable. As others will say, it is a hard pill to swallow. Are you sure you want to know?"

"I do," Mara said.

Morgan closed her eyes. "Despite being equal in power, Kallisto never saw Kratés as a king or a husband, let alone a god." She opened her eyes. "So, he turned his gaze elsewhere."

"And he saw Amara?" Mara asked.

Morgan nodded. "According to Khan, the king invited them to get close to Amara. Then Kratés threw him out and kept her. It had been a year since Khan last saw his daughter."

"Then the divine awoke and almost destroyed Ardana," Aspen added.

"And it was the seven who defeated Aazalith," Mara said. "Is that when you found her?"

"One soul connects all of the undying," Morgan revealed. "When I approached Amara, I sensed her agony."

Mara's hands curled up as she listened.

Morgan took note yet continued. "She suffered the same fate. When I gazed into her soul, I learned the truth."

Mara looked at her with anticipation. "What did you see?"

"Kratés took her," Morgan answered.

The huntress gazed down at her clenched fists. Her anger was building while her nails dug into her palms.

"You mean he raped her?" Mara demanded, her voice breaking down.

"Kratés kept Amara for a month before Kallisto discovered her," said the original undying. "After having her imprisoned, Kallisto tortured and murdered Amara many times. She demonized an innocent girl, while Kratés did nothing. One day, Amara managed to escape and fled deep into the Dark Labyrinth. She kept running, unaware she entered Aazalith's dormant body. The divine captured Amara and fused her to the core. The process was not pleasant."

Mara began to shake as tears welled up in her eyes.

"Why? Why didn't you kill her? You could have ended her suffering!"

"It was not in my place."

Mara shot a glare at her. "Then, whose place is it to kill her?"

"You already know the answer," came the older woman's reply. "Harold sent you on this quest. Only you can put an end to this."

"Then answer me this," Mara said. "Will I cease to exist?"

Morgan refused to answer her question, but her silence was very telling. Mara shot up and stormed away without saying goodbye to her hostess. The Watcher put her visor back on while following her out. Morgan sat alone while watching them leave.

"Mara," Aspen called.

She glared at Aspen. "It's true, isn't it?" Mara asked in a shaky voice.

The Watcher gazed at her. "Yes, it seems that way."

"Isn't there another way? There has to be."

"Harold believes only Thalia can defeat Kallisto," Aspen said. "He sent you on this quest." Then, "What shall we do next?"

Mara looked down. "I just want to go back to the laboratory."

"What about Morgan?"

"I'd rather find another way," Mara murmured.

Aspen nodded. "Very well, I'll take you home."

The Watcher held out her hand. Mara gazed at her hand before taking it.

* * *

In a bright flash of light, they returned to find Allen's laboratory in disarray. It seemed like a group of people came here and trashed the place.

"Heretic," Mara read the word in silence. It adorned a wall in bright red. After hearing some groans, she found James lying on the ground.

"James!" Mara called. She and Aspen helped him up. Looking at him, Mara noticed a few new bruises on James.

He opened his eyes. "Mara?"

"Are you okay?" Mara then noticed someone was missing. "Where's Allen?"

James' eyes widened as he recalled what happened. "The Holy Blades attacked us! They took Allen to the temple!"

She gaped at him. Mara shot up, grabbed Godstruck, and dashed out the door. She left the Silver Thorn long sword behind.

"Don't go!" Aspen warned. "It's a trap!"

Mara ignored her and continued to run.

* * *

Mara did not know how long it took to reach the temple. All she could think about was saving Allen, so she ran like the wind. She hoped she was not too late. The Holy Blades did not see her rushing up the path. In a blind rage, Mara killed anyone who dared to get in her way. She did not know how many she cut down. She needed to save Allen.

Storming the temple, she saw Commander White, his father, Kallisto, and Allen. Allen walked towards the unveiled goddess, intoxicated by her beauty.

"Allen! Don't look at her!"

Mara's cries fell on deaf ears. Allen stumbled towards Kallisto while she took possession of all his senses. The goddess had her arms open as he tumbled into them. They stared into each other's eyes and leaned in.

"Allen!" Mara screamed. It was too late.

Kallisto pressed her lips to Allen's. He did not pull away. After a few seconds, Allen lost his balance and began to crumple. He fell to the ground and became motionless.

Mara dashed to him, ignoring the others. It was like Dad all over again. Kallisto and her followers watched while Mara held Allen's body in her arms. She tried to wake him, but it was futile. Nothing could bring him back. Her vision became blurred by tears.

"Allen... All—"

A powerful force smashed into the back of her head, throwing her to the ground beside Allen's body. While grieving the loss of her friend, one of the Holy Blades struck her with a metal sledgehammer. She felt disoriented as her whole body went numb. Another powerful force smashed into her skull. Blood and pieces of brain matter splattered onto the floor.

The last thing Mara saw was Allen lying beside her.

Chapter Nine

Frail Hope

The tingling sensation touched every nerve in her body. It soon became a scorching heat rushing through her veins, pulling Mara from her death-like sleep. Returning to life, she heard two male voices, but they were unfamiliar. Opening her eyes, she saw the Holy Blades dragging her through a dark place. She could not move, for the brutal hit to the back of her skull left her paralyzed. She was helpless while they dragged her away to who-knows-where.

After hearing a low howl reverberating in the passage, the Blades stopped and dropped her. They went to investigate the growls. The sounds came from everywhere. After a few seconds, the men screamed in terror. They took on a creature way beyond their abilities. Then it grew silent.

Lying in the darkness, Mara remained paralyzed. Would she be stuck like this forever? Moving her eyes, she found herself back in the Dark Labyrinth, though in a different location. Not surprising, considering that the underground labyrinth spanned throughout all of Ardana. Sensing a presence beside her, she tried to move her head the best she could to see who it was. Eventually, her head rolled to the right, allowing her a glimpse of Allen's corpse. The Faith had tossed his body down here to rot. Seeing his lifeless face was horrifying because she could not look away. At least he looked peaceful.

Mara wanted to apologize, though a raspy moan was all she could produce. Deep down, she knew it was the consequence of discovering the truth and seeking revenge. She wanted to kill Kallisto and save Karl, only to lose a dear friend.

Another low growl grabbed her attention. Mara saw a wolf-like creature emerging from the doorway. She thought it was a werewolf, but noticed its thin legs, humanoid torso and arms, and the horns protruding from its head. The black fur and glowing yellow eyes identified a shadow beast, which possibly killed the Holy Blades. The wolf-like creature released another growl as it approached. The metallic scent of her blood attracted it. As the monster towered over her, Mara could see its bared fangs glowing in the dark. It gave another snarl before grabbing her right arm. It dragged her away to another part of the Dark Labyrinth. She could not do anything. At least Allen's body was left alone.

As the creature dragged her down the dark halls, her body began to tingle again. The sensation had returned to her limbs. Mara felt relieved, for she thought the paralysis was permanent. The creature seemed unaware. When the shadow beast reached its destination, it dropped her. Pain shot throughout her body. The monster leaned towards her face, opening a mouth of razor-sharp teeth. Before the wolf-like creature could take a bite, she drove her hand through the creature's chest.

A red haze blinded her while a brief screech escaped from the monster. She pulled something out of the beast. Coppery-tasting liquid filled her mouth as her fangs pierced flesh. She was hungry. Food was all she could think about at the moment. After a few bites, Mara felt better. But a question arose in her mind—where did she get the meat?

Clarity began to set in as the red haze faded away. Mara's gaze drifted onto her right hand to see a half-eaten heart. Then her eyes wandered onto the shadow beast's corpse, where it possessed a gaping hole in its chest. Her mind began to reel. Mara wanted to vomit, but her stomach had no intention of releasing its contents. Her body needed sustenance.

The taste of the blood reminded her of the mysterious illness she almost died from as a child. She recalled the strange ritual performed by Dad's home village. The chanting in a foreign tongue and the pounding drums echoed in her mind. The shaman, Alkina, approached her with a bowl of mysterious red liquid. She painted it on Mara's face before making her drink it. The coppery taste matched the blood inside the heart.

"Fight poison with poison," Mara recalled the shaman's words.

What was that ritual? Why did they perform it on her? With Dad gone, she might never get her answers.

Now she needed to find the exit. Examining the monster nest, she found many carcasses of victims claimed by the shadow beast. Using the moon water, which remained on her person, Mara investigated the pile. The two Holy Blades, who dragged her down here, never stood a chance. Deep claw marks shredded the golden armour as if it was parchment.

She began to pillage the bodies. Every time she was captured, she always lost her essential belongings. Although she was allowed to keep her flask of moon water and the number of useless trinkets, including the tarnished comb, the faded letter, and the withered flower—obtained from the three undying she slew. The enemy took her weapons, gold, and things of value. Before, it was her trusty Silver Thorn straight sword and Saskia's bestiary.

This time, it was Godstruck and her crossbow. She needed an alternative. The Holy Blades' weapons were out of the question, due to being broken. Talon had mentioned their weak nature. No wonder why the shadow beast won! All she got was a thousand gold from pillaging their corpses. After some searching, she found a sharp and sturdy sickle made of steel and silver. Mara was unfamiliar with sickles but had little choice. She walked back to the area where Allen's body was.

* * *

Upon returning, Mara noticed the absence of her friend's body.
"Mara…"
Mara's ears perked up to the familiar voice of Aspen, but she remained alone.
"Aspen? Where are you?" Mara questioned.
"I am unable to teleport to your location," Aspen spoke. "The magical essence flowing through this particular area is interfering with most of my powers."
"Mara," James called, "are you okay?"
"James?"
"I am letting him speak through me," Aspen explained.
"Is my brother okay?" James asked.
After a long pause, Mara shook her head. "No, he's not." She took a deep breath. "He's gone."
A long pause of silence greeted Mara. She figured James was upset by his brother's passing. She stared at the ground where Allen's body was. Thanks to the light of the makeshift lantern, she spotted some drag marks leading to another area of the labyrinth. Eyeing the path, Mara took a step forward.
"I suggest you make a swift exit," Aspen recommended. "I can meet you at the entrance. My powers will not be limited."
"No, I have to find him," Mara said. "I won't leave him here."
"That is inadvisable," Aspen responded. "There is nothing more you can do for him. He's already gone."
"This is my fault!" Mara argued. "He's dead because of me."
"No, this isn't your fault," James told her. "Just come home."
She stared at the doorway. Mara had two choices, but her decision was final. She took another step towards the entrance.
"I would not advise you to go down that path," Aspen warned. "That is a particularly dangerous area of the Dark Labyrinth."
Mara did not care. She was willing to retrieve Allen's corpse, even if it meant descending into a nightmarish hell.
"Mara!" James and the Watcher called her name in unison, trying to persuade her to leave, but Mara ignored them as she made her descent into the darkness.

* * *

As always, Mara saw darkness. The dark even choked out the light from the moon water. She walked until she stepped on something soft. She looked down, trying to see what she stepped on. She took her flask and shook it. In the growing light, a corpse deformed by lacerations appeared before her. The victim bled to death. Mara glanced up, finding herself in a large circular room filled with corpses. The frozen bodies lining the walls looked as if they were trying to scale them and escape through the hole in the ceiling. A faint chime of a bell and a white glow drew her attention.

She turned to the right and saw a glowing feminine figure. Mara watched the ghost-like entity with apprehension. Judging by the white dress, it looked like Kallisto. Mara grew wary, clutching her sickle. She followed after the glowing figure, her pace growing faster. Suddenly, the woman in white stopped and turned around.

Mara had seen the ghost before during the procedure to protect herself against Anna's powers. Allen had dismissed it as a hallucination, yet here she was again. The woman in white continued to gaze at her before lifting her left hand. She pointed to the doorway in silence. Mara was baffled. Who was this woman? The undying could not see anything past the hood and veil. As she approached her, the ghost vanished from her sight. Mara glanced around in confusion but knew she should not dally long. She still needed to find Allen and leave this place. She looked to the doorway before entering another room.

Allen's body was being dragged across the floor by an undead creature in rusted armour and wielding a long knife. The muscles were unaffected by time. The skin was pale, and it possessed stringy white hair. The eyes glowed an icy blue colour. Glowing blue tattoos decorated the left arm and torso. Upon further inspection, she saw that it had masculine features. Some kind of magic or an unknown type of embalming created this creature. He appeared lucid.

Based on Harold's information, she assumed this was a Labyrinth Guardian. According to the decree of the Order of Aazalith, guardians joined their purifiers in the tombs below. Yet he seemed to be alone. The guardian fastened a rope around Allen's ankles, then he yanked on it, hauling the corpse up. After securing the line, he approached the hanging cadaver with the large knife. He made a deep cut across the neck. Blood gushed from the wound to the floor.

Mara saw red. After seeing Allen's body treated with indecency, she ran at the creature. The labyrinth guardian stared at her with an eerie glow in his eyes. She heard inhuman growls and stopped. The smell of the red liquid spilling from her friend's body attracted monsters from deep within the labyrinth. Soon, another shadow beast appeared.

Knowing what the creature came here for, Mara needed to kill the shadow beast. She could not allow the terrible monster to eat her best friend. She swung her sickle, but it disappeared before her eyes, leaving behind a plume of black smoke. Mara forgot about the creature's ability to teleport. It was not fair, considering she was supposed to be part shadow beast. The monster reappeared behind her to take a swipe, but Mara spun around and countered its attack. She parried the shadow beast, allowing her to land a critical hit. Her hand disappeared into its hide, tearing the flesh apart and ripping its heart out. She stared at the fallen monster while gripping the heart, drawing the pungent ooze from the organ. A strange euphoric sensation rushed through her brain as she crushed the creature's heart. She dropped it before targeting her next prey.

While Mara stormed over to the labyrinth guardian, the creature tilted his head to the right before cutting the rope. Allen's body plummeted to the bloodstained ground. She dashed to catch his remains, not wanting to see him more damaged. Mara saw the ugly gash on his neck, and his pale face took on the characteristics of a deceased person. She looked at him with sorrowful eyes. He was so cold, but at least she got his body back.

She switched her attention to the guardian, who was now approaching her with his weapon. She glowered back at the undead creature while lowering Allen's body to the ground. While standing up straight, Mara gripped her sickle tight. Her eyes began to glow. She wanted to kill the guardian for desecrating the body of her friend. The creature slashed at her with his blade. She backed off and countered.

The two clashed with their weapons. During the brawl, Mara noticed the speed and strength of her opponent. These traits were kept even in death, allowing the labyrinth guardian to dodge and counter effectively. He parried one of her attacks, knocking her to the ground. As Mara fell backwards, she had very little time to react to the knife driven into her chest. Even though the knife had missed her heart, nothing could stop the bloodcurdling scream from escaping Mara's lips. The guardian pulled the blade out of her body.

Unable to stand, she rolled onto her stomach and crawled away from him. Her slowness allowed the guardian to plunge the knife into her body again. She cried out in pain, coughing up blood. She looked at Allen's body and tried to reach for it, but the guardian kept stabbing her. She had enough. Rolling onto her back, Mara grabbed the blade, stopping the attack. The tip of the blade was three inches away from her chest. She wanted to leave this place with Allen's body. Dying was not an option. The guardian kept pushing the large knife towards her chest, hoping to deliver the fatal blow. The creature showed no signs of tiring.

Mara clenched her teeth while struggling to keep the blade from penetrating her heart. The tip of the weapon came closer, inch by inch. What was she thinking, trying to take this creature on? But she refused to give up. A faint white glow grabbed both of their attention. It was beneath Mara, growing brighter by the second. She glanced around, seeing more black and gold coffins glowing in a similar white light.

An unseen force threw the guardian off of her in a bright flash. Ten glowing orbs flew around and entered Mara's body. The familiar searing pain surged throughout her veins, but it was not enough to knock her out. Instead, she felt her flesh regenerate. Mara lifted her gaze to the guardian, revealing a more human face. With her strength restored, she could stand again. The guardian recovered and dashed towards her. She gripped the sickle tight. Once he got close, she aimed for his neck and struck once. A single slash was all she needed. Blood gushed from the guardian's wound as he fell to the ground. His cold eyes watched her as the blue glow faded away. Mara gazed down at the guardian's knife. Taking her prize, Mara also spotted a healing stone on the creature's person. It was very convenient since she lost the one obtained from Harold. Although she didn't need it now, she took it anyway.

Rising to her feet, Mara stared at the guardian and sighed. She survived the fight but remained curious about the light. Those were the souls of the undying. There was no mistake, though she noticed how absorbing them did not knock her out. They seemed weaker compared to the three she slew on the surface. And unlike Evelyn, Aria, and Madeline, none of their names emerged in her mind. Perhaps it was by sheer will Mara remained awake. She fought a strong enemy and could not afford to pass out. She turned her attention back onto the casket, unearthed from the earlier force. Mara approached it, then placed her hands on the lid. The coffin was easy to open. Whatever was inside was trying to get out.

Opening the casket, she froze. It was her. No, someone who looked like her, but in an advanced state of decay. She was another reincarnation of Thalia. Judging from the state of the mummified corpse, she might have existed in the years between Amara and Evelyn. Embedded in her chest was a green dagger with a golden hilt. Gazing at the other coffins, a sense of dread washed over Mara. She found the remaining undying Harold mentioned.

Ten caskets later, Mara came to a horrifying conclusion. She knew the Faith hunted the reincarnations since Amara but had no idea how dire the situation was. The victims ranged in age and size. Two never grew up to become teenagers. Three never reached adulthood. Four were adults. One stood out from the rest, possessing a large, bulging stomach. She appeared to be at least seven months pregnant. The life growing inside of her was the target. Mara grew numb. She could not believe the lengths Kallisto would go to stop Thalia's return. Mara recognized the casket, for one of these was her prison. She was one of the lucky ones to escape. But she was unsure about being blessed to learn of Kallikratés' dark secret. All the corpses had identical daggers embedded in them.

A weak moan drew her attention. Mara looked behind and noticed Allen standing on his own two feet. All she saw was his silhouette. How was he alive? Allen saw Mara and shuffled towards her. He only made raspy moans. Both his hands were up, reaching for her. She realized this was no longer Allen once the zombie-like creature lunged at her. Dark circles surrounded his white eyes. His lips were dark grey. It pained her to see him like this, but she no longer had a choice. The reanimated corpse lunged at her again, unaware of the knife before him. He released a stuttered moan while the blade penetrated his heart. The magical essence left his body quicker than it reanimated the cadaver. Allen stared at her with his dead eyes before falling backwards.

Mara froze as her mind went numb. The knife tumbled from her hand. It hit the ground with a clang, jolting her out of her frozen state. She shuddered with each breath. Falling to her knees, Mara kept gazing at Allen's corpse. She trembled as pain and sorrow overwhelmed her. Lifting her shaky hands, she buried her face in them and sobbed. Mara broke down. Her eyes burned from crying.

A glowing hand touched her left shoulder. Mara lifted her head and looked at it. She calmed down, though her breathing remained hitched. The other hand rested on her right shoulder. Mara grew calmer as she sensed a presence behind her. She looked behind, but the woman in white disappeared. She was bewildered but had an epiphany.

Hope kept Mara from caving in, believing there was a cure to the curse. Despite the lies and being used, she never gave up. Mara came this far, and there was no turning back. She gazed at Allen's body and stood up. She also picked up the large knife and tucked it under her belt. Approaching the corpse, Mara crouched down and took him into her arms. After lifting his body, she proceeded to leave the Dark Labyrinth.

Chapter Ten

The Third Truth

It was past midnight on December 14 by the time Mara emerged from the Dark Labyrinth. It took a while to appear because she was hauling some precious cargo. Aspen was waiting outside the entrance on Golden Mountain. As the huntress came out, she noticed the unconscious Holy Blades surrounding the Watcher. She suspected that Aspen had knocked them out with her psychic powers.

"It was unnecessary to take his body," the Watcher told her. "It slowed you down."

Mara shook her head. "He is my friend. I will not leave him in there." Then, "I remember now. For thirty years, I hunted in the Dark Labyrinth to become stronger, so I could avenge my family."

The Watcher stared at her. "My powers are no longer restricted." Aspen offered her hand. "I can take us home."

Mara remained still while gazing at her hand. "You haven't been honest with me," she said, looking back at the Watcher.

Aspen tilted her head to the right. "What are you talking about?"

"Why did you erase my memory?"

Despite the visor, Mara could tell Aspen was surprised. The Watcher lowered her hand.

"How did you know? When did you find out?"

"I knew for a while," Mara admitted. "If you can restore my memory, then you can erase it."

"You're telling me this now?"

Mara nodded. "We should be honest with each other if we're to save this world and survive."

"Very well." Aspen then confessed, "I did seal away your memories. And only I could retrieve them until you fought Anna. The serum Allen injected into your brain allowed you to regain them without my help."

The Watcher stared up into the starry sky. Mara opened her mouth to speak, but Aspen glanced back at her.

"You want to know why I did this?" Aspen asked, taking the words right out of Mara's mouth. The Watcher already knew what she was thinking. Aspen turned away. "It was the only way to seal away the Huntress."

"The Huntress?" Mara thought she was given the name due to her reputation. There was also her past, in which she worked for her father's business.

"Yes, that is what I've come to call you as the sixth known undying," according to Aspen. "You already succumbed to the curse upon seeing your father die. Despite mending your mind, there was little I could do about your inhuman appearance. So I advised against showing your face." Then, "The Huntress was very dangerous, even the Faith feared her."

Mara was surprised to hear this. "Why?"

The sound of two horses neighing drew Mara's attention onto the road. Under the bright full moon, a wagon was heading towards Mirahyll before it stopped abruptly. Something about this scene was familiar to Mara.

"We should leave," Aspen told her.

Mara looked back at her, then glanced down at Allen's body before gazing up at the wagon in the distance. "I should help them."

"We should not get involved. What about Allen's body?"

She turned on Aspen and glared at her. Mara shoved the corpse into her arms. "Fine, take it home!"

Mara took off, ignoring Aspen. She made sure to avoid Ozin while getting on the road.

* * *

Approaching the wagon, Mara saw the two horses and the driver, who was an aged man. She came closer but stopped upon seeing six black shadows dashing towards it. Six men wore brown and black leather armour. They looked rough. Each wielded either a sword or an axe. A part of Mara's mind told her they were bandits. The older man was pulled from the wagon by two men while the other four pillaged the transport for goods.

"No!" cried the older man. "That's my livelihood!"

"Well, I'm sorry," the head bandit said unapologetically. "I'm afraid this is our livelihood. It is what we do, but don't worry." He brandished a dagger. "We shall make great use of your goods once we take them and kill you."

The other brigands noticed Mara and pointed at her. "Boss! There's a witness."

The leader sighed and walked to where his men stood.

Mara watched them, hearing everything they said. The bandits saw her as well.

The leader placed his hands on his hips.

"Hey!" he shouted. "If you want to live, turn back!" His voice echoed down the road.

She responded by moving towards them.

The leader sighed again before looking at two of his men. "Deal with the witness."

The two bandits brandished their weapons. They walked down the road to deal with Mara while the leader went back to deal with the old merchant. One of the thugs ran at her, but challenging an undying was the biggest mistake. With a single swipe of the guardian's knife, she sliced his head off with no effort. The other bandit stood paralyzed as she cast her glowing gaze onto him. Realizing that she was inhuman, the bandit turned and ran. Mara closed the distance and stabbed him in the back. The thug cried out in pain but stopped as soon as the large knife sliced through his neck.

Once more, Mara drew the other bandits' attention, approaching them with two round objects in her left hand. In her right hand was the blood-stained knife. Stopping before the highwaymen, Mara raised her left arm, presenting the severed heads of the two men sent to kill her. Both the bandits' leader and the old merchant were stunned. A glimpse of her inhuman appearance made them realize who and what they had provoked.

"Shit!" shouted one of the brigands. "It's the Black Smoke!"

Mara dropped the heads, then held the knife before her. The other three ganged up on her, thinking there was strength in numbers. The huntress disappeared in front of them as they were about to attack her, leaving behind black smoke. They stopped and looked around.

"Where did she go?"

Before another could reply, his head toppled from his shoulders. The huntress stood behind him with fresh blood on her blade. Another took out a crossbow and aimed.

"You bitch!" He took a shot at her.

She grabbed the body of the decapitated bandit and used it as a shield. The corpse took shot after shot while she charged at the thug, knocking him down. The undying stabbed the stunned bandit through his heart and killed him. The last brigand lost his nerve and ran.

The leader was none too pleased. "Where the fuck are you going?"

The bandit ignored his boss and continued to run. The huntress grabbed the crossbow and aimed. After pulling the trigger, the steel bolt flew towards the fleeing man. It embedded itself into the back of the bandit's neck, severing his spinal cord. He fell to the ground motionless.

The leader looked astonished. All of his men were dead. He gazed at the huntress, who stared back with glowing wolf-like eyes. He had no choice but to face her alone.

Brandishing a large hammer, he ran at her. The huntress vanished, then reappeared in front of him. He got a good look at her face. Her mouth was wide open, showing her elongated canines. He also noted the dark markings around the eyes and her glowing irises. Her nearness startled him, so he swung his hammer at her in fright. She vanished in a wisp of black smoke. He glanced to the left and right. Unable to see her, he began to relax, only to feel a sharp pain in his back. The bandit leader glanced down to see the tip of a knife emerging through his chest. He fell to his knees while the huntress pulled the knife out. She swung again and lopped off his head.

The older man stared in astonishment. He could not believe what happened. At one moment, he was in danger of losing his life while being robbed. And now he witnessed the brutal slaying of his aggressors.

"Ah, can it be? The Black Smoke has returned!"

She looked at the old merchant before approaching him. The glowing eyes and the bloodstained blade did not make her appear kind.

Fearing for his life, the older man bolted to his wagon and grabbed the reins. The horses neighed while galloping to Mirahyll.

She watched him flee to the city, feeling confused by his words. Knowing she was safe, Mara changed back. The huntress glanced down at her left hand. She still held onto the crossbow. Mara decided to keep it since she needed a new one anyway.

"Now, do you remember?"

Hearing a familiar voice, Mara turned her head and saw Aspen without the body. The Watcher had sent Allen's remains home. James received it and was preparing his brother's funeral. Mara glanced at the brutal scene she created.

"I did this," she murmured.

"It was not your first time," the Watcher said.

"So, you knew as well?" Mara asked. "I was the Black Smoke."

"Yes, but I also played a role," Aspen revealed. "Five years ago, I made contact with you, and unleashed the Huntress upon Ardana."

Mara gazed back at her. "You decided to unleash a dangerous undying?"

"You were different, only killing when provoked or endangered." Aspen glanced at the grizzly scene. "You were here before, wandering the roads at night and came upon a bandit attack. They tried to kill you to prevent witnesses, but the same thing happened. Your actions earned you the title of vigilante."

"Yet I was called a murderer," Mara muttered.

"The Faith wanted to portray you as such. They saw you as a threat."

Mara was baffled. "How was I dangerous to them?"

"Your actions undermined Kallikratés' efforts to control Ardana," Aspen revealed. "The bandit attacks grew to a point where the middle and lower class wanted something done. But the Holy Blades prevented anyone from investigating while offering an escort service only the rich could afford. It never solved the problem. When you appeared and began to kill the bandits, many praised you. You did what none could be bothered to do."

Mara placed her hands on her hips. "What happened afterwards?"

"The Faith condemned the attacks. Commander White took to the podium and declared you as a murderer. He announced he would capture you, thus provoking you. You took the bait and got captured in a hunt led by him. While setting up camp, the commander sought you out."

Mara found this familiar. The dream she often experienced in the previous month—it was a memory from five years ago. Still, she wanted to confirm what happened.

"How did it go?"

"The Holy Blades captured you, but the commander made a mistake, thinking he could defeat you by himself. You made him squeal like a pig after impaling him into a tree, and drank his blood."

Mara raised an eyebrow.

"No wonder why he hates my guts," she grumbled. She looked at Aspen and began to understand why she erased her memory. "I am grateful. If not for you, I would've ended up like the others, but please don't do that again."

"Sorry, but it was the only way to bring you back. And I couldn't restore all of your memories at once without the risk of you succumbing again." The Watcher looked north on the road to Mirahyll. "We should go."

Mara gazed in the same direction and spotted a group holding lanterns. They were guardsmen, who remained far away for the two to make their escape. Mara put away her new crossbow and took Aspen's hand. The two teleported back to the Moen residence.

* * *

The next thing Mara saw was James looking at her. She gazed back at the younger twin, unsure what to say to him. What could she say after what happened to Allen? Silence filled the room. James stormed over to her and pulled her into a hug. She never expected him to do this.

"I thought I lost you again." James hugged her tighter.

"I... I thought you'd be mad," Mara murmured.

He pulled away. "How could I be mad at you?" James demanded. "This is not your fault!"

The huntress felt relieved that he did not blame her. But a lingering question surfaced in her mind.

"Where is he?" Mara asked.

James' face fell into a frown. He looked away and gestured to a closed door. Looking at the door, Mara had an awful feeling in the pit of her stomach. Mara began to approach it.

"It is best if you didn't see," the Watcher said.

She ignored Aspen. Opening the door, Mara saw his body lying on the bed, wrapped in white sheets and prepared for a funeral pyre. A cloth cloaked his face, hiding the ugly gash across his neck. Mara felt numb as she drew closer. Before the bed, she fell to her knees while staring at Allen's body. Closing her eyes, Mara could sense James' approach.

"Kallisto kissed him," she said. "He died within seconds, like Dad." Mara opened her eyes and looked at James' astonished face. "I tried to save him but failed. They dumped our bodies into the Dark Labyrinth, where I resurrected. A labyrinth guardian took Allen. Eventually, the magic resurrected his corpse." She gazed back at Allen's remains. "I had no choice."

"I'm sure you did what you had to do," James replied, grabbing a chair and sitting down. He watched Allen's body and sighed. "This is just like the day our father died," he said. "My dad was a brilliant man, yet critical of Kallikratés. The Faith invited him to the Temple of Kallisto, to change his views. But it was the last time we ever saw him. Allen believed they caused our father's death." He looked back at her. "What will you do now?"

"There's only one thing I can do." Mara rose to her feet. "I'm going to find Amara and kill her. If I do this, I can stop Aazalith."

Aspen watched her. "So, you're going to do it, even if it means ceasing to exist."

James looked perplexed. "What are you talking about?" He glanced at Aspen and Mara.

"Harold sent her on a quest to collect the souls of the undying," the Watcher revealed. "She believed it would help lift her curse, but its true purpose was to revive Thalia. All of the reincarnations are fragments, containing her power. Once the soul is complete, Thalia will take over. And Mara will cease to exist."

James gawked at Aspen. He seemed horrified to hear this. He looked back at Mara.

"Why didn't you tell us?"

"I learned about it a few days ago from Commander White," Mara said. "At first, I didn't believe him, but something happened."

"What is it?" James asked.

"Harold nearly defeated me, but something took over. For a brief moment, my body acted on its own." Mara paused. "He said Thalia would never let any harm come to me."

"Oh, Mara," James said solemnly. "If we knew this would happen, we would have never allowed you to do this. You are our friend."

Mara gave a sad smile. "Thanks, but I don't have a choice."

"You lost Godstruck upon your capture," Aspen stated.

"I know—how stupid of me. It's probably destroyed by now. My only choice is to obtain the last few pieces of Thalia's soul." Mara glanced at her Silver Thorn long sword sitting in the corner. She was smart enough to leave it behind. A regular sword would be enough to deal with Amara since Mara had slain other undying with such a blade. She gazed back at Aspen. "I'm out of options."

"What about the other undying?" James inquired.

Mara looked back at him. "Found them in the Dark Labyrinth. Most of them never reached adulthood, and one died before she could be born! I have to break the cycle and end this nightmare!"

"I'm sorry." James glanced down at the floor. "There has to be another way." After a moment of silence, he glanced up with a spark of determination in his eyes. "Only four undying remain, right?"

Mara and Aspen gazed back at him and nodded.

He then asked, "Three of you have your humanity intact?"

The two women nodded again.

James gave a resolute look. "What if you three combined forces?"

Mara looked uncertain. Aspen tilted her head to the right.

"It could work," Aspen spoke, then gazed at Mara. "Since you cannot bring yourself to kill any more undying, I believe this would be the best alternative."

"What do you mean?" Mara asked.

"We could defeat the Forlorn by combining the power of us three," Aspen said. "We might be able to withstand Aazalith's power and put Amara to rest."

Mara nodded. "Okay, but I want you to absorb her soul," she said. "Amara will be the last undying I hunt."

"Very well," Aspen replied.

James' eyes were wide with surprise.

Seeing his face, Mara sighed. "I'm sick of being used. But I'm not going to sit here and watch my home get destroyed. I will save this land and stop Kallisto, but on my terms."

James and Aspen looked at her.

"If we stop Aazalith, not only would the world be spared, but it may weaken Kallikratés further," Aspen spoke.

Mara and James watched her.

"However, it'd be best if we approached the divine while the remaining seal is intact," the Watcher continued. "This way, she won't be at full power. I'll help you, but we must find Aazalith first."

"How long will it take to find her?" Mara asked.

"It depends," Aspen replied. "The divine exudes immense magic—the kind that interfered with some of my powers. It may take a couple of days."

"That's fine, as long as the Faith doesn't know what we're planning," James said. "It could also give us some time to let Morgan know about our plan and ask for her aid."

"What if the Faith comes after her?" Mara questioned. "She has the final seal."

"I think she'll be fine," James replied. "I hear Morgan is the most powerful sorceress in all of Ardana. Unless the Holy Blades stole another anti-magic field generator, they would never dare harm her."

"Okay," Mara said as she nodded. "I guess I could use the time to recover."

* * *

Mara headed to her room. She was about to open the door when James approached her. He held an envelope in his hands.

"Allen left this for you in the event of his death," he said.

She took the envelope. Looking back at James, Mara nodded.

"Thank you."

After James left her alone, Mara entered her room and sat on the bed. She opened the envelope to read Allen's final farewell.

'Dear Mara,

If you are reading this, then I am already dead. I'm sorry our time was cut short, but nothing in the world could bring back those years. I admit to being disappointed when you forgave Karl for all the things he did to you. I'll admit my jealousy when you accepted his marriage proposal. I thought we could be together, but I lost hope and never believed I could be happy. Your death crushed my heart once again. And that man never cared. He chose a fake goddess over you, and they killed you! You didn't deserve any of it!

When I became Chancellor Davis' advisor, I had to see him most days. Seeing his face reminded me of what happened to you. Sometimes, I wonder if he knew what he did. And I hope he regrets his actions one day.

I have always loved you. And no one can replace you. I'm grateful to have known you in the short amount of time we've been together.

Sincerely,

Allen Moen'

Mara looked away from the note. Tears were already streaming down her face. She would have been happy to know Allen loved her, but now he was gone. She lay down and closed her eyes, hoping the tears would stop.

* * *

The next day, they took Allen's body and created a funeral pyre for him. It was painful watching the flames consume him, but it might draw more suspicion if they buried him. And after the incident in the Dark Labyrinth, it would be the last thing they would want. The three did it far away from any populated areas, making sure to keep watch in case the Holy Blades were around.

As Mara watched the embers, she recalled her first day of college. At the time, Mara was the only Stone Mage to attend. She stuck out like a sore thumb; everyone gawked at her like she was some freak show. Also, Karl attended college the same year. He never hid his disdain towards her, asking why a savage was attending college. The nobleman had a circle of friends who shared the same social class as him. But they were more like sheep, being guided by Karl to bully her. It got to a point where she considered dropping out. Then she met Allen and James. The twin brothers were from the middle class—commoners who worked hard to get to where they were. She could relate because she worked for her father's business and saved money to afford the tuition fees. The three became friends who withstood whatever anyone threw at them.

As she finished looking back into her past, Mara could feel tears forming in her eyes. Allen had been a true friend, regardless of what happened.

Once his body became ashes, the three friends gathered the remains and placed them in a box. They went to a spot not too far from where they cremated him. Mara took a shovel and dug a hole for Allen's grave. Upon finishing, she and James took the box and laid him to rest. Exiting the pit, Mara looked at the receptacle. It was hard to look because this was once a close friend. James took over and buried him. She watched while Allen's remains disappeared into the earth. After they said their final goodbyes, they went back to Allen's home laboratory, now owned by James.

* * *

The Watcher sat on the floor and got into a meditative pose. She became frozen as her eyes glowed. Mara watched her in curiosity.

"To find Aazalith, I will search for the Forlorn," Aspen explained. "Since we share the same soul, I can use it to find the other undying. As I've said before, the magic may cause interference, and it could take a couple of days."

Mara was intrigued. "Is this how you found me?"

Aspen nodded. "Yes, this is how I made contact with you."

"Okay, what do I do?" Mara asked.

"Your help is not required."

Mara was a little surprised. She got to sit there and do nothing, and it made her feel anxious. "Shouldn't I do something?"

"You could relax," James suggested. "You've been through a lot."

Mara gazed at him. "Oh…"

So she spent the first day thinking. Many thoughts ran through Mara's mind. She had an uneasy feeling about having to kill Amara, even though it was the best thing to do. She also hoped James' idea would work. She gazed in the mirror, remembering the life she once had. Thoughts of her lost humanity made her think of Karl. She wanted to rescue him but began to wonder if it was worth it.

All she had to do was remember her friendship with the Moen twins. The more she thought about it, the more Mara realized she knew Allen better than Karl. There was a time when she felt much closer to the older twin than the man who became her fiancé. Graduation was when things fell apart. Mara attended the ceremony after her mother went through the trouble of buying her a dress. She didn't ask for it and made herself clear that she was not going. But Dad persuaded her to go. When she attended, everyone watched her. Like the first day of college, they gawked at her the same way. And Karl was there, watching her. At least Allen and James were present, making the night more bearable. For much of the night, she stayed near them until Karl somehow got her alone. He apologized for all the things he did to her and asked for a dance. That moment had created a rift between Mara and Allen, and ultimately Dad.

Mara returned to her room and sat down. She studied Allen's note again. After placing the letter back into the envelope, she noticed another piece of paper inside. With curiosity, Mara took it out and inspected it.

"This is from Dr. Simon in Hema," Mara noted to herself. "Why is this here?"

While continuing to read, Mara noticed some extra notes left by Allen. According to these notes, he did some experimentation involving her and Commander White.

"Took some blood from the commander while he was recovering from Anna's brain drain," Mara read out loud. "Unusually high amounts of magic within the subject's blood."

She wondered if Allen knew about Commander White's immortality before she did. She continued to read.

"Introduced a drop of the female creature's black blood to a sample from the commander. I can't believe it—the black blood extracted the magic from the sample of the subject. Subject's blood became normal."

Mara tried to understand what it meant, then remembered biting the commander in Hema. Drinking his blood could restore her human form, but the effects lasted less than twenty-four hours. Mara also remembered the look on the commander's face. The ordeal left him shaken, requiring assistance from his father and Dr. Simon.

Once, Mara believed Commander White to be a demigod because he was both Kratés' reincarnation and a descendant. But after everything that happened, Mara realized she was wrong about him. Aazalith's soul contributed to his immortality, as well as his superhuman strength and speed. Could it also explain the high amount of magic in his blood? The wheels began to turn in her head.

She put the notes back into the envelope and went to bed.

Chapter Eleven

A Dire Situation

On the morning of December 19, Mara awoke to four knocks on the door. She opened her eyes and noticed that the sky remained dark. The sun had yet to rise. It had to be past midnight or very early in the morning. Another four knocks came. It seemed urgent. Despite being in her room, she could hear someone answering the door.

"Chancellor Davis," James greeted. "I wasn't expecting you."

After her ears perked up, Mara rose out of bed and got dressed. She even donned her hood and mask. While unsure what to expect, Mara left her room to witness James inviting the chancellor. It had been a while since she saw Davis. The regular middle-aged man still had greying hair and pale blue eyes. His full beard and moustache, however, had gained a few more strands of grey. Also, he seemed to have obtained more wrinkles, as dark circles sat below his eyes.

"Yes, I'm looking for Dr. Allen Moen. He hasn't shown up to the office for about a week," Davis said, entering the living room. He glanced around before looking at the middle-aged doctor. "Do you know where he is?"

James' face fell to a frown. "My apologies, Chancellor, but Allen passed away."

Davis' eyes bugged out while he briefly froze.

"Oh, I... I'm very sorry," the chancellor responded. "We didn't always agree on many things, but I always appreciated Allen's character and mind." Then, "If you don't mind me asking, how did he die?"

Before James could answer, Mara came forward. The Watcher was also awake and followed suit. The chancellor took notice and watched them with apprehension.

"The goddess killed him," Mara answered. "I saw him die."

Davis gaped at her. "Killed?"

"It's all my fault." Mara shook her head. "All because I wanted to find the truth."

James sulked at her. "Quit being so hard on yourself! For many years, Allen questioned the control Kallikratés had over Ardana. Everything he stood for went against their ideologies. He was already an enemy before we met you."

Everyone watched James.

"They planned to kill him anyway?" Mara inquired.

The Watcher removed her visor. "I would not be surprised."

Davis could not help but notice how inhuman Aspen's face was. It was his first time seeing the creature behind the visor.

"Well, Dr. Moen always encouraged others to think for themselves," said the chancellor. "And speaking of reincarnations…" Davis gazed at Mara. "I've been looking for you, Miss Mara Ashwood."

The huntress furrowed her eyebrows. "You know my name?"

"Well, that is your name, is it not?" Davis asked. "I've learned of Mrs. Daniella Ashwood's passing. I hear she was a well-known and upstanding citizen until the incident."

"What incident?" Mara questioned. She looked around for an answer.

James turned away.

She noticed this and gave a questioning glance. "James?"

James gazed back at her. "It's nothing."

Mara suspected he was hiding something judging by the tone of his voice.

"So, why were you looking for her?" James addressed Davis.

After an awkward moment of silence, the chancellor cleared his throat. "Well, there's something I need help with." He gestured to Aspen. "Originally, I intended to use Dr. Moen's creation for an important task." Then Davis switched his attention to Mara. "But I think you'll be much better for it."

Mara and Aspen exchanged looks before gazing back at him.

"It depends," the huntress replied. "What's in it for me?"

"I knew you would ask," Davis sighed. "There is a monetary reward if you help the city, and all of Ardana."

"Sounds great," Mara mused. "Yet, I'm unsure if the money is worth it." She pointed to James and Aspen. "We are searching for the Dark One, so I can stop her from destroying Ardana."

The chancellor looked astonished. "What did you say?"

"We found a way," James revealed. "An undying is fused to the creature's core. Only Mara, Aspen, and Morgan can kill her."

Davis gawked at them. "So, if you kill the undying, it will stop the Dark One?"

"Yes," Aspen answered, "but we need to find the creature first."

Mara folded her arms. "Besides, I don't think I'm the right person for the job you're offering."

The chancellor gave her a questioning look. "What do you mean?"

"In case you haven't realized, I have one of these faces." Mara removed her mask. "I'm the reincarnation of someone guilty of a crime she didn't commit. As a result, I'm now an enemy of the Faith."

"Well, this is why I think you'll be perfect for the job," Davis replied. "Are you aware of the mass arrests across Ardana?"

His words drew their attention.

"I am," Mara replied. "Thought I stopped it since I'm the one they're after."

"Well, Mirahyll and Hemal made a formal request to have those imprisoned returned to their homes," Davis explained. "The Faith did comply, but…" He reached into his pockets and produced a piece of paper. The chancellor handed it over to her. It appeared to be a letter.

Mara took the letter and began to read. James and Aspen watched while she read the words on the paper. Her eyes widened as she paused.

"What is it?" James questioned.

Mara stared at the paper, then to the chancellor. "This is a ransom!"

James gaped at her before turning his bewildered gaze onto Davis. The Watcher also looked at him.

Davis trembled. "We received this a few hours ago," according to the chancellor. "The convoy was taken by the Blackthorns while it was en route to Mirahyll. And they killed all of the Holy Blades accompanying it. If we don't pay them a hundred thousand gold by sundown, they will kill the women."

"So, you're asking me to find them and kill the bandits?" Mara asked. "You're not asking the Guardsmen to do this?"

"The Holy Blades are investigating, and demanded that we don't get involved," Davis claimed.

"They said this before," Aspen said, "and so far, they have done nothing."

The chancellor sighed. "It always seems the Blackthorns are a step ahead." He gestured to Mara. "But she, who can lurk in the shadows, can strike when least expected." Davis then mentioned, "I know about the attack at the temple, as well as the recent massacre on the southern road. Rumours of a certain vigilante are beginning to circulate, and I have reason to believe you are that vigilante."

Mara nodded. "I am the Black Smoke, or I was." A question crossed her mind. "Why don't you let the Holy Blades rescue them? They claim to be doing something about it."

"He no longer trusts them," Aspen replied, gazing at the chancellor with glowing eyes. The extra eyes on her face were open.

Davis gawked at her with a dropped jaw.

The two friends glanced at her.

"Not after what the Holy Blades and the Faith did," the Watcher continued.

Mara and James switched their attention to the chancellor.

Davis looked flustered. "I wish you wouldn't read my mind! It's an invasion of privacy!"

Aspen kept gazing at him until the glow faded, then closed her extra eyes. "I'm sorry, but at least you are honest." She placed her visor back on and entered another room.

Mara watched her before turning her gaze to the chancellor. "Really? You don't trust them?"

The chancellor took a deep breath. "For a long time, I've questioned how they have handled their investigation. It's been at least five years, and I have not seen any results. I had suggested combining the forces of the Guardsmen and the Holy Blades, but Commander White refused."

She raised an eyebrow. "Or they couldn't be bothered?" Mara sighed. "Fine, I could kill some time."

"Good," Davis said. "I hoped you would agree." He took out another piece of paper and handed it to her. It was a pass of some sort. "A little incentive for your willingness to help the city," he explained. "In addition to the guardsmen leaving you alone, you can also invoke the right to self-defence should the Holy Blades cause you trouble."

"Okay," Mara said. "So, where should I start?"

"Check the roads near Golden Mountain," Davis suggested. "I believe the convoy was travelling on the southern road at the time of the attack." Before leaving, the chancellor had one more thing to say. "After you do this job, meet me at the Council Hall. I shall reward you."

Then he left.

Mara looked at the pass, then to James.

"Well, I guess I'm on my way," she spoke. "Will you be okay here?"

"The Faith is unaware of our plan and should not bother us. Oh, and one more thing…" James left to get something. He returned with a familiar-looking pendant.

Mara remembered Allen using it before.

"This is a communication stone." He handed her the pendant. "Its wavelengths can be picked up by Aspen, and she'll be watching you. Once you find them, she will let Chancellor Davis know, and he'll send the Guardsmen to retrieve the hostages."

She stared at the stone before lifting her gaze to him. Mara nodded before heading to her room to get her sword. She left to find the missing women.

* * *

Mara roamed along the road near Golden Mountain while keeping a vigilant eye on any potential enemies. The sun began to rise, offering some light to help in her investigation. Checking the roads for any signs of the convoy, she found some tracks belonging to a large wagon as well as several hoof prints. But there was no blood or any signs of an altercation, contrary to what Davis had claimed.

A horse neighed in the distance. Looking up, Mara spotted a black mare with a white diamond in her forehead. As the horse galloped towards her, Mara recognized her as the little lady. Mara never expected to see the horse here. The last time she saw the lady was when she went to Haranta Village to slay the Marionette. The huntress had an idea. Mara could use the horse to help her find the hostages by sundown.

However, whenever she approached the horse, the animal bolted. The mare remained uncooperative.

"I don't have time for this!" Mara refused to go through this again, especially with lives on the line. She noticed the tracks leading towards Hema. The bandits' lair was likely in the northern realm.

As Mara followed the trail, the mare trotted behind her. Growing annoyed, the huntress stopped and scowled at the horse. The mare froze. The two ladies watched each other for a while before Mara returned to her work. The horse followed again, picking up speed. The little lady dashed past the huntress and stopped before her. She stared at the horse. Mara thought about ignoring her, for she had no time to waste. The horse watched her, then began to kneel. Mara was unsure what to think of this new development. The mare whinnied as if telling her to get on. With caution, she approached the animal and mounted the saddle.

On the huntress' command, the horse galloped down the main road to Hema.

* * *

Much of the day had passed by the time Mara entered Hema. She went east, riding along the foot of Ghost Mountain. The tracks led her into a thick forest. Following the trail, she spotted an orange glow deep in the woods. Four men in leather armour surrounded a fire. Judging by their rough appearance, she suspected they were Blackthorns. She dismounted her horse in silence and approached them. Reaching for her crossbow, she loaded a bolt and aimed.

The first bandit fell as soon as the bolt penetrated his skull. The others saw the steel tip emerge between his eyes before going into a panic. They stood up and unsheathed their weapons. They looked around, searching for the aggressor. She watched them while reloading her crossbow. Another man was shot in the head and fell to the ground dead. The other two saw where the bolt came from and approached her. She saw them coming. Mara's eyes began to glow as she disappeared in a wisp of black smoke.

She reappeared before one of the bandits and stabbed him in the chest. The sword went through his heart, killing him instantly. The last one tried to rush her, but she pulled the sword out and swung the blade across his neck. His head toppled down his back. Mara watched as the headless body fell to the ground. Approaching the fire, she found the convoy. It was empty as several footprints led into a cave. Mara decided to investigate. She still had some daylight remaining.

The bandits used a part of the Dark Labyrinth as a dwelling. Entering the hideout, she could hear the voices of men and women. The huntress found the hostages and their captors. Around the corner, she saw one of the women being grabbed by a thug, who held a weapon in his other hand. Mara arrived not a moment too soon. In a flash of silver, the bandit no longer had a grip on the woman's arm. He froze upon seeing his forearm fall to the ground. Blood squirted from the stump as he released a bloodcurdling scream. She grabbed his head and slit his throat, reducing his cries to a loud gurgling sound. The undying dispatched the other, though his screams drew attention to her location. Two more appeared, but Mara slew them. After dealing with the fiends, she felt confused.

'That was it?'

Despite their numbers, she found the bandits easy. She checked the corpses and found a key to the cells. The huntress turned to face the women. While walking towards them, she saw their petrified looks. She thought they were aiming the stares at her before noticing a looming shadow. Mara turned to see a great hulk with a sledgehammer raised over his head.

She raised her sword and blocked the hit, but was caught off guard by the immense strength of the brute. The muscular brigand towered over Mara with biceps bigger than his skull. The huntress doubted she could reason with him. His strength overpowered Mara, knocking her to the ground. It seemed to be over when he raised the sledgehammer again, ready to deliver the final blow.

Mara refused to give up yet. Looking at his legs, she swung her sword across his shins. The giant screamed as he fell onto his back, his feet no longer attached to his legs. The huntress could not believe that she pulled it off without her sword breaking. It was like slashing through two thick tree trunks. She would need to visit Talon soon.

Rising to her feet, Mara stared at the brute. The big muscled man was still screaming in pain, though the loss of blood from his severed feet made him weaker. No one else came to his rescue, for only he remained. His screams died down while he grew paler. She towered over his head. Taking her sword, Mara positioned the tip of her blade to his forehead. He never fought back. The sword went through his skull, and he stopped moving.

After removing the sword from his head, she turned to the hostages. The women looked startled while some were put off by the blood and gore. As Mara approached them, her face returned to normal. The hostages were like frightened rabbits locked in a cage. She removed her mask to show a human face. Some of the women grew calmer, but some remained apprehensive. They knew she was not human.

"I was sent by Chancellor Davis to save you." She took out the pendant and gazed into it. She saw the Watcher's face within the stone, nodding to her. Then the image disappeared. Mara lifted her gaze to them, seeing the curiosity in their eyes. "The Guardsmen will arrive soon, and take you home."

Mara opened the cages. The hostages remained frozen. Eventually, one of them stepped forward, watching Mara while walking past her. When the others realized there was no more danger, they began to exit the cage. As the women left their confines, the huntress noticed something on the dead giant's person. A piece of paper caught her eye. Mara reached down and took the folded paper. There was a seal on it, indicating an important document. She opened the letter and began to read.

'Theo,

I would like to thank you on behalf of the Faith for your outstanding services. I regret that our relationship ended on a bitter note. We understand the losses you incurred during the Black Smoke incident. Yet we still upheld our agreement—the death of the Black Smoke, and the continued payment for your cooperation.

We also acknowledge our debt to the Blackthorn Guild. However, the Faith has fallen on lowly times. As a result, we are unable to pay the previous instalment but offer another solution. We offer forty women to do with as you please. You can use them as slaves or sell them, and whatever you do is none of our concern.

We hope this transaction pleases you, and we can work together again in the future.

Praise Kallikratés,

P.V.'

Mara lowered the paper and stood frozen while waiting with the rescued hostages.

* * *

After a few hours, Mara spotted the transports. The Guardsmen had arrived to take the hostages home. Much to her surprise, Chancellor Davis was among the rescue party. He approached her.

"Thank you for helping Ardana," Davis began. "Your actions shall be remembered…" His voice trailed off when she stormed past him, shoving the letter against his chest. He grabbed the letter, making sure not to drop it. He was baffled with her behaviour. "What is the meaning of this?" He then looked at the letter and began to read. His eyes widened. "This cannot be!"

He gaped at her. Mara watched him and shook her head.

Davis looked back at the letter. "I can't believe this!" He saw the seal and inspected it. "This is their official seal." He gazed at the writing. "This writing… I recognize it." He saw the signed initials.

Studying his face, Mara reckoned Davis was familiar with whoever wrote this letter.

"I found the hostages," she said. "About my payment?"

The chancellor glanced back at her. "Ah, yes… I'm sorry, but could you come to the Council Hall tomorrow morning?"

"Excuse me?"

The chancellor frowned. "I'm sorry, Miss Ashwood, but this is very serious!" He raised the letter to his face. "I must find out what's going on. I shall pay you, I promise."

"Fine, I'll go tomorrow." Mara hoped this was not a trap.

While riding home with the rescue convoy, Mara saw the vast field north to Mirahyll. She caught a glimpse of a male form, standing before the forest at the foot of Ghost Mountain. The huntress could not discern any details, for it was too dark. For some reason, Mara couldn't help but feel someone was watching her. She took her eyes off for a brief second. When she looked back, the figure was gone. Her eyes scanned the field, but could not see anything. She shrugged it off and returned to Mirahyll.

Once she reached the city, Mara dismounted from her horse. The two ladies parted ways for now. The black mare galloped away while the huntress walked the rest of the way to the Moen Residence.

* * *

James was pleased to see Mara's return.

"You came back," he chimed.

Mara gave a strange expression. "Of course, I did. Why wouldn't I?"

"Oh, it's just… Ah, never mind. How did it go?"

The huntress' face became frozen.

James took notice and frowned. "It didn't go well, did it?"

The Watcher approached the two.

"It went well," Mara replied. "Everyone is safe and sound. No innocent lives were lost. Mirahyll is in the process of returning everyone to their rightful homes."

"That's good, but what's wrong? You are a hero, yet you don't act like it."

She stared at him. "The Faith sold those women."

James looked surprised. "What?"

Mara nodded. "Kallikratés hired the Blackthorns to terrorize Ardana over five years ago," she revealed. "I was the Black Smoke, responsible for almost decimating the Blackthorn Guild. The Faith sought my recapture as part of their agreement with Theo. Much of their gold was also spent on keeping him silent until they could no longer pay him, so they decided to sell the women they arrested." Then, "Chancellor Davis wants to know what's going on. He asked me to come to the Council Hall tomorrow morning, but something isn't right."

The shock faded from his face as he frowned.

"It could be a trap," James suggested. "Maybe we should go with you?"

"I don't know," Mara replied. "The last thing I need is to drag you two down with me."

"No, it'll be fine. If we lose you, our plan would be in vain."

"I agree," Aspen said. "Our plan would be less successful if we lost you."

Mara nodded in agreement. "Better to have strength in numbers."

"That is true," the Watcher responded.

"Okay, then it's settled," James said. "I got something for you." He gestured to the table.

Mara spotted two urns sitting there. They appeared to be funeral urns.

"Are those…?" Mara paused. A strange sensation washed over her.

James gave a sympathetic look. "After your mother's passing, the hospital cremated her body. While you were out, I managed to retrieve her ashes without drawing much suspicion." He gazed at the urns before looking at her again. "I believe you, of all people, deserve some closure. You lost your life and your family. I also lost my family, but I got Allen back because of your selflessness."

Mara was stunned by his generosity. "You didn't have to do this."

Approaching them, she noticed the other urn. One of them contained Mom's ashes, but what about the other one? A thought crossed her mind, but it couldn't be.

James looked at the urns. "While retrieving your mother's ashes, I saw this old box sitting in the morgue. It sat there for thirty years. No one had claimed them, and there was no name. So, I checked the records to find out whose ashes these belonged to." He turned to her again. "I found a name: Mathias Ashwood."

Her heart skipped a beat.

"Dad," Mara uttered.

She reached for the jars. While holding them close to her bosom, a single teardrop fell on one of the urns. Aware she was crying, Mara held them with one arm and wiped the tears from her eyes with her free hand. She looked at James.

"How? He died in the temple."

"Davis mentioned an incident about your mother," James revealed. "At the time, I couldn't tell you, even though you deserved to know."

"Know what?" Mara asked.

"Thirty years ago, your mother dragged your father's body through the streets of Mirahyll," he confessed. "She claimed the goddess killed you and your father, then made her drag his corpse back from Golden Mountain as punishment. No one believed her and thought she murdered her husband."

Mara shot a glare at him. She grew angry upon learning what her mother went through. It was much worse than it seemed.

James glanced down. "There was nothing the doctors could do. Allen and I witnessed this, but neither of us had the heart to tell you," he continued. "Your mom was put on trial for his murder, but was committed to the hospital's psychiatric ward after the judge deemed her insane." He lifted his gaze to her. "It was the last time we ever saw them until I became a doctor. By the time I began work at the hospital, she already fell into a catatonic state."

She gazed back at the urns. Despite being reduced to ashes, Mom and Dad were now together after being separated for thirty years. The suffering they endured was over. She closed her eyes while James and Aspen watched her.

"Maybe we can find a place to bury your parents," James suggested, "after we meet with the chancellor."

She looked back at him and nodded. The three called it a night.

Mara sat on her bed and gazed at the jars sitting on the small table. Swearing Kallisto would pay, she lay down and drifted off to sleep.

Chapter Twelve

A Father's Gift

Mara tossed and turned, unable to fall asleep. It was past midnight when a hand rested on her shoulder, shaking her awake.

"Mara," called a male voice. "Mara, wake up. Let's go and practice."

Her eyes shot open. That was Dad! Upon sitting up, she spotted a shadow form standing before her. She blinked, and the black mass vanished. She stared at the space for a while, then heard a horse neighing. Looking at the window, she got out of bed and walked towards it. It was still nighttime as the stars shone in the dark sky. The little lady was galloping in the clearing north of Mirahyll. Mara watched the mare in confusion. She should investigate. After getting dressed, she went outside without waking anyone up.

* * *

The huntress stood alone in the clearing. The horse vanished as if she were never there in the first place. Mara looked around. Then the shadowy figure appeared. It stood on the other side of the clearing, just before the forest at the foot of Ghost Mountain. She recognized the entity from earlier when she was heading home. The figure turned around and disappeared into the woods.

"Wait!" Mara ran across the clearing, chasing after it.

As soon as she entered the woods, Mara lost sight of the mysterious figure and became lost. After wandering for minutes, she found a path. The snow was beaten down by footprints. Soon, she found herself in familiar territory. A brief memory flashback showed a younger version of herself as she followed Dad. For one moment, Mara thought she saw him as he walked away from her. She followed after his image while travelling on the trail.

At the end was an abandoned house surrounded by overgrown trees, tall grass, and frozen vines. The familiar sensation continued to grow within Mara. The more she gazed at the building, the more she began to remember. She had been here before.

"Dad's workshop…"

Her eyes widened as she almost fell to her knees before her old family home and birthplace. After her birth, Mom wanted to move to Mirahyll. But Dad built this house and was not ready to let it go. Instead of selling it, he transformed it into a blacksmith's workshop—a place where he could continue his trade as a hunter and forge his weapons.

She remembered coming here as a child. Dad often brought her here to train or show off the workshop. He intended to leave this place for her when it was time, but that day never came. Despite being old and derelict, Mara was astounded the workshop remained standing. Taking a few steps towards it, she heard voices coming from within. It sounded like three men who didn't belong there. She reached the door and saw three bandits who found the workshop and decided to rob the place. Mara recognized their black and brown leather armour. It did not take long for the Blackthorns to notice her. They unsheathed their weapons in response.

The first bandit asked, "Who's there?"

"Ah, it's just a woman," said the second brigand.

The third looked at her and questioned, "Hey, isn't she the Cursed Herald?"

The first bandit had an idea. "Hmm, if we present her head, we'll get paid."

They began to approach her with their weapons. Knowing they intended to kill her, Mara responded by unsheathing her sword. Her eyes glowed as she stared at them.

The first fool ran at her, but she sliced through his neck with relative ease. His head toppled to the floor, startling the other two bandits. They thought she would be easy. The second had enough courage to challenge her, only to be impaled through the heart. She kicked him off of her sword.

The third brigand lost his nerve and ran. Mara drew her crossbow and aimed at him. After the huntress pulled the trigger, the bolt flew. It punctured his spinal cord, paralyzing him. He hit the ground, crying in pain as she approached him. Using her foot, she rolled him onto his back.

He whimpered as tears rolled down his face, but he was not fooling her. Reloading her crossbow, Mara aimed at his head.

"Please," he begged, but his pleas fell on deaf ears.

After she pulled the trigger, he was no longer whimpering or moving. The huntress gazed at his lifeless body before returning to her old home. She dragged the other two bodies out and burned them together with some matches found inside.

Using the moon water in her flask, Mara looked around. Thirty years had not been kind to the old Ashwood Workshop. Other than time degrading her former family home, it had also fallen victim to vandalism and theft. All sorts of weapons used to adorn the walls and tables, but now the displays were empty. It seemed the bandits she just killed were not the first to come here. Only the grindstone and the wooden table in the dining area remained. Dad showed her how to use the grindstone when she was a child. She hoped she still remembered how to use it and planned to fix her weapon. While examining the grindstone, she noticed a person standing in the corner of her eye. In a swift motion, Mara unsheathed her sword. She stared at the figure with glowing eyes. Upon taking a closer look, she realized this was no thug. Her eyes widened as they stopped glowing.

"Dad?"

The ghost-like vision of her father stood before her. He looked the same as the last time she saw him alive. Another memory flashed in her mind. Dad was busy in his workshop when his daughter walked in. His hair was black, indicating a very early memory of her childhood. His large burly build sat before a metal anvil while he hammered a weapon into shape. She knew to be silent while he worked. He knew she was right behind him. He looked back at her with dark eyes. His face grew into a warm and bright smile.

"Mara," her father greeted.

Snapping out of the flashback, Mara found herself alone. Dad had vanished, leaving behind a small letter and a key. The moonlight illuminated them, drawing her attention. Picking them up, Mara began to read the note.

"To my daughter, when she returns… Look under the table."

She studied the note before searching the wooden table. Examining it, she could not find anything. She walked around it, noticing how the floorboards made a different creaking sound. Moving the table and the rug away, she found a trap door underneath. The bandits had missed this. The door was locked, though the key was a perfect fit. Opening the door, she saw a ladder leading down. She had never seen this before.

Mara descended into a small room that contained a single chest. Upon opening the chest, she found two books. One was a journal, while the other was full of notes and diagrams. Every creation Dad forged was inside this book, either for recreating the weapon or passing his knowledge onto a successor. Inside was another box, wrapped in fancy paper and a bow. Holding the glowing flask to her face, she first read the journal.

"I went to see the shaman today," Mara read out loud. "She told me about my future. I will marry a woman from beyond Andel's gates and conceive a daughter. The daughter will bring the downfall of the false goddess. And the false goddess will seek the child's death."

She stared at the entry. It seemed there was some prophecy telling of Kallisto's defeat. She read more of his journal.

"I left Andel behind. It was the only way to protect everyone and the child."

The words written by her father made her more curious. Mara was surprised to learn that he left his home village to protect her. It might explain why Dad hardly talked about Andel. As she continued to read, an entry caught her eye.

"Daniella took our daughter to a doctor, but her condition grows worse. I returned to the village to see Alkina. She claimed it was the work of the false goddess. The vile witch is casting a spell on Mara to kill her, making it look like an illness. The shaman gave me a moonstone necklace and instructed me to put it on my daughter." Mara reached for her necklace. "Alkina has decided to perform the Melding Ceremony, to give Mara the strength to fight the false goddess. She must drink the blood of a shadow beast, the dark hunter. I shall have Daniella think I invited a healer from my home village. Daniella is not to know the truth."

Everything came together—the terrifying sickness, the strange ritual, and all the things that happened afterwards. Naturally, Mara was astounded to know Kallisto caused her illness. Then again, the deranged goddess would do anything to destroy Thalia.

Mara remembered the ritual happening after her recovery. According to the journal, she was some witch. Both Lady Lorelei and Morgan had mentioned the Thoron Witches. This Melding Ceremony somehow gave her the power of a shadow beast.

Her mind went back to the bouts of rage she sometimes experienced, or the moments of joy after a successful hunt. Dad likely took her out hunting to vent her aggression on to some beast. When the anger subsided, she came home with a strange calmness. Mom was often disturbed whenever Mara returned blood-soaked, and not caring what anyone thought.

After closing the journal, Mara drew her attention to the long box wrapped in elegant paper. Gold ribbons held it together along with an attached card. Taking the card, Mara opened it and began to read.

"Happy Birthday…"

Mara's eyes widened, for it was a birthday card addressed to her. December 21 was the day of her birthday, which was tomorrow. Recalling the last time she celebrated her birthday, Mara realized there was no celebration for her twenty-fifth because of the wedding that never happened. The card appeared to be written by Dad alone.

"I hope you like it," Mara read, then went silent.

The rest was a final plea. Mara knew Dad hated Karl, but never expected him to write his true feelings in the card. He hoped she would say no at the altar, and this gift would remind her of their bond. To remind Mara of everything she worked for, and how she was turning her back on it. All the days they spent training, him offering her an opportunity to take over his business, and the hopes that she would continue his legacy. Dad wanted to give her a chance to turn back and embrace her fate. The training was to prepare her for the day of Kallisto's defeat. She stared at the card before turning her attention to the box. She reckoned that Dad wanted to give this to her either before or during the wedding.

Mara opened the gift to reveal a beautiful, curved sword with a golden hilt and guard. Three rings of gold formed the pommel with a hollow opening. Two golden metal ribbons formed the knuckle bow. Wrapped around the black leather grip was a thin gold wire.

On the sword's guard was a carving of a golden bird. Lighter pieces of gold decorated the black sheath. Unsheathing the sword revealed a long cutlass of gold and silver gleaming in the light of the lantern. Silver blends dyed the sharp blade, while the central ridge and spine were a darker shade of gold. Lighter gold etchings adorned the dark golden edge.

The quality and craftsmanship were like nothing she had seen before in her father's work. She doubted he used real gold and pure silver. Dad likely used steel and carbon, with a little bit of silver, for the blade's forging. As she recalled, he often used a solution to create that golden colour. On its guard, she saw its name—Nightingale.

Nevertheless, it was a remarkable gift from the father to the daughter. Holding the grip, she promised to make good use of this weapon. She would not let Dad down. The huntress sheathed Nightingale, then strapped it to her belt. Taking Dad's journal and the diagram book, she left the Ashwood Workshop.

The sun was rising as Mara emerged. Ignoring the charred corpses of the bandits, she returned to whence she came. After leaving the forest, she stopped and watched the sunrise. The clouds in the sky appeared to be on fire. The horizon had an orange glow as the sun rose to the sky. She once stood here with her father during their days of training. They used to watch the sunrise together. Now she stood alone. Mara held onto the last vestiges of her father's possessions, trying hard not to cry. She missed her father and never got to say goodbye.

Knowing she could not stay long, Mara returned to Mirahyll.

Chapter Thirteen

Secrets Unveiled

Mara returned to the Moen Residence. The others had to be awake by now. As she entered the home, the younger twin greeted her with confusion.

"Where did you go?" James asked, eyeing all of her possessions. "Where did you get this stuff from?"

She gazed back at him. "I got these from Dad's workshop."

He was mystified. "It's still around?"

"Yes, but this is his last weapon." Mara gestured to Nightingale strapped to her belt. "The workshop was stripped bare by thieves."

"I'm sorry," James murmured.

"Don't be," she said. "It's been many years." Mara gazed down at the books in her hands. "At least I got these and his final gift. Not all of his work is lost."

"Well, I suppose we should go to the Council Hall," he suggested.

She nodded in agreement. After putting the book and the journal away, the three left for the Council Hall.

* * *

They encountered Talon along the way. The old blacksmith spotted Mara, but his eyes fell upon her new weapon.

"Hey," he greeted, gawking at Nightingale. "Where did you get that sword?"

She gave an odd expression, then looked at her blade.

"This was a gift from my father," she replied, gazing back at Talon.

The blacksmith kept gawking at the sword like a lewd man would ogle a beautiful woman. She also noticed an older balding man standing before a nearby door. Edwin was opening his workshop for the day. They walked by his building to get to the Council Hall. He turned his head to scowl at her through round glasses but dropped his facial expression upon seeing the sword. Even the miserable old fart was gawking at Nightingale as well.

"Really?" Talon seemed curious by her answer. "Who is your father?"

Mara took her eyes off Edwin and addressed Talon. "Mathias Ashwood, but others called him Bear."

Talon's jaw dropped as his eyes bugged out. "You… You're his daughter?" He was stunned by this revelation. "And you said nothing?"

"You realize I had amnesia, right?" Mara asked.

"Well, I knew that! Still…" Talon paused as a thought crossed his mind. "The Ashwood Workshop—is that where you got it?"

"Yes," she answered, "but the place was robbed. Found three bandits last night. Killed them before they could get away with anything. Only Nightingale remained."

The slamming of a door drew her attention to Edwin again, but the other blacksmith had vanished. No one else seemed to notice. She looked at the workshop with suspicion.

"Very sorry," Talon said. "If you don't mind, can you please tell me where the workshop is? I want to see if I can absorb some of the inspiration behind the Ashwood Weapons. It could help revitalize my business."

She turned to him and shrugged. "I guess it wouldn't hurt to tell you. It is north of Mirahyll, at the foot of Ghost Mountain. Keep in mind, it was once my family home, and I might move in."

"Okay. I need to run a few more errands, but I'll be sure to come by and take a look around," Talon said. "I'm almost done setting up the new workshop, though it's eerie being next to an abandoned village."

"After dealing with the Marionette, I'm sure Haranta will be inhabited," Mara responded. "There should be no reason why people wouldn't want to return."

"Very well. I'll see you later then." With that, Talon walked away.

Mara rejoined James and Aspen. They went to the Council Hall.

* * *

Upon arriving at their destination, Mara noticed several people on the higher levels looking down at them. Ten guardsmen surrounded her and her friends. Chancellor Davis stood before a podium. Even Evan, the interim chancellor of Hema, was present. The young dark-haired man stood at the side with some of Hema's knights as he watched her. Mara did not expect to see Lady Isabella's former steward. Little had changed with Evan, who still wore his ensemble of red, black, and gold. His blue eyes and pale skin remained drained of colour. Also standing before Mara was at least two Holy Blades and a middle-aged man wearing gold and ivory robes. He was a priest of Kallikratés.

"Welcome, Miss Ashwood," Davis greeted. He gestured to the priest. "I don't know if you're acquainted, but this is Father Petyr Vernon. He runs the Grand Cathedral in Mirahyll."

The name rang a bell. She saw the priest turn around to give a dismissive look. Mara recognized the overweight man by his greying hair and blue eyes. He was the one who spread those lies about Amara. Mara took a deep breath and stepped forward.

"I met him after rescuing Commander White from Anna," Mara said. She kept her eyes on the priest. "Dr. Allen Moen helped me, yet the Faith murdered him."

Some of the crowd murmured to each other, expressing surprise to hear about the good doctor's passing. Father Vernon, however, kept his dismissive look. He showed no remorse for what happened to her friend.

"How nice of you to show up," Father Vernon said coldly. The priest glanced at his Holy Blades. "Arrest the Cursed Herald."

Mara looked daggers at him. The Holy Blades approached her with their swords drawn.

She was about to reach for Nightingale, but then she noticed two guardsmen stepping forward. They drew their weapons as they stared at the Holy Blades and the priest.

The Faith's disciples appeared stunned by their actions.

Looking around, Mara noticed the other eight guardsmen approaching the priest and the Holy Blades. She was astonished by the outcome.

Displeased, Father Vernon scowled at the chancellor. "What is the meaning of this? You told me she would be here!"

"Yes," Davis spoke, "but Miss Ashwood is not on trial. She's to be rewarded and thanked for her role in the rescue last night."

Two men appeared with five bags of gold. When they handed her the bags, she took notice of their weight.

"How much is this?" Mara questioned. Never in her life had she ever received a bag this heavy, let alone five bags weighing around the same.

"Each bag is worth two thousand gold, Miss Ashwood," the chancellor replied. "Just don't spend it all at once."

Mara and James were stunned. She knew there was a monetary reward, yet never thought it would be worth this much.

"Chancellor Davis! Not only are you paying money to an enemy of the Faith, but you are letting her go?" Father Vernon demanded. "This does not bode well for you or the city."

Terra's chancellor turned to the priest. "You are mistaken if you think I'd let her go now. She is important to a case," Davis explained, "which is the real reason why I called you here."

"What do you mean?" Vernon asked in a cold tone.

Evan took a step forward. "We have discovered some disturbing allegations about Kallikratés." He glanced at Davis. "The Chancellor of Terra has called for an emergency meeting."

Davis nodded. "I sent some guardsmen to Hemal and invited Evan to this meeting. He rode overnight." Then he addressed the priest. "Care to explain the Faith's recent actions?"

The priest appeared surprised but kept his composure. "I have no idea what you are talking about."

Aspen stepped forward. "They are talking about the brutality the Faith demonstrated across Ardana." She looked at the chancellor. "Kallikratés arrested and killed several innocents in search of the so-called Cursed Herald." She looked back at the priest and removed her visor.

Father Vernon and the Holy Blades expressed apprehension upon seeing her inhuman visage.

"Despite knowing what she looked like," she finished.

The crowd began to shout and yell at the priest and the Holy Blades.

A middle-class man aimed his anger at the priest. "You bastards killed my daughter!"

Many of the people present were families and friends of the victims. Even some of the rescued women were there.

"We committed no crime, yet we were either arrested or slain!"

Mara knew Kallikratés was losing power, and this moment made it more evident. Folding her arms, she approached the priest. Father Vernon took notice and glared at her.

"Stay away from me, vile woman!" Vernon hissed.

She raised an eyebrow. "I'm vile?" Mara asked. "At least I did not sell forty women to a group of brigands."

The priest looked shocked while the Holy Blades frowned at her.

"What? Kallikratés would never do such a thing. You are lying!"

"I'd be careful with my words if I were you." The chancellor raised two pieces of paper. Then he held them before the priest. "Take a look. Do you recognize your writing on both of these letters?"

Father Vernon frowned as he came closer and studied the letters.

At first, Mara believed this meeting was a trap for her. But it was meant for the priest. The huntress also gazed at the letters, recognizing one of them.

"I found this on the large brute last night," Mara said, pointing to the letter. "According to this, Kallikratés hired the Blackthorns to terrorize the people of Ardana over five years ago. I assume you did it to get people to pay for an expensive escort service, and some of the profits went to them."

The priest glared at Mara. "That is untrue."

"You wrote both letters," Davis said, taking the letters away. "This one has the official seal of Kallikratés." He looked down at the two pieces of paper. "At first, I didn't notice the similar writing." He glanced at Mara. "After she rescued those women, I began to notice."

Mara gazed at the chancellor. "I think he set us up to destroy the Blackthorn Guild. They're a major liability, knowing Kallikratés' true nature. It wouldn't be the first time the Faith used others to achieve their goals." She frowned at the priest. "Unfortunately, Theo was not present, just his lackeys."

The crowd was surprised by the revelation. Their blood began to boil. They yelled and screamed again, demanding the arrest of the priest and his men. Father Vernon trembled, his hand tightened into a fist as he clenched his teeth.

"Lies!" Father Vernon shouted.

Everyone grew silent.

He made one more attempt to save his hide. "I did not write that letter! It is all a fabrication!"

The chancellor sighed. They were getting nowhere despite their evidence. His eyes drifted onto Aspen, giving him an idea.

The Watcher sensed his gaze, then turned to look at him. They stared at each other.

While the two never saw eye to eye, something in Davis began to change. In this situation, the Watcher's powers could prove invaluable.

"Watcher," Davis addressed her. "Has Father Vernon been truthful?"

The Watcher cast her glowing gaze onto Father Vernon. The priest froze, then his expression turned to horror upon seeing the extra eyes opening on her face.

"He is lying," she replied. "Kallikratés hired the Blackthorn Guild to terrorize the people of Ardana. Then the Black Smoke appeared and slaughtered members of the guild. Theo threatened to expose the Faith unless Kallikratés agreed to his terms—the death of the Black Smoke and the continued payments for his silence. The Faith complied. But in the end, Kallikratés sold those women, for they could no longer afford Theo's silence."

Everyone gawked at Aspen except for Mara and James. The priest clenched his teeth. Reaching into his robes, he pulled out a dagger while glaring at Aspen.

"How dare you speak blasphemy, devil woman!" He dashed at her with the dagger poised to strike. "In the name of Kallisto, die!"

All of a sudden, Mara teleported in front of Aspen and stopped the priest from attacking. She grabbed his wrist and held it tight. The crowd gasped. Everyone saw the wisps of black smoke surrounding her as she reappeared. The huntress saw the dagger, noting the familiar green blade. She had seen this before upon discovering the sealed undying. Mara turned her glare onto him while her grip tightened. The sounds of bones cracking echoed in the Council Hall. The priest cried out in pain as he dropped the dagger.

Some people managed to get a glimpse of her face.

"Is that the Black Smoke?"

Before anyone else could speak, the chancellor shouted, "May I have silence!"

His voice silenced everyone. Mara's face returned to normal as she loosened her grip on the priest. Father Vernon yanked his arm back and held his wrist.

Davis scowled at the priest. "I'm very disheartened to know Kallikratés would commit such atrocities. I wonder if the Faith even stands for what the gods represent."

Mara heard his words and wanted to say something, yet chose to stay quiet. If only Davis knew the gods were as fake as the Faith worshipping them.

The chancellor gazed at Mara and her friends.

"You and your friends may go, Miss Ashwood. Once again, thank you for helping Ardana in her time of need." Davis glared at the priest. "Guards, arrest Father Vernon and his lackeys. Mirahyll will no longer allow the Faith to do as they please."

Still, the priest had one last thing to say while the guardsmen apprehended him and his men.

"When the Dark One awakens, this city of heathens will be the first to go!"

Mara shook her head. "Not if I get to her first," she hissed.

The priest looked mystified while she turned her back and walked out. James and Aspen, who placed her visor back on, followed after her.

* * *

A couple of hours had passed when the three left the Council Hall. On the way home, Mara spotted Talon standing before Edwin's workshop. He was knocking on the door with ferocity.

"Open up!" Talon yelled. "I know you're in there!"

Mara watched the old blacksmith in confusion. "What are you doing?"

Talon turned to face her with a flustered expression. He stormed up to her with a crumpled note in his hand.

"Oh, I'm so glad I found you!" Talon cried.

She looked concerned. "What's going on? What's wrong?"

Her two friends also gazed at him.

"Well I... I went to—"

"The Ashwood Workshop?"

"Yes, I went there and it... it's on fire!"

She froze. It took a while to process those words, though the shock hit her hard.

"What?" She shot a glare at the blacksmith, then noticed the black smoke rising beyond the city. It came from the same location where the Ashwood Workshop stood. Before she could do anything, Talon handed her the crumpled piece of paper.

"It was already on fire when I got there! I saw Edwin running away and chased him back here, but he locked himself inside." The blacksmith gestured to the note. "This was found near the burning workshop." Talon looked at James. "Help me open this."

"Okay." James helped Talon open the door.

While they were trying to break into the workshop, Mara read the crumpled note.

"The Blackthorn Guild will transfer Edwin of Mirahyll weapons from other blacksmiths and workshops, based on the terms and conditions," she read out loud. "For every weapon sold, half of the profits will go to the Blackthorn Guild. A representative will come by and collect payment every month. If payment is late, the Blackthorn Guild will demand full compensation. If full compensation is unable to be paid, the Blackthorn Guild will expose Edwin of Mirahyll for the fraud he is."

Mara looked up as her brain attempted to process the words from the contract. She recalled Corlin cutting ties with Ardana due to the rampant attacks on transports carrying goods. Weapons were the main targets. The thefts were also a massive issue for any blacksmith who did not have a shop in the city, forcing many to close up and quit. Even Dad's workshop fell victim. She snapped out of her thoughts upon hearing Talon and James break the door down. The huntress stormed inside.

"Mara?" James asked.

Mara could not hear him, for the display racks held her full attention. The last time she was here, Mara found the abhorrent prices shocking. Now coming back here, she grew disgusted. Edwin never forged a single piece of weaponry in this shop. Earlier, she had flipped through Dad's diagram book. She recognized five armaments, right here in this workshop. A hefty price tag sat next to each one. How many of Dad's weapons did this crook sell?

She heard a click from another room. Mara dashed towards it and saw a trap door in the floor closing. She tried to open it, only to find it locked. Talon, James, and Aspen entered the workshop. Mara emerged from the small room, shaking her head.

"That bastard got away!" Mara cried.

"Hey! What's going on?"

They all heard an unfamiliar male voice calling out to them. Two guardsmen came by and noticed the busted door. It looked suspicious.

"Okay, everyone. Out!"

The four came out of the workshop.

"We're not thieves," Mara said as calmly as possible. "If you're looking for one, you just missed Edwin."

The guards gave a peculiar look.

"That's quite the claim," the guardsman told her.

"It's no claim," Talon responded. "We have proof!" He glanced at Mara.

Remembering the contract in her hand, she passed it to the guardsmen. One of them took it and began to read. After a few seconds, his eyes widened in response.

"So, our master blacksmith sold stolen weapons?" He looked at the four. "Where did you get this?"

"I found it during my visit to the Ashwood Workshop as it went up in flames," Talon said. "I saw Edwin flee from the area and followed him here. I tell you, he was the weasel who set fire to the workshop to get rid of the evidence!"

The other guardsman questioned, "Why doesn't he get rid of the weapons instead?"

"Weapons are valuable!" Talon exclaimed. "They will never betray you!"

"He might've been after the diagrams," Mara answered. "Whenever my father forged a weapon, he made a diagram in case he needed to recreate it or pass on the knowledge to another blacksmith. I have the book, and it can identify the weapons made by Dad." She then pleaded, "Please, let me get it. It won't take long."

The guards allowed Mara to retrieve Dad's diagrams, while Talon stayed behind to keep watch in case Edwin returned.

* * *

Soon, Mara and her friends returned with their proof. The diagram book confirmed five weapons that belonged to Dad. Upon further investigation, the guardsmen managed to open the trap door, revealing a passage leading out of Mirahyll through the sewer system. Inside was an enormous stash of armaments, every one of them stolen. It became evident that Edwin used it to transport stolen weapons without anyone knowing.

However, Edwin was long gone. The slippery weasel took all the gold he could carry and ran, leaving everything else behind.

"We will have to report this to the chancellor's office," the guardsman declared. "We will also send out a notice to the rest of Ardana. Should Edwin be found, we shall arrest him without question."

They went to retrieve a wagon to transport the weapons out of the workshop. Many people arrived and watched as the guardsmen cleaned out the place. Some came to see the blacksmith, only to discover the truth.

It was then Mara spotted Dad's weapons loaded into the wagon as well. "Excuse me, but what about my father's weapons?"

"I'm sorry," said the guard. "All stolen weapons must be processed. But we shall return them within the next few days."

While the guardsmen took them away, Talon walked up to her.

"Hey, you don't mind if I could borrow your father's book?" Talon inquired.

Mara and her friends looked at him.

"What?" Mara never expected such a request.

"If I study those diagrams, I can reproduce the Ashwood Weapons," the old blacksmith explained.

"You can do that?"

"It'll take some time, but it is possible," he said. "What do you think?"

She glanced down at the book, feeling hesitant about parting with one of her father's possessions, but decided to hand it over to Talon. "I guess it can't hurt."

It seemed right to give him Dad's diagrams. Talon had been a great help to her by providing reliable weapons.

Thrilled, Talon looked at the book with a twinkle in his eyes. "Thank you. I promise you will not regret it. Come by my workshop later."

With that, he left. As soon as he was out of their sight, Mara gazed back at her friends.

"I suppose we should get back and continue our search for Aazalith?"

James smiled and nodded in agreement. They headed home.

* * *

After a long day, Mara returned to the Ashwood Workshop with the urns containing her parent's ashes. She had persuaded her friends earlier to let her come here alone because this was a very personal matter. It was already snowing by the time she reached the burnt building. Mara intended to make this her home since it meant something, but Edwin made sure nothing remained. After putting down the urns, she walked inside to survey the damage. A lone family etching somehow survived the fire. It was a little burnt around the edges, yet intact for the most part. She picked up the picture and looked at it. It was of Mom and Dad. A younger version of herself stood in front of them. They were all smiling. To Mara, it was a distant memory of a happier time. Tears formed in her eyes as she gazed at the image.

Mara swore to avenge them by defeating Kallisto. She would make sure everyone involved would pay. Tears rolled down her face as she took the picture with her. Mara went outside and dug a deep hole. Placing the two urns inside, she buried her parents together. After finishing, the huntress made two small hillocks using stones. She stood there in silence before the gravestones.

"Hi, Mom and Dad..." Mara paused. She glanced down at Nightingale strapped to her belt. She took the sheathed weapon and held it tight in her hands. "I want to thank you for the birthday present. It's beautiful."

She breathed in the frigid air, then exhaled. Watching her breath, she wondered what good it was to talk out loud. Could her parents even hear her? Taking another breath, she spoke again.

"I'm sorry." She closed her eyes. "I did love Karl and wanted to save him, but I don't know anymore. Now I lost Allen forever. I wish I never met Karl or said yes to marrying him. And I never got to say goodbye."

At the corner of her eye, Mara thought she saw two people. A man and a woman stood together, smiling at their daughter. She turned her head to look at them, but the image of the two vanished. Beams of the afternoon sun shone into the charred remains of the workshop. Chickadees sang in the distance. She glanced around, sensing a calmness within her heart. Mara had a feeling they heard her.

"Goodbye, Mom and Dad," she said, then strapped Nightingale back onto her belt.

After finishing what she needed to do, Mara returned to Mirahyll. The snow fell like sparkling crystals from the sky.

Chapter Fourteen

The Discovery

On the morning of December 21, Mara woke up and joined James for breakfast. It was a quiet morning. Today was her birthday, yet she never said anything. No one else said a peep about it either. It was possible her remaining friends forgot, but it was okay. She missed thirty birthdays. With her family and close friend gone, it was not worth celebrating. Mara's birthday also coincided with the Winter Festival, but the impending apocalypse had cancelled the event. Then again, a cancelled festival also meant little to Mara since she would not be able to celebrate with family. Instead, they were searching for Aazalith so they could stop her from destroying Ardana.

Mara watched while Aspen meditated. The darkling was still as her many eyes glowed. She stayed like this for a few hours. Mara turned away briefly, but James remained to watch. He was the first to know what Aspen discovered.

When Mara returned, she saw James approaching her.

"We have some good news and some bad news," he announced. "Aspen found them."

"That's good," Mara responded. "So, what's the bad news?"

"Aazalith has partially awakened. The recent earthquake was her leaving the Dark Labyrinth. I guess it's no surprise since two seals remained when it happened, but it does make me wonder if she awoke as soon as the seals began to fail."

Mara remembered her previous encounter with the divine. While hunting the Siren, she came into contact with the creature. Aazalith opened her eyes and looked right at her.

After thinking about the memory, Mara gazed at James. "I think you're right." Then she asked, "Where is she?"

"She is deep in the ocean," the Watcher answered, rising to her feet. "As long as the final seal remains intact, she will not fully awaken."

"Okay, but this is what we want, right?" Mara asked.

"That's just the thing," James murmured. His face grew solemn.

"The final seal must fail," Aspen revealed.

The huntress gawked at the two. "I thought we weren't going to kill Morgan?"

"She will return to life as long as her soul is not absorbed," Aspen replied. "She can still help us put Amara to rest."

"This is risky," Mara argued. "We don't know what kind of destruction Aazalith will bring once awakened."

"We are running out of options," James told her. "Even with our current technology, there is no way to reach her."

"There has to be some way," Mara said, returning to her room.

Looking to her father's belongings, she reckoned there had to be something about stopping the divine without awakening her. Going through Dad's journal, Mara glanced at Nightingale. The sword seemed incomplete, thanks to the hollow opening at the pommel. Her eyes drifted back to the notes. Turning the page, she began to read an entry.

"The Thoron Sages defeated Dragon Goddess Aazalith, using a mystical rock called moonstone. Moonstone can siphon magic, ultimately removing Aazalith's soul. Upon absorbing her soul, the stone crystallized and exploded, shattering into several pieces of varying sizes."

She stared at the page with a questioning glance. Turning the page, she continued to read.

"Fearing the soul would fall into the wrong hands, our ancestors produced weapons for the Order of Aazalith. Magical daggers, mounted with moonstone, were granted to the keepers. Then there was Godstruck, forged by our ancestors?" Mara never knew she was related to those responsible for the sword's existence. Now everything became connected. "When used, the soul of Aazalith shall be removed, taking away the host's immortality."

She snapped her gaze back onto the opening in Nightingale's pommel. That was its purpose! Now she needed a moonstone. Mara took her necklace off and then unsheathed her sword, revealing the dark gold and silver blade. Taking the blue gemstone, she inserted it into Nightingale's pommel. Not only was it a perfect fit, but she also sensed a change within the sword.

The dark golden fuller was a conduit that carried magical energy, spreading it throughout the blade. The gold etchings shone in bright blue hues. She stared at Nightingale in shock while the sword came alive. Now she understood why Harold gave her a fake sword. She removed the moonstone, and the glow faded. Nightingale became an ordinary sword once again. Mara gawked at it, knowing that she now had a weapon capable of defeating Kallisto.

Mara put down the notes, sheathed Nightingale, and placed her necklace back on. She needed to tell James of her findings, so she dashed out of her room in excitement.

"James! I—"

She stopped upon noticing James with a guest. She never heard him arrive. Looking at the short and plump man, Mara recognized the snow-white hair, moustache, and beard. Mr. White stood with a frozen expression. As Mara gazed back at him, her anger began to flare.

"Mara," Mr. White began.

"Why are you here?" Mara snapped.

James glanced at her. "Yes, even I'm surprised to see him," he said calmly. "Let's hear what he has to say." He looked back at the former college professor with folded arms.

Mr. White held his hands behind his back. "Hello, Mara. It's been a while."

She kept staring at him. Despite everything, he had the nerve to show his face. "I'm amazed you are here," she said, "considering Father Vernon's arrest."

"Yes, we are well aware of his incarceration," the old gentleman said, "but the rest of us were not involved."

Mara and James exchanged glances before gazing back at him.

"So, you're telling me the Faith had nothing to do with the Blackthorn Guild?" Mara questioned. "What about those women?"

"The Faith was never involved," he insisted.

She could not believe his words. "How could you stand there and say that?" Mara gestured to James. "After what the Faith did to us?"

"Please, I'm sorry!" Mr. White pleaded. "I never meant for any of this to happen."

"I don't believe you." Mara approached him while her friends looked on.

James was worried that she would kill Mr. White.

The older man backed away in fear. "Please, I beg of you! Hear me out. I need your help once again!" Mr. White cried. "You're the only one I can rely on."

Mara stopped. She was a little surprised to hear that he needed her help again, considering they were enemies. But she was also curious. "Out with it. What do you want this time?"

Mr. White regained his composure. "Karl has been abducted again."

She folded her arms. "Again?" Mara shook her head. "I don't know. Every time you asked me to save him, someone got killed. Heru, Lady Isabella, and Anna died because of him, yet the Faith had no problem shifting all the blame onto me. Besides, shouldn't Kallisto save him? He is the reincarnation of her husband, is he not?"

Mr. White's jaw dropped. "Don't you still have feelings for him?"

James and Aspen looked at the older man, then to her. Mara gave a stunned expression.

"No," Mara replied. "How could I? Because of you, my parents…"

Mr. White appeared startled, though remained silent.

105

His reticence agitated her. Was he even sorry for what he did? Mara was not expecting an apology, for Mr. White was a devoted member of the Faith. Other thoughts went through her mind. What if this was another plot to get her captured again? Or some scheme to separate her from her friends and get them killed? Losing Allen was the breaking point. She began to move away from him. Her right hand tightened into a fist.

"I'm not saving Karl. Get someone else to do it!"

She stormed into her room and slammed the door shut. James and Aspen gazed at Mr. White. The former college professor stood dumbstruck.

* * *

Later in the evening, Mara heard a knock on the door.

"Someone came to see you," James called. "And no, it's not Mr. White."

Answering the door, she saw James on the other side. She grabbed her cape, in case she had to go anywhere. Mara left her room to greet whoever came to see her. On the way, she saw Mr. White still here. He glanced up at her as she stopped and stared at him. James caught up to her.

"Why is he still here?" Mara whispered to James.

"He's too frightened to go back," James revealed. "He fears Kallisto will kill him for failing to return with Karl."

She could have felt some pity for her former college professor, but he brought this all upon himself. In the end, she was unmoved by his plight.

Mara answered the door and saw a young man standing before her.

"Good evening, Miss Ashwood," the young man spoke with his hands behind his back. His blue eyes, black hair, and goatee were familiar to her.

"You're Morgan's butler, Kai," Mara spoke.

"That is correct," Kai replied. "My mistress has invited you to dinner." The butler gestured to a carriage already arranged for her.

Mara never expected this. Her friends expressed curiosity while Mr. White watched from the background.

"An invitation?" James asked.

The butler glanced at him. "Yes, that is correct. My apologies, but the invitation is only for Miss Ashwood."

Mr. White stormed over to them. "I wouldn't trust him," he warned.

Kai gave a dismissive expression. "It is just a dinner," he said flatly.

Mara took a step forward.

"Morgan is not to be trusted!" Mr. White cried. "She abducted Karl!"

Mara snapped her gaze onto him. She was astounded to know Karl's abductor was the original undying. A sense of dread washed over her.

"So, this is your angle?" Mara demanded. "You're trying to trick me into killing Morgan and break the final seal."

The older man gaped at her. He appeared stunned that she would implicate him of such a thing.

"I know about Kallisto's plan to awaken the divine." Mara scowled at him. "Have you no shame? You don't even care if millions die! If anything, you'll be far away in Corlin, living in a luxurious mansion while Aazalith slaughters millions!" She looked at James and Aspen. "Are you two going to be okay without me?"

Her friends nodded their heads in unison.

"Yes, we will," James replied.

"If anything happens…" Aspen gazed at Mr. White with glowing eyes. "I will turn you inside-out."

The older man gazed at the Watcher with apprehension. He seemed terrified of her claim.

Mara watched the three before storming into the carriage. She put on her hood and mask. Once settled, the butler got on top of the coach, then directed the horses to move. Leaving for Désir, Mara saw Mr. White giving chase, only to be stopped by James and Aspen. Her friends took the older man inside.

Chapter Fifteen

The Deal

Mara looked out the window, watching the winter scenery as Kai steered the horses. She had second thoughts about going alone. Though after hearing about Morgan having the commander, she needed to go there. In truth, the huntress wanted to make sure the worst-case scenario did not happen. With Morgan possessing the final seal, Mara was well aware of the target on the original undying's back.

Once they reached the manor, the carriage stopped. The door opened, revealing the butler.

"We are here," Kai said, offering his hand.

Mara took his hand before walking out into the cold. She then released it upon standing before the mansion as two other men took the coach away. The butler led her into the manor, directing her to the main living room and offering her a seat. The huntress pulled down her mask and took off her hood. She sat there and waited, unaware of the presence behind her.

"I am glad you could come," Morgan began.

Mara turned her head to see the hostess approaching her. Despite the dark veil, the huntress could see a smile on Morgan's face. The original undying appeared to be in a pleasant mood. She sat adjacent to where Mara sat. The older woman leaned over to get a closer look.

"I've heard you had a very rough time with Kallikratés," Morgan said. "It must be painful to lose loved ones. So much tragedy during a time of festivities and joy, especially during your birthday."

Mara watched her with an odd expression. She never told anyone about her birthday.

Morgan reached for Mara's left hand and touched it. "I wanted to have you over," the original undying spoke. "No one should ignore their birthday."

The huntress gazed back at her hand, sensing a strange but familiar power. She recalled the sensation before in the Dark Labyrinth.

The older woman gave a questioning look. "Or perhaps you came looking for him?"

Mara glanced back at her. "So, he is here?"

Morgan removed her hand, then reclined back in her seat. She gave a small but very confident smile. "Yes, if you wish to see him." Then she called, "Karl, my dear, please come in."

As if on command, he entered the room.

Karl walked to Morgan's side before facing the huntress. The first thing Mara noticed was his blank face and glazed eyes. At least he was not glaring, nor did he reek of alcohol. He wore an outfit similar to the butlers and servants—a white dress shirt and a black vest with golden buttons decorating it. The tie, dress pants, and shoes were all black. Morgan reached for his arm and stroked it. Karl smiled while she petted him as if he enjoyed being touched by her.

Glancing back at his face, Mara could not get over his unnatural expression. "I hear you abducted him," Mara said.

Once Morgan withdrew her hand, Karl's face reverted to a blank expression. "He came to me of his own free will," Morgan explained.

Mara pointed at him. "Then why is he in a trance?"

Morgan frowned, realizing that Mara caught on. The older woman stood up and walked past her. "Okay, perhaps I was a little dishonest," she admitted, gazing at him. "He and the Holy Blades came to Désir to capture me, and break the final seal."

The huntress shot up to her feet, staring at the older woman in shock.

"After sending his men away, I showed him the truth," said the original undying. "But he could not handle it, and Kallisto's hold over him remains strong."

Mara grew more puzzled. What did Morgan mean? The older woman gazed back at her while heading towards a hallway.

"Come with me," the hostess beckoned. "I wish to show you."

Mara followed her.

Morgan led her down the hallway, where they came to a dead end. The older woman pulled on a light fixture, and the wall opened up, revealing a new passage.

"Did Harold tell you about the Legend of Kratés?" Morgan inquired while leading her guest to a room on the other end.

Mara nodded. "He confirmed it was a fabrication. The real heroes were you and the other six, assisted by the Stone Mages, the Silver Thorns, and the Aristocracy."

"That is correct," Morgan said. "We were able to communicate with Aazalith, hoping to reason with her. The divine demanded her soul back and threatened to destroy the land. We had no choice but to stop her. With the Stone Mages' magic, seven seals were placed on her, suppressing access to Amara's soul, as well as her magic."

Stopping before the door, the hostess placed her gloved hand on the doorknob. Before opening the way, Morgan looked back at Mara.

"We were the unsung heroes the world never knew. We were feared and hated while Kallikratés lied to humanity."

The original undying opened the door to reveal a large circular room with a glass and golden casket in the centre. The contents caught Mara's attention, for there was a body submerged beneath a glowing blue liquid. The hostess gestured to Mara to take a closer look. The huntress complied and approached the casket. Her eyes went wide upon gaining a clearer image of the figure inside.

He looked almost identical to Karl, save for his slightly longer hair. His body was well built, though he was not too muscular. Her eyes drifted down to his bare chest. A tattoo began from the left side of his neck and spread over the entire length of his left arm. The strange markings were also present on the left side of his torso. She had seen the tattoos before on the labyrinth guardian. All he wore was a pair of dark blue pants with leg wrappings below the knees. Sandals adorned his bare feet. He looked as if he were merely asleep.

Mara was mystified. "That's…"

"Kratés," Morgan interrupted.

The huntress snapped her gaze onto the hostess with a dumbfounded expression. At first, she was at a loss of words but found her voice. Mara looked back at the body of the former king.

"Why is he here?"

"After neutralizing Aazalith, I returned to my domain," Morgan revealed, watching his body. "Kratés followed me home."

Mara glanced back at her. "Did he know who you were?" She saw Morgan nodding. "You let him into your home?"

"Yes," Morgan replied. "Kallisto abandoned him while Aazalith tore their palace down. Thanks to us, he survived but became upset by Kallisto's betrayal. The tension between the two had finally broken. He never wanted to see her again and became my lover once more."

"You let him back into your life? After what he did to you? To Amara?"

"He changed," Morgan insisted.

"I find it hard to believe."

"Please, listen and understand," the older woman pleaded. "After regaining his senses, Kratés wanted to make things right. But Kallisto found us. She stabbed Kratés with a keeper's dagger, which once belonged to Harold. I believe she kept it, in case he turned on her." Morgan kept her eyes on the empty vessel. "He didn't need to die. The dagger could make him human again, but Kallisto could not stand to see us together. So, she took him away again by stabbing him in the heart, robbing him of his life. She fled with his share of the divine's soul before I could defeat her. Since then, neither Kallisto or her followers dared to return to Désir until recent times."

Mara did not know what to think. It was much to take. She looked down and saw all the proof she needed to believe Morgan. The scar from the dagger was almost faded, but it remained visible. She stared at Kratés' body for a while before being escorted to dinner.

* * *

Dinner was ready by the time Mara and Morgan arrived at the table. While being served, Mara glanced up from her plate to see a servant come with a different dish. With so much food on the table, she could not eat it all. Staring down at her dinner plate, she began to think of her plan.

The original undying watched her.

"There appears to be something on your mind," Morgan said. "Did you truly come here to rescue Karl?"

Mara looked back at her. "No," she admitted. "If anything, I was more worried about you, possessing the final seal and such."

"Is that so?" Morgan asked. "How sweet…"

"We have a plan," the huntress revealed. "We're going to confront Aazalith and put Amara to rest. We are going to break this vicious cycle."

"We?"

Mara nodded. "With the three of us combined, we can do this. Aspen already agreed to help."

"And now you're asking me?" Morgan questioned.

"Yes," Mara replied.

"You're not going to honour Harold's wish?"

"I already found the others," Mara said. "I got captured while trying to save Allen and was tossed back into the Dark Labyrinth. While trying to retrieve his body, I found them and absorbed their souls. Ten victims—more than half never reached adulthood, and one hadn't been born yet."

"I know," Morgan responded.

Mara gave a curious expression. "How do you know?"

The older woman gazed at her. "I saw them myself."

"You have?" Mara soon realized what was going on. "The apparition—that's you?"

Morgan nodded. "Psychic projection is one of my powers."

The huntress kept staring at her. "You've been watching me all along?"

"Ever since I discovered you were cursed," Morgan replied. "When I first saw you, you were frail, and your soul was a tiny spark. At first, I could make myself invisible to you. But with each soul claimed, you grew stronger." She changed the subject. "I knew of Kallisto's hatred towards me, but never thought she would stoop so low to murder innocent girls." Keeping a cool and calm demeanour, Morgan watched her. "Very well, I'll help you. I will also aid you in stopping Kallisto and the Faith."

Mara's eyes grew wide. "Really?" Then her excitement faded when she wondered about the final seal. "But to make Aazalith appear…"

"I can break the final seal myself. I shall die, then return to life." Morgan paused. "Although I will admit—I did not expect your unwillingness to slay me."

She watched Morgan. "Considering the circumstances, I don't think you want to die."

"What circumstances?"

"The fact that you have the perfectly preserved body of your former lover."

Morgan froze. It seemed like she never expected Mara to say those words. After a few seconds, a smile crept upon her face.

"You are much more observant than I thought," she said. "I plan to resurrect Kratés, but I'm missing one thing to complete the ritual."

"What is that?" Mara asked.

"His soul," Morgan answered. "So, it was very convenient for Karl to come to my domain."

Those words caught the huntress' attention. "Are you going to kill him?"

"I just need to stop his heart for five minutes. Believing Karl has died, Kratés will return to his own body. Not only does the alchemic potion preserve him, but it'll also draw his soul back. He will return as a human. Once Kratés has been resurrected, I shall revive Karl. No harm will come to him. You may be unaware, but there are two souls within Karl—Kratés' as well as his own. Kratés was quite special, being able to father many children. His spirit can ride the current of his bloodline, allowing him to be reborn within one of his descendants."

"How do you intend to do this?" Mara questioned.

"With a spell," Morgan replied. "However, his mind must be free, and Kallisto's hold over him remains strong."

"How long will it take to free him?"

"I cannot say, but the longer he is away from her, the better off he will be." Morgan fixated her gaze upon Mara. "Once I free him, I shall return Karl to you."

Mara frowned.

The older woman took notice. "This is what you desire?"

Mara remained quiet. It was Morgan's turn to frown.

"You two were together," the older woman said. "You were engaged to be married."

Morgan's words reminded the huntress of Karl's proposal in the garden.

"I know," Mara said. "When I entered a relationship with Karl, it created a rift between Dad and me. If I never met him, none of these things would have happened."

Morgan watched her. "When Kratés betrayed me, my feelings for him had diminished as well. But he regained his mind and begged for my forgiveness. Karl, on the other hand, has not been fortunate."

"What do you mean?" Mara questioned.

"Even though a small fragment is enough to make him powerful and immortal, it's not enough to let him keep his mind. I can revert him to his former self."

Mara pondered her words. How was Morgan going to free Karl? Other thoughts surfaced in her mind. Should she let Morgan resurrect the former king? It would be weird to meet the one who harmed Amara. And what about Mr. White? He likely remained at James' home, still waiting on her to save the commander.

"What will you do?" asked the original.

Mara gazed at her. "Let's make a deal. I'll let you keep Karl for Kratés' resurrection if it makes you happy. And I want you to revert Karl to his former self. If you can remove the divine's soul from him, it'll be one less opponent to deal with."

Morgan smiled. "Very well."

While eating a slab of roast beef, the huntress could not help but quiver. It was rare to eat a well-cooked meal. When she glanced up from her plate, the huntress noticed the looks of the hostess and the servants. Mara figured she had transformed again.

"Sorry," she murmured, concentrating on changing back.

Morgan stared at her, then smiled. "That is perfectly fine," she told her. "I had seen it before in Thoron Witches, though it's been thousands of years since I've been there. To be honest, I do miss Thoron."

Mara gazed back at her. "Thanks for the birthday dinner."

The original undying nodded, and they continued to eat.

* * *

Once dinner was over, Mara was ready to return to James' place. She put her hood and mask back on while heading for the exit. The original undying accompanied her.

"I hope you had a good time," Morgan said.

She looked back at her. "Yes, I did."

Morgan smiled. "I'll need a few more days. Once ready, I will come to you."

"Okay, I'll see you then."

Once Morgan left her alone, Kai appeared to escort her out of the manor.

"Please wait here," said the butler. "The carriage will be here soon."

He left to get the coach.

While waiting, Mara heard the faint groans of a man. At first, she thought nothing of it until she heard it again. Turning around, she saw a window. The room light was on. As she came closer to investigate, the groans grew louder as if a man was experiencing pleasure. She had second thoughts and decided not to go any further, remembering her night in Har' Yhan. Before turning away, she saw Morgan's shadow. Growing more curious, Mara gazed through the window to see Morgan and Karl together.

Karl was lying in bed, naked and paralyzed. Morgan was still clothed while approaching him. She began to remove her veil and hood. Mara watched while her older look-alike cast her gaze upon Karl, keeping him paralyzed. She was unaware of Mara's presence as she kept her eyes locked with Karl's. Then her face transformed. Her eyes glowed blue while her scleras darkened. The mermaid-like creature emerged as blue and green scales decorated her body. Karl remained paralyzed while watching her. Parting her full lips, Morgan released a soft tune. The notes passing through were like warm honey.

Karl grew more relaxed. His brow became smooth as his eyes were further glazed over. The original undying approached him while the mesmerizing sound flowed through her lips and invaded his ears. Coming closer, she removed her clothes. The dark bustle dress fell to the ground around her ankles. Morgan moved with grace and fluid, walking over her dress without tripping. Once she reached him, she placed her hands on his thighs. They roamed up his body, making him aroused. Then she mounted him, taking his gender into her own.

Realizing what they were going to do, Mara looked away. She heard them groaning with pleasure. It was just like Har' Yhan all over again. She wondered about Morgan's plan of opening Karl's mind. How was this supposed to free him? Or was this something else? She remembered her confession to Morgan. Did she just hand over Karl's heart to another? Then again, did she ever have his heart?

Gazing back, she watched as Karl rose and held Morgan in his embrace, never letting go as he thrust into her repeatedly. Even the way he kissed seemed genuine. Something in Mara began to change. No longer did she see Morgan and Karl, but Thalia and Kratés. She thought about the tale of the two lovers torn apart. And they were finally reunited. Where did this leave Mara, who watched as her former fiancé made love to another? However, it wasn't just some woman. It was Thalia, who created the reincarnations, including Mara. Karl once said she was an incomplete copy and nothing more.

Deep down, Mara remained upset at the sight of them together. Even though her feelings for Karl waned, and her relationship with him had cost her a dear friend. Yet she could not shake off the feelings of betrayal.

But Mara needed to think about the bigger picture. They had an agreement, and this was their best chance of saving the world. And Kallisto no longer had her commander.

She moved away from the window and waited for the carriage to take her home. In time, the transport arrived. Mara boarded it and returned to Mirahyll.

Chapter Sixteen

True Colours

Mara sat in the carriage while being taken home. The image of seeing Morgan and Karl together was burned deep into her mind. Though the further she travelled away from Désir, the less upset she felt. She was still weighing the pros and cons of leaving him with the original undying. It was one powerful enemy out of the way, but Morgan might have gained a new lover if her plan to resurrect Kratés failed. Any future visits could be awkward.

As soon as the carriage arrived at James' place, she got out and dashed to the door. As she drew closer, the door opened to reveal James. He stood at the side and invited her in.

"How did your night go?" James inquired.

Without saying a word, Mara stormed past him and entered his house. James looked shocked and concerned. Mara walked into the living room and saw Mr. White. The former college professor watched her as she stopped and stared at him.

"You came back," Mr. White spoke.

"What happened?" James asked, walking up to her.

Aspen stood in the distance.

Mara pulled down her mask and glanced at everyone. "I made a deal with Morgan," she said. "She agreed to help us, but needs a few days."

While this was encouraging news, they grew curious about the deal.

Mr. White approached her. "Did you see him? Is Karl there?"

She looked at the older man. Mentioning Karl's name made the huntress think of the last time she saw the commander.

"Yeah, I did."

"Why didn't you save him? He's in danger!"

Mara grew annoyed with Mr. White, who still maintained that she had to save his ward.

"What sort of deal did you make?" James questioned.

The huntress dropped her scowl and gazed at her friend.

"For helping us, Morgan will keep Karl for now," Mara revealed. "After we deal with Aazalith, Amara, and Kallisto, she will let him go."

"How could you?" Mr. White cried.

Everyone watched as the former college professor lifted a quivering finger, pointing at the huntress in an accusing manner.

Mr. White glared at her. "How could you side with that devilish woman and let her have her way with Karl?"

The scowl returned to Mara's face. "Then would you like to explain why the Faith made up the Legend of Kratés?"

Mr. White's face turned pale as he dropped his menacing gaze. He grew silent, showing his awareness that the tale was false.

Mara gazed at her friends. "Kratés never fought Aazalith. Kallisto killed him!"

James looked stunned while Aspen froze. Even Mr. White's mouth dropped open.

"What happened?" James questioned.

"Thalia and Kratés were lovers before Kallisto stole the soul of Aazalith," Mara said. "At the time of the calamity, Kallisto abandoned him. But he survived. Recognizing Morgan as Thalia, he followed her home, where they became lovers once again. But Kallisto found them and killed Kratés. She stabbed him with a moonstone-enchanted dagger, ending his life. She stole his share of Aazalith's soul and fled before Morgan could kill her."

James stood frozen. "The Legend of Kratés is a lie," he murmured. "I wish Allen could hear this..." He looked at Mr. White, then folded his arms. "Speaking of lies and truths, we discovered some things from him."

Mara figured this, yet wanted to know what they had discovered. "Like what?"

"Two days ago, Commander White led a group of Holy Blades to Désir, intending to capture Morgan and break the final seal," Aspen revealed.

"Two days ago?" Mara questioned. "I was dealing with the Blackthorns." She turned her scrutinizing gaze at Mr. White. "So, they sold those women to create a distraction as well?"

"Yes," Aspen replied. "However, they underestimated the original undying's power. Morgan enslaved them. She kept the commander and sent the Holy Blades back to Golden Mountain, where they eventually snapped out of the trance." The Watcher gazed at the former college professor. "Yesterday, Morgan appeared before Kallisto to explain why the Holy Blades returned without their commander. The goddess demanded his return, but Morgan claimed he had no desire to leave. Kallisto attempted to strike her down, but the original undying used a psychic projection. In anger, Kallisto ordered the execution of the commander's group for losing him. Then she ordered Mr. White to retrieve him or else he'll suffer the same fate."

Mara gave a wry smile while folding her arms. To be honest, she found it amusing. Morgan was toying with the goddess. No wonder why she was in a happy mood when Mara visited her.

The older man looked at the huntress with pleading eyes. "You must help me. Who knows what she will do to him!"

The smile faded from Mara's face. She closed her eyes. "I already know what Morgan is planning for Karl."

Everyone watched her.

"What is she going to do?" James asked.

She let out a sigh and opened her eyes. "She's going to resurrect Kratés."

James and Mr. White gaped at her.

"That's impossible!" Mr. White cried.

"I saw the body." Gazing at Mr. White, Mara saw his mouth drop open in shock. She then revealed, "Morgan needs Karl to complete the resurrection. She has no intention to harm him, only to stop his heart long enough for Kratés' soul to leave his body. After Kratés returns to life, she will revive Karl."

"Really?" James questioned.

Mara nodded. "That is our deal."

"How could you?" Mr. White demanded.

Everyone looked at him.

The older man pointed at Mara again. "You must go back there and save him!"

Mara rolled her eyes. "I'm not saving him."

"You must!"

His sudden outburst took Mara by surprise. She could not understand his aggression but grew to a point where she had enough. The huntress stormed up to Mr. White with glowing eyes.

"Why should I save him?" Mara demanded. "Because of you, I lost everything! Then you used me, even though I saved you and your damn ward." She pointed to the door. "Now, get out!" The huntress kept scowling at him. "I never want to see you again!"

She turned her back and folded her arms. The older man's mouth dropped open. He looked as if he didn't know how to retaliate.

"But, Mara," he squeaked.

She ignored him, not caring for anything else he had to say.

Aspen watched him. The eyes on her visor began to glow.

"She is watching us," Aspen said.

The older man gazed back at the Watcher with horror. Mara turned to look at her. She was perplexed but noticed Mr. White's face when she glanced at him. James also took notice and dashed into another room. He returned with a small black box. Mara watched while he placed it on the ground in front of them.

"What are you doing?" Mara asked.

In silence, James activated it. The box opened up, revealing a glowing blue gem inside. The glow grew brighter, releasing a powerful flash of light, blinding them for a short while.

When her vision cleared, Mara saw circular runes on the floor glowing in a bright blue colour. Then they faded away. She looked at James.

"What's going on?" Mara inquired. "Was that...?"

"Anti-magic field generator," James replied. "While we're unable to use any form of magic in the generated field, it also prevents any outside magic."

"Like magic used to spy," Aspen added, gazing at Mr. White. "He was linked to Kallisto, allowing her to spy on us through him. She was watching us the entire time."

Mara gawked at Aspen before turning her attention to the former college professor. The huntress looked daggers at him.

"You knew the whole time?" Mara questioned sharply.

"What was I to say to you?" The older man began to tremble. "In case you haven't realized, Miss Ashwood, I am kept on a short leash! They already suspect me of conspiring against them."

Mara grew bewildered. "What do you mean they suspect you?"

"For many years, I watched Karl turn into a monster," Mr. White confessed. "No longer can I stand back and watch!"

Mara gave a strange expression. It was as if the older man became a different person. She folded her arms. "What are you talking about?"

"Do you remember the time when Karl fell victim to Anna?" Mr. White inquired.

The huntress nodded. "Yes, I do."

Mara recalled the day Mr. White begged her to save Commander White from Anna. It was a difficult rescue with the first attempt ending in death. The second attempt was possible with the help of Allen and the Watcher.

"I believe that was the real Karl," the older man said. "After the incident, he became a different man. He was free before he saw Kallisto again. And when he challenged you at the temple, he regained his mind temporarily."

"Must have been the generator the Holy Blades stole earlier," James said. "It might have weakened Kallisto's hold over him for a brief moment." He gazed at the Watcher. "It may also explain why Aspen couldn't teleport into the temple."

Mara glanced at the middle-aged doctor with intrigue before looking back at the former college professor.

Mr. White gazed at her with a softer expression. "I want to save him, and I need your help."

The huntress furrowed her eyebrows. "Well, if you want him to be free, then he's better off being with Morgan. She's attempting to free Karl from Kallisto's control."

"It may not be enough," Mr. White claimed. "Thalia's power was divided among her reincarnations. Thus, she may not succeed."

"You have a better idea?" Mara asked.

"Yes, I do." He looked at the Watcher. "I know what you are," Mr. White addressed Aspen. "I know it was you who sealed away Mara's memories and restored her humanity. If you can do that for her, then Karl can still be saved."

Mara and Aspen exchanged glances before looking back at Mr. White.

"Aspen?" Mara asked the older man. "Why her and not the original undying?"

"I am part-darkling," Aspen answered. "The experiments augmented the latent psychic powers within me."

The former college professor cleared his throat, then gazed at Mara. "Will you please save him?"

Mara folded her arms. "I still don't know if I should trust you."

"I don't blame you," he told her. "Still, I need you to place your trust in me again."

"Why should I?"

"I'm leaving the Faith of Kallikratés. I shall leave for Corlin, and take Karl with me once we free him. I know of your plan to slay the goddess, and I wish you well in your endeavour."

The three friends looked at him in confusion.

"You have no problem with me killing Kallisto?" Mara questioned.

"That is correct," Mr. White said. "As I've said before, I can no longer watch as his soul darkens." Then he revealed, "When Karl was five years old, his real father passed away. My family took him in, raising him as one of our own. Despite the greatest privileges and the best education, it did not change the fact that he was from one of the old bloodlines. Started by Kratés when he was human."

Mara gave a peculiar look. "You just admitted to Kratés being human."

The older man cleared his throat, then placed his hands behind his back. "That is correct."

"Isn't that going against your beliefs?"

Mr. White walked past her. "Maybe, if it had anything to do with my beliefs or even religion." He looked back at Mara. "You, of all people, know that the Faith has very little to do with religion and more to do with power."

"Can't argue with that logic," Mara mused. "Still, you haven't given me a reason why I should help you. You can't expect me to do this out of the kindness of my own heart."

"I have something you want."

"Like what?" Mara asked.

"A way to stop Thalia from taking over," Mr. White said.

She stared at him in shock. "What?"

Mara glanced at Aspen, but the latter just gazed back at her.

Mr. White saw this. "I'll tell you more once you return with Karl. Do we have a deal?"

Mara frowned. "Do I have a choice?"

The older man sighed. "I'll give you an hour to decide." Then he went to sit in the living room and picked up a book to read.

She looked back at Aspen. "You couldn't read his mind?"

James approached them. "Sorry, this generator is fully functional. And it will block all of Aspen's powers if she's in it." He moved the device closer to the former college professor so he could have some protection from the watchful eyes of the goddess.

"It'll be a while before I can regain my powers," Aspen explained. "I must avoid further contact with the anti-magic field."

"Oh, I see," the huntress murmured. "Guess I have to make a choice."

Aspen looked at Mr. White. "I don't know if he was telling the truth, but it seems too much of a coincidence for him to bring this up." She gazed back at Mara. "If you decide to do this, Morgan may be unwilling to part with Karl. You did make a deal with her."

"I don't want to go back on it," Mara grumbled. "Especially since she's willing to help us."

While turning away, Mara sniffed a strange odour. At first, it smelled like chocolate and flowers before becoming the stench of blood and smoke. The scent grew overpowering. She looked back and saw the whole room on fire! Her eyes went wide with shock. The suffocating smoke caused Mara to collapse.

Chapter Seventeen

Morgan's Salvation

"Mara," Aspen called. "Mara, wake up."

Mara's eyes fluttered open. The first thing she saw was Aspen staring at her. The huntress was in her room. James and Mr. White were also present. She looked around. The Moen Residence was no longer on fire.

"What's going on?" Mara asked. She glanced around again. "What happened to the fire?"

Everyone looked baffled.

"What fire?" Aspen questioned.

James gave a concerned look. "You blacked out for a couple of hours. Are you okay?"

Mara sat up. "There was a fire," she insisted. "The house was burning."

James shook his head. "There's no fire. Everything is fine."

They heard a knock on the door.

"Who could it be at this hour?" James wondered out loud. Even though it was past midnight, he decided to answer the door.

Mara got up and followed him to the front entrance. Every step she took, the knocking grew more urgent. When James opened the door, a young black-haired man tumbled through. He collapsed as soon as he came in. The young man was covered in ashes while his clothes reeked of smoke. James crouched down to turn him over.

Mara recognized his face. "Kai? What are you doing here?"

Morgan's butler gazed up at her while coughing. "Miss Ashwood," Kai spoke. "Milady is in danger! The manor is burning!"

Everyone was stunned to hear this. Mara thought about the disturbing vision, wondering if it was a warning or a distress signal.

"How did this happen?" Mara demanded.

"Karl stabbed Lady Morgan," according to the butler. "Somehow, he overcame her power and retrieved one of the weapons we confiscated from him. Milady fled into the woods. We tried to stop him, but he killed many of us. He set fire to the manor and went after her."

The huntress gaped at him.

"Kallisto might be responsible," Aspen suggested. "Rather than going after Morgan personally, she took control of Karl and made him attack her."

Mara snapped her gaze onto Mr. White. "Can Kallisto do this? Control a person's mind from a distance?"

The older man gawked at her with a slack jaw. Even he was surprised by Kallisto's actions.

Mara shook her head. Morgan was in grave danger.

"I have to find her," Mara murmured, rising to her feet. She went to her room to retrieve her cloak and Nightingale.

"I will go with you," the Watcher said.

James looked at Kai. "He's suffering from smoke inhalation," he said. "I'll take him to the hospital to make sure he's fine." He helped the young black-haired man to his feet.

Mr. White took a step towards the door. "I'm going to look for Karl." Then he left.

Mara heard the older man's plans while walking out of her room. Watching him leave, she wondered what would happen when he found Karl.

The Watcher approached her. "We can teleport there. My powers have returned." Aspen held out her hand.

Mara took her hand, and they disappeared in a flash of light.

* * *

When the light dissipated, the two stood before Morgan's manor. Ash and snow fell around them while flames engulfed the mansion. The heat of the fire threatened to burn them should they come too close. The scent of smoke and blood was overpowering. Mara was surprised at the carnage Karl had caused. Bodies were scattered around, but Morgan was not among them.

"I don't see her anywhere," Mara said, gazing at Aspen.

The Watcher lifted her right hand and pointed past her. The huntress turned to see traces of blood going into the woods. Suppressing her dread, Mara began to follow the trail. The Watcher accompanied her.

"Morgan?" Mara called. But she got no reply.

"She is ahead," the Watcher said, "but her vitals are waning."

During their search, they discovered a green dagger with a golden hilt. They stopped and studied the blade.

"There's blood," Mara said. The huntress had seen the dagger before, growing aware that Kallikratés had been responsible. She lifted her gaze to the dark forest path. The blood remained visible on the frozen ground. Mara rose to her feet as they resumed their search.

"Morgan, where are you?" Mara called again.

The lack of replies was not a good sign. Morgan's injuries had to be very significant. The two wandered deeper, searching for the original undying. The air was still as the snow fell in silence. It was then a weak moan drew both of their attention. They looked ahead and found someone lying on the ground.

"Morgan!" Mara cried, running to her.

Morgan was barely recognizable. The black veil had been removed, revealing pale skin and blackened veins. Upon closer inspection, two vertical slits sat on her chest where the poison entered. Black ooze seeped from the wounds as well as her mouth. The snow was stained black around the fallen undying.

The older woman stared up at the sky, appearing to be dead. She switched her gaze onto Mara, realizing that she was not alone. "Oh, has the little wife returned to save her husband?"

Confused, Mara shook her head.

"No?" Morgan asked. "Are you the sweet songbird who was silenced and driven to suicide?"

Mara shook her head again.

Morgan frowned. Tears leaked from her eyes as she grew weaker. "What about the kind herbalist, murdered by those she helped?"

The Watcher looked at Morgan, then to Mara. "She is talking about Evelyn, Aria, and Madeline—the undying whose souls you absorbed."

Mara removed her hood and pulled down her mask. "No, it's me. Mara." She glanced down at Morgan's body. "I heard what happened."

Morgan watched her for a while before giving a weak laugh. "I'm afraid I underestimated Kallisto." She coughed up some blood. "I don't think we'll be able to keep our agreement. Everything I worked for is gone."

The Watcher gazed down at the original undying. "She is dying."

"She'll come back to life, right?" Mara asked. "She is the original."

"It wants my soul," Morgan said just above a whisper.

Mara was baffled by her words. "What are you talking about?"

"It took all of my powers, and now it wants my life." Morgan's skin began to decay.

Mara looked horrified. "What is it?" She surveyed the area around the original undying. "I don't see it."

Morgan lifted her left arm, reaching for the huntress' sword. "Kill me."

Unsheathing Nightingale, Mara gazed at the blade before looking at the older woman.

"What about you?"

"You must claim my soul," the original undying insisted. "If my soul is lost, so shall all your hopes to lift this curse."

Mara gaped at Morgan. "What about—"

"No, listen to me," Morgan interrupted. "This is a fate I would not wish on anyone." Then, "I wanted to be with Kratés, but we could never be together. So, I planned to take the soul of Aazalith for myself."

Mara looked puzzled. "Why?"

"I sinned by stealing the rose. The Thoron Sages would never help me, but I knew they wanted the soul back. If you wish to be free of this curse, reclaim the soul of Aazalith. Trade it for the rose." Morgan looked around. "This is where I created the reincarnations. I had cast Banish to free my soul from my own body, but I never meant to kill them." Tears continued to fall from her eyes. "They captured me and planned to send me back. I had no choice."

Mara gave a sympathetic look. "Morgan, it's okay."

"No, it's not," Morgan argued. "I became a monster, the very thing people saw me as—a witch and a succubus. I know you saw me take Karl. You must hate me."

Mara froze, then regained her composure. "No, I made myself clear. My feelings for him are not as strong anymore. I lost so much because I loved him."

"Love... I tried to remind him of the love he once had. I wanted to save both him and Kratés, but I failed." She struggled to breathe. "Please end it."

Morgan closed her eyes and lost consciousness. Her body was shutting down. Mara and Aspen knew she would not last long. Taking Nightingale, Mara positioned the sword over her chest, ready to pierce her heart. Morgan released a loud gasp while the huntress put an end to her suffering. The original undying's eyes were wide as a glowing orb emerged from her chest. A smile formed on Morgan's face upon seeing her soul rising from her body. Tears poured from her eyes as she glanced back at Mara. It was over.

"Save him," Morgan whispered her last words, then closed her eyes forever.

Death and decay reached her face. Within seconds, Morgan became a dried mummified corpse. Unlike the previous undying Mara slew, the original was unable to keep her human form. The body was bereft of blood, and her skin was dry and brittle. Not only was it disturbing to see Morgan like this, but it also reminded Mara of the sealed undying. She reckoned the poison dagger was responsible for the state of the corpse. Mara glanced up at the glowing orb.

"You did the right thing," Aspen said. "Now, claim her soul."

Mara lifted her hand and touched the orb. As soon as it shot into her, the familiar jolt of pain and the burning sensation returned. This time, it was more intense. Mara collapsed and cried.

Aspen held out her hand. "Are you okay?"

Mara could not hear her as a seizure took hold. For a brief moment, she found herself standing in a vast meadow where wildflowers bloomed. Some of the flowers glowed in the moonlight. A sea of stars flooded the night sky. The moon was close, revealing every crater and detail. Towering mountains capped with snow stood before her. A mysterious blue glow sat on top of one of the peaks. Not too far into the forest was a little house obscured by trees.

It was very similar to what Morgan had. Before the house was a woman in white—the same one Mara saw before. The woman did not seem to notice her while staring up at the moon. After a few seconds, she looked at Mara. She froze upon seeing the woman's gaze on her. The huntress blinked a few times, and the woman disappeared. Mara was back in the woods again.

In the distance, someone approached them. At first, Mara could not tell who it was since her vision remained blurry. As her vision cleared, she saw a man walking towards her. He stopped and picked up the dagger. Green eyes glared back at her. It was Commander White, who hid nearby and saw everything. He wore his commander's garb, and all of his weapons were in his possession.

He began to approach them. Mara tried to get up but was too weak to stand. Aspen stood between them. Commander White didn't care. Seeing the look on his face, Mara knew that he intended to kill them both. She took deep breaths while her right hand tightened into a fist. She pushed her hands against the frozen ground and forced herself to stand. As soon as Mara rose to her feet, a strange sensation rushed through her head. Intense vertigo almost made her collapse, but she remained standing.

Without warning, her body took a step forward. Mara was stunned. No longer was she in control. Even Aspen took notice. Mara wanted to ask what was going on, yet could not move her lips. Her body took a few steps and stopped. Her eyes remained on the commander, who was still approaching them. From the corner of her eye, Mara saw her right hand rising, her palm facing inward. She kept her glare on him and closed her hand as if she were gripping something invisible. Another unknown force flowed through her.

Commander White stopped and gripped the side of his head with his free hand. He hissed in pain while his face twisted in agony. Mara had no clue what was going on.

"Mara," Aspen called, but Mara could not respond.

The commander removed his hand to reveal a bloody palm. Blood seeped from his ears. He looked back at her in bewilderment as his body trembled. Commander White dropped the dagger, then fell to his knees. He clutched his head and released a pathetic cry. His face grew more twisted with pain. It was an expression Mara had never seen since his abduction by Anna. He could not bear it anymore and began to scream. Tears leaked from his eyes.

Mr. White showed up. The round nobleman saw them and approached. He expressed surprise and horror at seeing the raw emotion radiating from his ward. He gazed at Mara with a look of dread.

"Are you doing this?" Mr. White questioned.

"Mara, you need to stop," Aspen told her.

She understood their concerns, but could not stop whatever was happening. Commander White's screams intensified as he clutched his head tighter. His fingernails dug into his scalp in an attempt to tear his head open. He stared back at Mara while his face remained twisted in agony. Tears spilled from his eyes as blood poured from his ears. Mr. White and Aspen looked back at her, begging and demanding for her to stop.

Mara tried with all her might to regain some form of control. Her mouth trembled. "I… I can't control… my body."

The older man stared at her in shock. "What do you mean?"

The Watcher stepped in front of her. "Thalia is taking over!"

Glancing at Aspen, Mara saw her reflection in the visor. No longer were her eyes brown, but bright blue. Mara's fears had come to life! The small amount of control she regained was fading fast. She tried to focus, yet the sounds of the commander's cries and the shouts of Mr. White and Aspen blended into a single noise. It prevented Mara from concentrating. Everything spun around her like a whirlwind. She wished she could tell them to stop, but no longer did she have any control over her mouth.

"Evelyn!"

It went quiet. The force possessing her weakened, to be replaced by another. Strong emotions of sorrow filled her mind. Mara wanted to cry, though she did not know why. Even Mr. White and Aspen stopped. All three looked at Commander White, who was on his knees. He removed his blood-stained hands from his head. There was a trail from his ears, down the sides of his face, and even down his neck. Even his clothes were stained. The commander raised his hands and gazed at her with pleading eyes.

"Evelyn, I'm sorry!" More tears spilled from his eyes. "I never meant to hurt you. Please forgive me!"

Mara stared at him in confusion. It was as if he were a different person. She wanted to say something, but could not control her mouth. However, whatever possessed her could and uttered out a name.

"Karl…"

Mara collapsed. Before blacking out, she saw Commander White also falling to the ground.

Chapter Eighteen

The Final Truth

Mara's eyes fluttered open on the morning of December 22. She groaned in pain, not wanting to get out of bed. Through the haze, the huntress spotted a dark bustle dress.

"Morgan," Mara called. She knew this had to be either a dream or a paranormal vision. She blinked a few times, seeing Aspen standing before her. Mara gazed at her and groaned again. "That was awful."

"Which part?" Aspen asked. "Being set ablaze? Or being possessed?"

Mara then glanced down at her body to see that she remained in control. The huntress began to remember what transpired the previous night. Morgan was the original undying and possessed the last seal.

Then the huntress gazed out the window. Much to her surprise, everything appeared okay. Everyone went about their everyday business, unaware of the great beast's unsealing. In truth, Mara believed the divine would awaken and destroy Ardana by now.

She looked back at Aspen.

"How long was I out?"

"All night and most of the morning," Aspen answered.

"My head is still pounding." As Mara sat up, her body protested against every move she made. Looking down again, she discovered that she remained dressed.

"I brought you here," Aspen said, "but I can see sleeping off the pain offered little help."

Mara lifted her gaze to Aspen, as the latter stared back.

"I'll admit I didn't know what to expect," said the Watcher, "if you would remain yourself."

"I could feel Thalia taking over. Her power flowed right through me. I could only watch." Mara then recalled what happened to the commander. "Did I gain her power?"

She looked at the crossbow on the dresser. Lifting her right hand, she tried to mimic Thalia. Mara focused for the next few seconds, but the crossbow would not budge. She furrowed her eyebrows, trying to move the object with her mind. After several moments of concentrating, the crossbow rose into the air and floated towards her. Her eyes widened as her jaw dropped. It was working; the weapon was floating to her! Before she could reach it, Aspen stretched out her hand and grasped the handle. Mara watched the crossbow in confusion, then realized what happened. The huntress stared back at the Watcher, growing very disappointed.

"It seems you do not have direct access to Thalia's power," Aspen said. "I suspect she needs to possess you." She handed the crossbow back to Mara.

Mara looked discouraged. "Really?"

The Watcher glanced at the door. "They knew this would happen." Aspen looked back at her. "The commander and his guardian are here."

"What? Why?" Then Mara remembered. "Oh, Mr. White promised to tell me how to stop Thalia from taking over. But what about her powers?"

"Why do you think he knew of a way to stop her?" Aspen asked.

Mara took a deep breath. "Because the Faith is seeking to stop her return." Then she asked, "You think he should not be trusted?"

"He has not been fully honest with you." The Watcher walked ahead. "Follow me."

Reaching the doorway, Aspen turned around and gestured to the door, as if Mara should be the one to open it. The huntress gave a questioning glance, even though she complied.

Upon entering the living room, Mara found the commander strapped to a chair by the wrists and ankles. An additional strap wrapped around his chest for reinforcement. An anti-magic field generator was nearby and active, containing him within the circle. She noticed and glanced back at Aspen. The Watcher did not follow, for she would lose her powers. Mara, on the other hand, did not care. She had little to lose. They were the only ones in the room at the moment.

Gazing back at Commander White, she approached him. Never once did he react to her presence. The commander just sat there in silence, staring ahead with glazed eyes. A blank expression adorned his frozen face. Mara watched him in confusion as she came closer. She stood beside him, but nothing happened. Taking her hand, Mara waved it in front of his face but got nothing from him.

"What's wrong with him?" Mara asked. "He's just like Mom."

"Do you remember what happened last night?" Aspen asked.

"Thalia took over and attacked him." Mara watched him. "There was blood everywhere. It looked like his head was about to explode. Then…" The huntress paused. "He called me…" She looked back at Aspen.

"Thalia broke Kallisto's hold on him," the Watcher revealed. "As Morgan, she could not do this on her own. But through you, she could, since you possess most of her soul."

"Okay," Mara responded, "but why is he like this?"

"He remembers everything, and the guilt overwhelmed him. He regained consciousness earlier but has been like this ever since. Mr. White wants to erase Karl's memories of his time serving Kallisto. He believes it will help him."

"You agreed to do this?" Mara inquired.

"Yes, but to help him, I must link with his mind," the Watcher said. "While gazing into his mind, I learned about the basilisk blade he used on Morgan. It is a dagger coated with a powerful poison. The Faith designed this weapon to weaken the undying." She glanced down. "The sealed undying, you encountered, had these embedded in them."

Mara gave a peculiar look. "I never told you about the dagger."

"I am the Watcher," Aspen responded. "I read your mind earlier and learned what you witnessed. I could imagine they suffered tremendously. All they could do was die over and over again."

After hearing the Watcher's words, Mara thought about the original undying in her last moments. "And the same thing happened to Morgan."

"The dagger weakened her, but it was not the cause of death."

Mara glanced at her in confusion. "So, something was trying to kill her and claim her soul?"

"I could detect a presence very close as if it were attached to her."

The huntress was intrigued. "Are you saying there is a Grim Reaper?"

"When I lived in Thoron, many had claimed to see such a creature," Aspen said. "Though I have never seen it myself."

The thought made Mara's skin crawl to know they encountered some unseen entity last night. It also made her wonder if she was right to take Morgan's soul. She wanted to be free of her curse, but at what cost? What if she angered this unknown creature?

Mara looked back at the commander and changed the subject. They had other things to worry about now. "So, about erasing his memories—will this help him?"

"Yes, but not until you learned the truth," Aspen told her.

Mara glanced at her. "What are you talking about?"

"Mr. White kept many things from you, and he had no intentions to tell you. In conscience, I cannot do this until you know the truth."

"What truth?"

"Kallikratés and the White Family orchestrated the death of Karl's father, to make sure he could not flee Ardana with his son," Aspen said. "The Faith put Karl in the care of the Whites. However, nobles looked down upon him, knowing his background as a commoner. His adopted sisters and brother despised him because they had to share their inheritance. The father and mother never loved him. No matter what he did, he could never please them. Ultimately, they were the cause of his alcoholism."

Mara knew about Karl's excessive drinking, but something did not add up. "Mr. White said he started drinking after his first wife died."

"He lied," Aspen said.

The huntress gave a questioning glance, though she believed her. Allen once said the Watcher was always accurate. "Okay, so what happened?"

"He got drunk at a banquet," Aspen revealed. "Humiliated, the Whites sent him to work at a farm as punishment. His siblings mocked him, for he was truly among his kind. One day he was tasked with delivering a sack of grain to a small house in Misty Valley. It was then he met the woman who became his wife. Over time, they fell in love. He bought her a gift—a silver comb with etchings of roses, to replace an old broken one."

As if by instinct, Mara reached into one of her belt pouches. She took out the tarnished comb and held it before her face. A sense of nostalgia washed over her. Looking at it, she reckoned this was the same comb the Watcher mentioned. It possessed etchings of roses but suffered from improper care. Mara remembered receiving this comb from Misty Valley. The monster who haunted the former village was its previous owner. She gazed back at Aspen, urging her to continue.

"However, the White Family discovered their relationship and threatened him with disownment and disinheritance. So, he ran away to be with the one who loved him and had no desire to return."

"But he did," Mara said. "After learning he was the reincarnation of Kratés, he left her. She took her own life."

"No," the Watcher said. "The Whites were devoted members of Kallikratés, who gave them their wealth and power. When Karl ran away, the Faith demanded the White Family retrieved him, or else. So, the patriarch tried to persuade him to return, but Karl refused. Not only did they discover his marriage to a commoner, but they were expecting their firstborn. Karl had cleaned up his act and stopped drinking. He was ready to be a father. But in a final attempt to separate the two, the adopted father revealed Karl's lineage as a direct descendant and the reincarnation of Lord Kratés. It was his destiny to reunite with Kallisto. At first, Karl did not believe it, but the White Family persuaded him to accompany them to the temple."

Mara watched her in confusion. "That's when he saw Kallisto?"

Aspen nodded. "Karl fell under her power and became her commander. For her first order, Kallisto demanded the death of the wife. Karl obeyed and returned to Misty Valley. He stabbed his wife through the abdomen, killing both her and their unborn child. Then he set fire to her home, destroying everything she had. The former wife returned from the dead, distraught at losing her child and her husband's betrayal. Her grief transformed her into a monster—a monster you killed."

Mara's jaw dropped. She glanced down at the comb, her mind reeling from the revelation.

"The White Lady," Mara murmured. "The first undying I killed. Her name was…" She thought back to last night, remembering the name Karl had called her. "Evelyn…" She gazed back up at Aspen. "He was her husband?"

"For murdering Evelyn, Kallisto granted him immortality," said the Watcher. "Karl served his goddess for the next two hundred fifty years, orchestrating the deaths of the next three reincarnations. He sabotaged Aria's voice, then drove her to suicide. He spread the rumour of Madeline being a witch, persuading Haranta Village to kill her." She glanced down. "He was already immortal before you met him." Aspen looked up at Mara. "I'm sorry. Karl never loved you. He only pretended so he could keep you and Allen apart. And Mr. White played a role by manipulating your mother into introducing you two."

Mara opened her mouth, but no words came out. She was confused. How could this be? She wanted to deny the truth. But the Watcher had no reason to lie. Her world came crashing down. Mara gazed at Commander White, who had not stirred from his catatonic state. The more she looked at him, the more she could no longer deny the truth. All she had to do was remember.

Her mind drifted to the time when Karl admitted to watching Mara confront the Marionette. The former herbalist, Madeline, saw him in the doorway and pointed at him. Mara could not understand back then, but now she knew. The Marionette still recognized him after all this time. Madeline was trying to tell her about Karl. However, her warning came too late.

Turning away, Mara saw James and Mr. White. The two men had entered the room. How long they stood there, she did not know. Mara glared at the former college professor and took a step towards him.

"You knew?"

Mr. White looked confused. "What do you mean?"

She took another step towards him. "Why didn't you tell me the truth?"

The older man gaped at her, realizing her awareness.

"I… I was going to tell you," he claimed.

She shook her head. "Really? You were going to tell me the man I was about to marry was already immortal?"

James looked stunned. He gazed at Mr. White. Even the doctor's trust in him began to fade.

Mr. White gave a sympathetic look, taking a step forward. He crossed the threshold of the anti-magic field. "It is true," he said. "The engagement was a plot to murder you."

Mara was speechless, for she never suspected the true nature of their marriage. Mom introduced them, hoping one day they would be married. And Mara accepted Karl's proposal. She remembered how excited she was to be marrying her prince. As she gazed back at the commander, all those happy feelings evaporated. The devastation broke her heart. Deep down,

Mara wanted to cry, but she kept her composure. Anger began to grow within. If she didn't hate the commander and his guardian before, she was about to now.

"But I never wanted you to die," Mr. White told her.

Her gaze switched to him.

The former college professor saw the rage in her eyes but continued.

"They took my idea and twisted it into a horrible plot." He glanced at Karl. "I hoped the sight of you would remind him of Evelyn. He would wake up and realize his errors, and turn against Kallisto." Mr. White gazed back at Mara. "She turned him into a monster. Not only did he murder his wife, but he also terrorized my family for a long time. Karl became the Lord of the Manor, obtaining everything we had. Yet the family fortune is in my name. We became his servants, obeying his every whim. He threw his adoptive sisters out in revenge but kept my grandfather around to pose as his father when the time needed. My grandfather wrote everything down in a journal so we would know the truth." He took a deep breath. "I want to believe he can go back to the man he once was. If it were up to me, I'd never want him to see Kallisto ever again!"

However, any remaining sympathy Mara had for the older man dwindled.

"We got him back," Mara said coldly. "How do I stop Thalia from taking over?"

"Ah, yes, the Binding Dagger," he said. "The Faith has been looking for this artifact, believing it can seal her away."

"Where is this dagger?"

"I'll tell you after erasing Karl's memories," Mr. White replied, gesturing to Aspen.

The huntress looked back at her friends before turning her glare onto the older man.

"That is not what we agreed on," she hissed.

"I'm afraid you'll have to wait," he insisted. "I will not leave Karl like this any longer!"

He was trying her patience. Mara released a low growl as her eyes glowed. Storming up to Mr. White, she grabbed the older man by the collar. He yelped in fright, but no one would help him. Exerting a little force, the huntress pushed him out of the circle. She kept glaring at him as she held his collar tight.

"Read his mind!" Mara ordered the Watcher. "Can you find the location of the dagger?"

Aspen's eyes began to glow. With Mr. White outside the threshold, he was now susceptible to having his mind read. "It is in Andel, in the Outer Frontier."

Mara switched her questioning gaze onto the Watcher. "Andel?" She heard the name before. "That is Dad's home village." She glared at the former college professor. "Where is the village?"

"I... I don't know!" Mr. White cried.

"He is telling the truth," Aspen confirmed.

Mara looked back at him. She released his collar as she stepped back. Mr. White cowered away. Pure terror adorned his face, and he had a right to be afraid. She wanted to harm the older man.

After calming down, Mara gazed at her friends. "Is there a marker near Andel?"

The Watcher shook her head. "No, and I cannot teleport to an unknown location."

Mara sighed. "I'll have to find it myself."

"What about Aazalith?" James asked.

"If she's going to awaken, she would have done so already," Aspen said.

"And I'm not going to let the Faith get that dagger," Mara added.

Upon returning to her room, Mara reached for Dad's journal. Hopefully, it offered a clue. She discovered a small map of Ardana, but nothing about the village. There was no sign of its location. Mara sat on the bed in defeat. It felt like she was back at square one.

Looking at the map again, she noticed something. A small black dot began to appear in the Outer Frontier by some unknown force. The name, Andel, appeared beside the marker. She could not believe her eyes, but the village's location revealed itself as if someone or something wanted her to find it. Studying the map, Mara reckoned it might take a day or two to find the village. She gathered the essentials, hoping she could do this before the divine fully awakened. Mara left James' home without saying a word or looking at anyone.

Chapter Nineteen

The Stone Mages

On the way out of Mirahyll, Mara spotted the familiar black mare galloping around and neighing. It was as if the horse was excited to see her. Either way, it was very convenient for Mara.

"Just what I was looking for," she murmured to herself.

The horse approached her, allowing Mara to mount her. As soon as she got settled into the saddle, the huntress directed the lady to the western road. To reach Andel, she had to go through Medulla Village, the abandoned City of Cerebell, and past the Black Tower. The ride would be long, but it was the only clear path. She didn't have much time to waste. With all the seals broken, Aazalith's awakening could happen at any moment.

* * *

It was already past noon by the time she reached Medulla. The inhabitants of the village were going about their business, unmindful of what was happening. Some glanced up as she rode by, but did not pay any more heed to her. The last time Mara was here was when she had to save the commander from Anna. The darkling had once enslaved the whole village with her psychic powers, making them attack anyone who came near. With Aspen's aid, Mara never needed to fight them. Everyone was back to normal, though she doubted if anyone remembered the incident.

The City of Cerebell remained abandoned. She figured none were aware of the darkling's death or were too afraid to inhabit the city.

She rode by until she stood before the Black Tower. It was another location she had not visited in a while. The marker allowing one to teleport through the Gateway was still standing. The tower remained deserted with a few crows or ravens flying around the top. It was eerily silent, enough to make her uneasy.

Mara continued to ride further until she reached the border of Lupine Woods, where the road stretched on. She reached the boundary to the Outer Frontier. She stopped to see the rough and rocky terrain. Vast mountains covered in mist stood before her while the road stretched on. Still, Mara decided to forge ahead for the village was nowhere in sight. A few hours remained until the sun went down. She did not want to waste any more precious time.

* * *

Travelling on the rough road, Mara encountered a tangled forest. She stopped before the entrance. Unlike Lupine Woods, the trees were twisted and deformed. Some had their roots exposed as if the trees came to life and uprooted themselves. Then she noticed the silence. No birds sang, and the lack of wildlife was strange. And the fading daylight offered little help. The horse grew nervous as if she could sense something. She stomped her hooves and whinnied. Mara could not blame her because she sensed it as well.

"This place is cursed," she murmured to herself.

However, the forest stretched over vast distances; the only option was to go through.

She glanced down at the lady. "Come on," the huntress spoke softly.

The mare was reluctant but went along. Entering the woods, Mara began to question if this was a good idea to travel alone. The deeper they went, the more aware they became of the dangers in the forest. It was very dark. The trees blocked out the sky. Mara reached for her flask of moon water and gave it a shake. The light grew brighter, illuminating her surroundings. She spotted some skeletal remains near the road. The bones were picked clean and broken in some places. The skull was fractured while teeth marks marred the bones. Whatever did this had to be huge.

Travelling further into the forest, Mara heard a twig snap. She snapped her gaze to the source of the sound, trying to see what caused it. She was going to stop and investigate.

All of a sudden, a loud screech broke the silence. Frightened, the little lady took off at full gallop. Hanging on for dear life, the huntress tried to calm the mare. But the horse had no intention of stopping, for she wanted out of this cursed forest.

The pounding of the mare's hooves drew the attention of whatever was hiding in the woods. Hearing a loud rustle, Mara looked back to see the trees shaking. Its loud footsteps almost rivalled the stomping of the lady's hooves.

The creature finally emerged, bounding through the air to swipe at the two ladies. The horse's speed allowed Mara to evade the monster. Glancing back again, all she saw was a grey blur. The beast was fast for its size and showed no signs of tiring. She would have no choice but to engage the creature in battle. If her horse dies, returning to Mirahyll in time would be impossible. She pulled on the reins to slow the mare down, enough to dismount safely. The horse continued to gallop away while Mara stayed behind to face the monster alone.

Unsheathing Nightingale, Mara stared down the beast, which stood at least twice her height. Decaying skin stretched over its bones, adorned in patches of fur. The head was like a deer's skull, sporting large antlers. The eyes were sunken into the sockets. At the end of its long arms were sharp claws on its hands, as well as its feet.

She never saw such a creature before, though it reminded her of the snow beast encountered on Grey Mountain. The creature's height rivalled one, making Mara realize that she could be in for a difficult fight.

The beast lunged at her and took a swipe. She dodged and countered. Even though Nightingale inflicted some damage, the monster showed little response. The creature screamed at her with a voice that could rupture eardrums. While fighting the beast, Mara discovered that it was fast for its size. She took another swing at it, only for the creature to dodge backwards. It also appeared very intelligent. The monster pounded the ground in front of itself, forcing Mara back.

As they fought, Mara heard the war cries of five people on horseback. Four dismounted and unsheathed their weapons, while one remained on their horse, watching the beast. Eyeing the mysterious fighters, Mara spotted their armour, which was reminiscent of the Silver Thorns. They also wore masks to hide their faces. Whoever they were, they appeared to be skilled monster hunters. One of them threw a firebomb which exploded on contact. The fire seemed to drive the creature away. The beast released another screech as it turned and ran back into the tangled wood.

With the coast clear, the four warriors drew their attention onto Mara. They removed their masks, revealing their faces. Like Dad, they had dark skin. Some were lighter, but it was rare to see these people outside the Village of Andel. Another thing she noticed was their cautious gazes. Some drew their weapons, unsure what to make of her. Was she a friend or foe?

"An outsider?" asked one of them.

Mara took note of their words. *'Guess they don't like outsiders.'*

When another reached for her mask and pulled it down, they grew surprised to see her face. She could fit in, though her skin was much lighter. Her skin colour used to bring up many discussions when she was younger. She was neither one colour or the other.

"I know this face," said a male voice.

He began to approach Mara while on horseback. Stopping, he removed his mask to reveal a round face with a prominent nose. Wrinkles sat on the corners of his dark eyes, and his long hair had several strands of grey.

"This is Mara Ashwood," he said, looking at her.

The others glanced at him, then to her. They all looked surprised. Mara was also astonished for this man knew her name. Another rider appeared on a horse. A black mare without an occupant was beside them, being guided by the reins. Mara recognized the little lady, feeling relieved that the horse got to safety. The man glanced at the horse, then to her.

"Is this your horse?"

Mara nodded. "Yes, she is."

"Very well," he said. "Perhaps we should return to Andel to talk."

Everyone agreed. The warriors returned to their horses and began to leave. Mara mounted the little lady and followed after them.

* * *

They reached the village by the evening of December 23. Passing through Andel's gates, Mara saw some people going about their business. Children played outside under the supervision of adults. After a few seconds, they spotted her and ran to their parents. They all took notice and watched her with wary expressions. Mara figured they had very few visitors from the outside.

Seeing the riders dismounting from their horses, she followed suit.

"Come inside," the man spoke. "There is plenty to discuss."

Mara followed them into a large home while ignoring the stares of others. She entered a great hall, where the middle-aged man stood. He looked down at the floor while his riders surrounded him.

"Welcome, Mara," he spoke, looking up at her. "We've heard so much about you."

She glanced back at him. "You know my name?"

He gave a light chuckle. "I knew your father."

"Well, since you know my name, care to tell me yours?" Mara inquired. "I'd like to thank those who helped me back there. If not for you, I wouldn't have made it here."

"I am Elder Ravenclaw," he said. "We are the Stone Mages, who descended from the ones responsible for defeating Aazalith. And to this day, the vile sorceress oppresses us."

The huntress smirked, for she knew who he was describing. "That's pretty accurate."

"Now that we've introduced ourselves, I must ask why you seek our village?" The elder gave a questioning glance. "I can tell that you are not human."

"I'm one of the undying," Mara told him.

"Undying? How did you become this undying?"

"The false goddess killed me," she revealed. "I was lured to the temple, unbeknownst to my parents. Mom and Dad confronted the Faith, only for Kallisto to murder my father. My mom spent the last three decades locked away in a hospital. And I've been a prisoner for thirty years until over a month ago. Since then, they've been trying to recapture me."

Everyone was bewildered by her tale except for the elder, who remained calm.

"I see," Ravenclaw said. "Thalia of Thoron was the first undying to walk this earth. Immortal but not invincible, and the immortality could not be shared."

"Unless someone inherits a piece of her soul," Mara replied. "Thalia broke her soul into several pieces. It's why I exist. I went on a quest to collect the undying souls, believing it would help lift my curse. Instead, it'll awaken Thalia. The Faith is seeking to prevent her return. Only three of us remain."

The elder was silent for a while. "Very well. So, why have you come here?"

"I came for a dagger," Mara revealed. "I hear it can stop Thalia from taking over."

"The Binding Dagger?" Ravenclaw questioned. "It can seal away powerful forces. How do you know about it?"

"The Faith is also looking for it," she replied. "They intend to seal away Thalia."

"They do?"

"They won't rest until they have it," Mara said. "Please, give me the dagger. I'll make sure it will never fall into the wrong hands."

"Maybe we can agree, for we have a common enemy." Ravenclaw gazed at her. "We've been hiding for many years. Our magic has protected this village for a long time, making it impossible for the Faith to find us, but it'll soon fade. Today, they spread lies of us being heretics and savages. Yet they seek to murder us."

"Why?" Mara asked.

"We know the truth," he replied, "how the gods and the Faith came to exist, and how to destroy them. Your ancestors created Lord Slayer Godstruck."

"Yeah, too bad the Faith destroyed it," Mara grumbled.

Everyone looked horrified to hear about the sword's destruction. However, the elder seemed less distraught as he spotted Nightingale strapped to her belt.

He glanced at her and said, "After learning about your family, we declared war on the Faith. We plotted to overthrow them by retrieving you. You are the only one who can stop the false goddess." He shook his head. "But they outmatched us. It was a massacre. The false goddess cursed the previous elder for leading the attack, transforming him into a wendigo—the creature you encountered. She tasked him to terrorize our people. And none had been able to slay him."

"If I kill the creature, will you give me the dagger?" Mara inquired.

The elder nodded. "I'll agree to this, but the creature will not be easy. One of our youths went to slay the monster, but he never returned."

"Think I found him just as I entered the forest. I'm sorry for your loss." Then, "I also noticed the forest was cursed."

"His curse bled into the woods, infecting it, and isolating us from the rest of Ardana," the elder said.

"I've lifted some curses," Mara responded. "If I go back there, will I find him?"

"Yes, but he also likes to frequent the graveyard."

Mara nodded. She then left the village to find the creature.

* * *

Wandering the dark forest at night, Mara questioned if this was a good idea, for the visibility was poor. Then she heard a familiar screech from the grave-yard. The huntress ran in the direction of the frightening howls and eventually found the towering creature. The wendigo was digging up graves for anything edible. With Mara's presence, the creature stopped and turned his attention onto her.

The monster released a high pitch shriek while lunging at her. Mara attempted to evade, but the beast's vast reach provided an edge. She received a nasty gash on her left arm. The huntress tried to fight the creature, though his speed was problematic. He leapt high into the air and pounced on her. Mara attempted to dodge, but the monster grabbed her.

The huntress tried to struggle out of the creature's grasp. Appearing annoyed, he smashed her into the ground at least four consecutive times. The beast's attack left her legs and pelvis shattered. He released her, knowing she was not going anywhere. Mara did not know how she remained alive. There was blood everywhere. She couldn't move her legs at all. The creature towered over her with his hand reached out, ready to grab and devour her half-broken body.

All of a sudden, Mara heard cries as two young warriors from the village came out of nowhere. One of the men stabbed his spear into the beast's hide. The creature retaliated by striking at the man, impaling him on the sharp claws. The wendigo proceeded to devour him. He bit off his head, causing the body to shudder briefly. The creature ate the remains and grew in proportion to the meal he consumed.

Then the wendigo turned on the other man and snatched him. Mara watched in horror as the warrior kicked and screamed. The creature fitted the young man's head into his mouth, then snapped his jaws shut. The man twitched for a few seconds before he stopped moving. While the huntress watched the beast devouring him, she had time to heal. Her bones and muscles managed to reset, but she remained unable to flee. The creature turned to her and grasped her body. The wendigo grew so much she could fit into the palm of his hand.

As the creature's fingers closed around Mara, she gripped her sword and slashed at his hand, cutting off all his fingers. The creature's roar echoed throughout the mountains. Then he lunged at her with a wide-open maw. The beast tried to bite her in half, but she managed to catch the jaws open with her hands. As she struggled to pry the beast's mouth open, her eyes began to glow brightly. With all her strength, she forced the creature's jaws open. The force she exerted snapped the monster's lower jaw off.

Gallons of blood sprayed onto Mara while the creature reared back. He held onto the massive wound where his jaw used to be, trying to keep the blood from gushing out. The wendigo staggered away from her, but the loss of blood made him weaker. He collapsed, the life slipping away from him. Standing before the creature's battered face, the huntress lifted Nightingale over her head. Then she hacked the monster to death, as a red haze blinded her view.

Once finished, Mara took deep breaths. She wiped the blood from her face as she continued to stare at his damaged head. Then she collapsed in exhaustion. Falling to her knees, Mara saw a shining stone. It was a healing stone. It was convenient, for her injuries were great. Staring up at the starry sky, Mara contemplated on what a clear night it was before the darkness claimed her.

* * *

A tingling sensation reached her fingers, making them twitch. Soon it became a burning sensation rushing through her veins. Mara jolted awake. She was right about dying from her injuries. But at least she obtained a second healing stone. Mara found herself lying on a bed. She was back in the village.

The sun rose on a cold winter morning. She reckoned the villagers found her and brought her back here. Chances were, everyone got a glimpse of her inhuman appearance. She took the healing stone and used it to restore her human form.

Glancing around, Mara saw the elder with his back turned to her. He sat before the fire, holding Nightingale in his hands. Mara glanced down to confirm that the elder took her weapon, sheath included. Looking up at him, she watched as he studied the blade.

"You have slain the wendigo," Elder Ravenclaw began.

She rose to her feet.

"I have," she replied. Mara glanced at Nightingale. Why did he take her sword?

"I hope the creature was not too much trouble."

She gazed at the back of his head. "It broke every bone in my legs and tried to eat me."

"You are still alive. That has to count for something."

"Why did you send those men?" Mara questioned.

"To buy you some time to heal and kill the creature." Then he looked back at her. "My father was the previous elder."

She froze while watching the grim expression on his face. The embers rose behind him.

"I'm sorry," she said. "I... I didn't know."

"Don't be. Thanks to you, my father is free." He then glanced down at Nightingale. "Your father forged this blade?"

She nodded. "It was a birthday present." She gazed at Nightingale. "Dad made it before he died."

The elder studied every detail of her sword.

"He was defiant to the very end." A small smile formed on his face.

Mara switched her attention onto him. "Why did Dad die?"

"Your father knew how to forge a Lord Slayer, being descended from the creators of Godstruck. They killed him to destroy the knowledge. However, they failed to stop him." He gazed at her. "This is a Lord Slayer, though he made it appear as if it were a normal sword. With a moonstone, it shall gain the power to defeat a god." He approached her and returned Nightingale. "The Faith must not know you have this."

As Mara strapped the sword to her belt, Ravenclaw retrieved a box from a dresser.

"By killing the wendigo, you saved the Stone Mage Tribe from many more years of pain and misery. You did what I had neither the strength or courage to do." He handed the box to her. "For that, we thank you."

Upon opening the box, Mara saw an ornate dagger with unique symbols etched onto the blade. She reckoned this to be the Binding Dagger the Faith sought. After taking the weapon, Mara gazed back at the elder and nodded.

"Wait," called a small female voice, which came from another room.

The elder looked behind him.

Mara heard the voice as well. "Who is that?"

Ravenclaw glanced back at her and said, "Our shaman, Alkina, wishes to speak to you. Go on. Go see her."

Mara walked past him and entered the other room. Inside was a lone woman surrounded by incense. She recognized the shaman, remembering the ritual performed on her. The one responsible for her transformation was now much older. The shaman had to be at least a hundred years old. Several wrinkles decorated her thin face. Her dark eyes had now become faded and glazed as if she had lost her vision. The hair was pure white like freshly fallen snow. She was dressed in white robes while a hood cast a shadow over her face.

The shaman kept her eyes on Mara. "You are the child of the one we sent away?"

Mara nodded. "Yes, I'm the daughter of Bear Ashwood."

"Such a beautiful woman you grew into," Alkina said. A smile formed on her wrinkled face. "I want you to know that it was never our intention to send him away."

Mara tilted her head to the right. The shaman was not as blind as she appeared to be. "I know. You did it to protect the village and my family. Though Kallikratés still found me."

"I remember it as if it were yesterday." The shaman's smile faded. "That witch tried to kill you with a spell, making it look like an illness. Your father returned to the village, desperate to find a way to protect you. I gave him a moonstone necklace and instructed him to place it around your neck."

Mara reached into her cloak and grasped the clear blue pendant. She showed the necklace.

"Ah, you're still wearing it! Moonstone siphons magic," the shaman explained. "This protected you from the false goddess."

A thought crossed Mara's mind. "But it doesn't protect me all the time. When I first encountered Kallisto, she killed me."

"Hmm, there's only so much magic they can absorb before breaking," Alkina said, gazing at the moonstone. "It might be enough to defeat her, but I recommend you find a new one. These moonstones can remove a divine's soul, although they are the rarest."

Mara examined the crystal blue pendant, rolling it around with her fingers. "So, I can still use this to stop her?"

"Yes, but keep this knowledge close to yourself," the shaman answered. "Surely you've heard of the discrimination against us. The Faith shepherded humanity, controlling how they think so none would stand up against them. We remain unshackled from their control. So they seek to destroy us." Alkina gazed at Mara. "Though we are fortunate to have you. We performed the Melding Ceremony to give you the power to challenge the false goddess."

Mara furrowed her eyebrows. "Dad's journal mentioned it, but I don't know what it is."

"It is a ritual sacred to the Thoron Witches," Alkina revealed. "Through the blood of Wolf Goddess Ulrika, the ritual creates a witch. We had to use a substitute, so we fed you the blood of a shadow beast, while I oversaw the ritual." She shook her head. "To be honest, we never tried it before, but we succeeded. You acquired some of the shadow beast's powers, as well as its temperament." She smiled again. "I heard you were quite the terror as a child."

Mara looked mystified. "Well, that explains the things I did."

She remembered those three incidents when she was a child. Once, she got in trouble for retaliating against a boy who threw a rock at her. Then she beat a girl, who stole her book, with a chair. And in high school, she attacked a pervert who tried to assault her.

"Do not worry about it," the shaman told her. "Most children are often a handful." She eyed the dagger in Mara's possession. "You intend to seal away Thalia, even though she is your main weapon against Kallisto."

Mara glanced down at the dagger. "Everyone says she's the only one who can defeat Kallisto, but at the cost of my existence?"

"Who said you'd cease to exist? The Faith?" Alkina snorted. "You are Thalia, and Thalia is you."

"She took over my body," Mara argued.

"Did she? Or was it you reverting to your true form." Alkina paused for a moment. "Thalia created the reincarnations to break free of her curse. Only an undying can slay an undying. You are a fragment of Thalia, but you are also her wish. The key to ending her suffering." She pointed at the dagger. "The Binding Dagger will not be enough."

"What do you mean?" Mara inquired.

"It can only be used once. And if you claim another fragment, the dagger's magic will be undone."

"So, you're telling me not to use this right now?"

Alkina nodded. "There are many factors to consider. As far as I'm concerned, the last reincarnation has not been born yet."

"How do you know?" Mara questioned.

"For many years, we've been watching for the return of Thalia," the shaman said. "Long ago, I performed a seance and predicted your birth as one of the reincarnations. The last reincarnation will appear to you sooner or later."

"So, what do I do?"

"Continue on your quest," Alkina said. "I assume you're going to challenge the one within the divine?"

Mara nodded. "Yes, Aspen and I are going to kill the Forlorn and stop Aazalith."

"Her armour is the body of a forgotten goddess. But you shall overcome this challenge." Alkina then asked, "After defeating the divine, you will challenge Kallisto?"

"Yes," Mara replied, looking at Nightingale.

"Very well. Then what? What will you do afterwards?"

Mara lifted her gaze to her. "I plan on going to Thoron. To remove my curse, I need to find the Blue Rose of Immortality. If it can make Thalia immortal, then it can make me human again. I need to find a way to get there."

"I see," the shaman said. "Thalia fled from Thoron because of her curse. I'm very sure she has some unresolved issues and lingering regrets."

A bell began to toll. Mara searched for the source of the sound. It reminded her of the warning bell in Ozin.

"Ah, the bell tolls," Alkina said.

Mara glanced back at her. "What is that?"

"Aazalith is awakening."

Mara's jaw dropped. Alkina beckoned a man and whispered in his ear. He nodded before entering another room. Soon, he returned with a strange lantern. Instead of having a chamber for a flame, it possessed a large moonstone.

"To get to the Forlorn, you will need the Moon Lantern," the shaman said.

Mara gazed at the lantern while receiving it. "Thanks… How do I use this?"

"It will respond to Aazalith's presence. Shine the light into the darkness," Alkina said. "Hurry home, my dear. Aazalith is coming. She will emerge from the eastern ocean."

Mara heeded her words, even if they sort of confused her. She left the house. On the way out, the Stone Mages bowed to her. The bell continued to ring as she left. The resonating sound lingered in her mind. She mounted the little lady and left the village.

While passing through the tangled forest, Mara sensed the lifting of the oppressive air. The trees appeared less twisted as the sunlight reached the forest floor. With the wendigo gone, the forest was reverting to normal. It would take a while, but it was a step in the right direction. The songbirds sang for the first time as squirrels chirped in alarm to her presence.

At full gallop, the mare took her home to James and Aspen.

Chapter Twenty

A Final Farewell

The huntress reached Mirahyll on the afternoon of December 25. Upon drawing closer, a thick fog rolled in as the clouds grew darker. Something was wrong; even the lady could sense it. The horse made an abrupt stop and reared up. The huntress attempted to dismount, only to land on her bottom. Even though the fall didn't kill her, it remained painful. While Mara recovered, the little lady galloped away.

"Damn horse," Mara muttered.

Then the huntress noticed the lantern in her possession. It emanated a faint blue glow. Aazalith was coming, just as the shaman had warned. Rising to her feet, she hurried home to Mirahyll.

* * *

She ran for the remaining portion. Aazalith could arrive at any moment. Mara gasped for air while dashing through the streets. Not many people were around. At least nobody got in her way. When she got to James' place, she knocked on the door frantically. James answered, appearing calm.

"Oh, you're back," he greeted.

Mara gasped for air while looking at him. "Sorry, it took longer than expected," she said between pants.

James looked concerned. "Did you run all the way here?"

"The horse left me just outside the city."

"Well, come inside." James invited her in.

Entering his home, the first thing Mara noticed was Mr. White in the living room. Aspen stood in the distance. The huntress looked at James with a questioning glance.

"What is going on?"

"We wanted to wait for you," James replied.

Mara gave a strange look. "Why did you wait for me?"

The round nobleman stepped forward. "I made the decision," he explained. "I wanted you to have a chance to say goodbye to him."

Mara turned her gaze to the former college professor and furrowed her eyebrows. "There was nothing between us. He never loved me."

"He would have if he were free," Mr. White insisted. "You saw what he was like when not under Kallisto's control."

Mara remembered Karl kneeling before her, wanting to tell her something important. She reckoned he wanted to tell her the truth, only to be stopped by his adoptive father and the Holy Blades. She also recalled the ride in the carriage where Karl kissed her. Mara snapped out of it, feeling embarrassed to even think about that moment.

"No, we have no time. Aazalith is about to awaken."

"It won't take long," James told her. "He's in the guest room."

However, Mara would not budge. Everyone took notice and frowned at her.

"Please," Mr. White pleaded. "Just say goodbye."

"Why?" Mara asked.

"Once I erase his memory, he will no longer remember you," Aspen said.

"I meant nothing to him," Mara argued. "What difference does it make if he no longer remembers me?"

"Because you have Evelyn's soul inside of you," Aspen said. "Evelyn was his wife. At least she meant something to him."

Mara glared at her. "In case you've forgotten, he murdered his wife and unborn child." She took a step towards her. "He was responsible for the Siren and the Marionette. He was the reason why I became cursed and lost my family. You said it yourself."

The Watcher nodded. "It is true. But you, of all people, knew he was under Kallisto's control. The only way he could ever be free was either through the power of Thalia or a darkling. He is already free from Kallisto's control but is unable to cope with his actions. The answer is to erase his memories, including those of Evelyn. So, this is why we are asking you to see him one more time."

"And I shall take him to Corlin," Mr. White added. "He'll be as far away from Kallisto as possible."

Mara gazed at him. "You think I'm going to let him walk away with a fragment of Aazalith's soul?"

"I promise to return with him after you slay Kallisto," the former college professor claimed.

"And we'll remove it without killing him," James said.

Mara raised an eyebrow. They had planned some things behind her back.

The older man stepped forward. "This will be his only chance at freedom. His one chance at starting over."

While his words rang true, it wasn't like Mara could feel sympathy in an instant.

"What if I refuse?"

Mr. White and James frowned. It was clear that their speech did not move her.

The Watcher stepped forward and removed her visor. "Then you are as selfish as Kallisto."

James and Mr. White gaped at Aspen. Mara's face grew hot.

"Excuse me?" The huntress became enraged. How dare Aspen suggest that Mara was anything like Kallisto? To be even compared to the goddess sent her mind reeling.

Aspen held her ground. "Jealousy and vanity drove Kallisto to steal the soul of a divine. Then she spent her whole existence trying to sever the bonds of Kratés and Thalia, even going as far as targeting their reincarnations. You are doing the same by keeping Evelyn away from him."

Mara glared at her. "What are you talking about?" she demanded.

"Evelyn's will is alive," Aspen revealed.

The huntress gawked at her with a slack jaw. Even the two men were shocked.

"What?" James asked.

"It can't be," Mr. White muttered.

The Watcher kept staring at Mara. "I always wondered how you could be so attracted to him despite your memory loss, or why you became upset whenever you saw him in Morgan's arms. You acknowledged that your relationship with him had created a rift between you, Allen, and your father. But in the end, you still loved him. You were determined to save him, even if it meant the goddess' murder."

"That's not true," Mara murmured, her voice began to break. "I wanted revenge."

"Did you, Mara?" Aspen questioned. "Or should I call you Evelyn?"

The two men gaped at the Watcher, then looked at the huntress. There was no denying the claims. Upon seeing Karl and Morgan together, Mara felt betrayed by him. Even though her feelings for him had diminished, a tiny part of her still loved him. She did not know why until discovering this revelation. The huntress shook her head while tears formed in her eyes.

"Why are you crying?" Aspen questioned. "Or are they even your tears?"

Fear overwhelmed Mara. In addition to the threat of Thalia's return, Evelyn had been influencing some of her actions. In fear of losing herself and her control, she reached for the Binding Dagger. One stab was all she needed to have her body back. Who cared if it was one use? However, her hand began to shake as her fingers loosened. She watched as the dagger fell to the floor. Evelyn was fighting her in her own body! Her mouth trembled.

"I just want to see him one last time."

Unable to control her body, Mara faced the door to the guest room. She knew what Evelyn was planning, but wanted no part of it.

"Mara, let her say goodbye to her husband," James told her.

She could not believe her friend told her to do this. Then again, she didn't have much say as her body moved towards the guest room. She would have no choice but to let Evelyn say goodbye to her former husband.

* * *

Mara saw him upon entering the room. Karl was lying in bed, not moving a muscle. He appeared to be sleeping. He wore a white dress shirt while the bedsheets covered the rest of his body.

She regained control of her body but continued to approach his side. Deep down, Mara wanted to leave. But she stayed, knowing Evelyn could take over again or her friends would scold her. Taking a deep breath, she came closer to him. He had not stirred or responded to her presence. When she reached him, Mara stopped and looked down. Some redness painted his eyelids. A single tear escaped from his left eye and rolled to the side. Karl was trapped within his broken mind, unable to cope with the guilt of his actions.

Gazing at his face, Mara parted her lips. She wanted to say something, yet unsure where to start. After pausing for a few seconds, the huntress found the words to speak.

"It was not my choice. I never wanted to see you, not after what you did. Because of you, I lost everything." Mara paused upon seeing another tear fall from his eye. It seemed he could hear her. "I am going to kill Kallisto. Surely, it'll be a great relief for you as it will be for me. I'm telling you this because you won't remember."

She glanced around before looking back at him.

"I cannot forgive you at this moment. But I'm sorry this happened. Kallisto took everything away from you, as she did to me." She turned away. "I wouldn't wish this on anyone."

Something warm came through her eyes. Tears began to form again as emotions rose from the depths of her being. Flashes of memory came to her mind. She saw a house near a waterfall. The huntress recognized the place from before; this was where she encountered and fought the White Lady. But the home was not burning and stood on a bright summer day.

A young man approached, holding a sack of grain. As Karl made his delivery, never once did he notice Mara. The huntress soon realized this was Evelyn's memory. She was able to peer into the past, yet stood at the side as a spectator.

He knocked on the door but got no answer. With a free hand, he rummaged through his pocket. He retrieved a small hand-drawn map and examined it. He arrived at the correct place, but nobody was at home. Nevertheless, he got the sack of grain here without spilling anything. He lowered it to the ground beside the front door. He finished his task, and it was time to leave.

Once he was twenty feet away, the door opened. Both Mara and Karl turned their heads and saw the owner. Evelyn looked identical to Mara. A beige tunic with a white cloth around the waist adorned her torso. Dark brown pants covered her long legs. Dirty brown boots went up to her knees. She bent over to reach for the sack of grain.

The huntress glanced back at him, spotting his gaze on Evelyn's chest. They remained stuck until he noticed her struggling with the sack of grain. It was no surprise since he struggled with it as well, but she was no match for it and needed his help.

"Excuse me," Karl called, walking towards her.

Evelyn stood up and watched as he came closer.

Once within distance, he crouched down to grasp the bag. "Let me help you."

With a firm grip on the bag, he lifted it to his chest. Evelyn gazed at him, appearing stunned by his strength. She stepped out of his way and let him into her home.

"Where do you want this?" Karl inquired.

Evelyn guided him to the spot to put down the grain. Upon finishing, Karl stood up and looked at Evelyn. The two gazed at each other for a long time. Love began to spark between them.

Fast forward into the night, Mara remained outside of Evelyn's home. Karl approached the house and knocked on the door three times. The door opened to reveal Evelyn. She stood on the other side, dressed in a simple long shirt for nightwear. The silhouette of her body was visible through the fabric in the light of the lantern. However, it was her eyes he saw. The huntress watched as their eyes remained locked, and suspected this was a memory of the night Karl ran away to be with Evelyn. Despite being disowned, he would rather be with someone who loved him.

Evelyn let him in. Mara watched from outside the window while Karl held Evelyn in his arms and kissed her. She did not resist. Some great force drew them together, and no longer could they deny their feelings. They removed all of their clothes before lying in bed together. Their bodies pressed against each other and their legs intertwined. Mara did not feel upset at seeing them together because she knew the whole truth.

There was one more thing Evelyn wanted to show her. Mara found herself standing before a great tree. She recognized the tree during her travels, often sitting beneath it. Karl and Evelyn stood underneath it. Another older man was present with them. No one else was around, but the two did not care. They looked happy.

"I now declare you husband and wife," said the older man. "You may kiss the bride."

The newlyweds held each other. Their faces leaned in for a very long kiss.

The man who married them appeared to be an alderman. Since many could not afford the Faith's wedding services, they sought out an alderman to perform the ceremony. It cost less than five hundred gold, which was ten times more affordable compared to only hiring a priest of Kallikratés.

Snapping out of the visions, Mara found herself leaning towards Karl's face. A final kiss—the last thing Evelyn wanted. Mara wanted to resist, but she felt Evelyn's grief and sorrow. The huntress wondered if she was aware of what happened. Could Evelyn see everything? She was the force behind some of Mara's actions. She did all these things for Karl. Whether he knew or not was unknown, but it no longer mattered. He would forget his former wife. So, Evelyn bid him farewell.

Mara pulled away, regaining control over her body, but the tears continued to fall. The huntress cried not for Karl, but the spouse who withered away. Would this be her fate, too? She tried to stop the tears from falling, yet it was futile.

"It's okay to cry."

Looking to the doorway, Mara saw the Watcher staring back at her. Aspen approached them. It was time. Without saying a word, the huntress stormed past her and left the room. Never once did she look at the Watcher.

Entering the living room, she saw James and Mr. White. They were watching her, but she ignored them. Mara saw the Binding Dagger on the floor. It remained there since being forced to drop it. She crouched down and picked it up. There was no need to use this right now. After strapping the dagger to her belt, Mara returned to her room.

* * *

Mara made her preparations. She had Nightingale, the Moon Lantern, her crossbow, and her necklace. It was time to face the divine. She hoped Aspen was also ready. By now, she should have erased Karl's memories. Looking out the window, the huntress saw the fog growing thicker. The blue glow from the Moon Lantern grew brighter. She saw the lantern and could not ignore the message it conveyed. Aazalith was coming.

The huntress entered an empty living room but did not have to wait long. Soon, the door opened to reveal Aspen and the three men. The Watcher stood beside Mara while James and Mr. White assisted Karl with getting the last of his attire on. No longer was he wearing his commander's garb. James lent a white dress shirt, a pair of black pants, and matching shoes for Karl. Mr. White provided a black coat to keep him warm. Gazing at his green eyes, Mara found them brighter than before. However, Karl looked befuddled. She wondered if the Watcher erased more memories than expected.

The former college professor glanced at his ward.

"Come along, Karl," said the older nobleman.

The younger man complied but remained very puzzled.

"Where are we going?" Karl asked softly.

"We are leaving for Corlin. You were in a terrible accident. Your adoptive family had perished. You survived, but lost most of your memories. You shall be under my care for now."

James nodded. "Yes, the doctors in Corlin will provide better help," he added. "I am sorry we could not do much, but I'm sure you will be fine."

Karl glanced at the middle-aged doctor. The look of confusion remained on his face.

Mara raised an eyebrow. The two men lied to him. Then again, it was the only way to hide the fact that he was immortal.

Karl remained silent until he noticed Mara. He stopped and studied her for a while.

"Who is she?" Karl questioned.

Mara stared back at him. Although she was a little sad at his inability to remember her, Mara knew this was for the best. Karl was no longer a threat, and Kallisto had lost her commander.

The older man glanced at her. "She came upon the wreckage, and found you passed out in the woods," he lied, then gestured to the three. "They all helped you recover."

"Oh, they did?" Karl kept his eyes on Mara while approaching her. "Thank you for your help." He offered his hand for a handshake.

Mara gazed at his hand, unsure of what to do. Glancing around, she saw everyone staring at her. The looks on their faces told her to shake his hand. Looking at Karl, Mara noticed a confused expression on his face. He was probably wondering why she had not shaken his hand yet. She had nothing to fear; it wasn't like touching him would make him remember. Before Mara could reach for his hand, a knock on the door drew everyone's attention. She looked away from Karl and watched James answer the door. On the other side was a familiar face.

"Greetings, Chancellor Davis," James spoke.

Chancellor Davis arrived with two guardsmen, who held onto some weaponry. They came to return the stolen property to their rightful owner, placing Bear's weapons on the floor. Mara looked up at the chancellor, noticing Davis' gaze on Mr. White and Karl.

"Commander White, what are you doing here?" The chancellor glanced at his attire. "I don't think I have ever seen you out of uniform."

Karl looked baffled. "Commander?"

Everyone glanced at each other, unsure of what to say.

The old nobleman stepped forward. "My apologies," he said. "My ward had been through a terrible accident. He has amnesia."

The chancellor seemed surprised. "Oh, is that so?" He gazed at Karl. "I am sorry to hear that. But it does explain why I have not seen you around lately."

"Yes, we shall be travelling to Corlin tonight," Mr. White said. "Given the circumstances, I believe their doctors will provide better care."

"And I recommended it," James added. "He'll be better off in Corlin."

Mr. White glanced at Karl. "Let's go home," he beckoned. "We must pack our belongings and prepare for the long journey tonight."

Karl nodded. As he followed the older nobleman outside, the chancellor had one more thing to say.

"I wish you well in your recovery."

Karl looked back at him. "Thank you."

Then the two left.

Mara folded her arms before glancing at the chancellor. "I'm surprised you did not arrest Commander White and his guardian."

Davis cleared his throat. "Given the circumstances and his amnesia, I'll let him go for now. In time, he will have to answer for his crimes." He changed the subject. "Now, the reason why I'm here—I wish to speak to you about the Dark One."

"What about it?" Mara asked.

"As far as I'm concerned, you're going to confront the beast. Am I correct?"

"Yes, if we can get inside and kill the undying fused to her core, we can stop her." Mara gestured to Aspen. "After all, only an undying can kill an undying."

"Well, I've spoken with Evan about your plan," Davis said, "and we wish to assist you."

"Assist us?" Mara looked intrigued.

"We shall provide a small army of guardsmen and Hema's knights to aid you. After studying the historical records, we determined that the creature will emerge from the ocean outside of Har' Yhan."

Mara gave a peculiar look. Alkina told her something similar. It seemed the shaman had the gift of foresight.

"I believe approaching the Dark One in the ocean may keep Ardana out of harm's way," said the chancellor.

"Confront her in the ocean?" Mara inquired.

"We will provide a fleet."

Mara watched the chancellor and folded her arms. "Seems like a great plan, though it won't be easy. I can't guarantee everyone will survive this night."

Davis gazed at her. "I am aware, but I'd be damned if we did not do something to protect our home."

She stared at Davis in silence. The huntress could use all the help she could get since she did not have a clue how to approach the divine other than breaking all the seals. Her respect for Terra's chancellor grew a little more. Then she looked at James.

He gave a sad smile. "Save Ardana. Please come back."

She nodded before turning her gaze onto the chancellor and the guardsmen. "We're ready to go."

"We can offer you two a ride to Har' Yhan," Davis said. He turned to the guardsmen. "Send transports to the town and oversee its evacuation."

The guardsmen left to perform their tasks.

Chancellor Davis looked back at Mara and Aspen. "Now, if you two come with me, I'll take you to your transport."

As they left, Mara glanced back at James. He gave a small smile, though she could tell he was very concerned for their safety. There was a possibility they would not return from this, but they had to try. She nodded before turning around. Mara and Aspen left with the chancellor.

Chapter Twenty-One

The Forlorn

Mara and Aspen sat in silence as their carriage drew closer to Har' Yhan. Looking out the window, Mara saw the town's evacuation. She also spotted five large ships beyond the buildings; the sails were visible. She figured the small army of guardsmen and knights were already there.

Upon reaching their destination, the coach stopped. After exiting, Mara gazed up to see the red moon hanging in the night sky. All the stars had faded. It was an ominous sign of impending doom.

Mara and Aspen followed Davis and his group to the port, where they got a closer view of the ships. Four of the five vessels were all outfitted with cannons and ballistas. Each ballista was equipped with a large spear four times Mara's height. The huntress was impressed. She knew the chancellors had a plan to help her and Aspen but had no idea how much they were going to offer. The two women ignored the stares of evacuees as they kept walking to their destination. Mara wondered if the townsfolk knew they came to save this land.

Approaching the port, Aspen stopped. Mara noticed this and glanced back at her.

"I'm sorry," Aspen spoke.

Mara gazed at her in confusion. "What are you talking about?"

Aspen looked down at the ground. "I shouldn't have said those words to you. You are nothing like Kallisto."

Mara frowned. "It's okay."

"No, I never considered how you felt. You've been through a lot more than anyone would ever face in their life."

"True," Mara said. "I was devastated and angry, but you were right. Evelyn deserved to see her husband one last time."

"What happened to Evelyn?" Aspen inquired.

"She went to sleep," the huntress replied. "After wondering why her husband betrayed her, Evelyn saw everything and learned the truth. I think the others were aware and found peace as well." Mara took a deep breath. "Now, we have to find Amara and put her to rest."

Aspen stared back at Mara. "Will we be able to do this? Amara is the oldest undying, protected by Aazalith. We may be no match."

The huntress placed a hand on her necklace. "Even after absorbing those souls, you think it's not enough?"

"I don't know, but we must try. We are the only ones who can stop this." Aspen walked ahead of her.

On the way to the ships, Mara spotted a familiar blacksmith waving to her. "Over here!" Talon called.

She ran over to him. "What are you doing here?"

"I've been searching for you. Heard you were facing the Dark One, so I wish to help by offering my services." He glanced at her equipment. "You won't last long if you don't use my services now!"

Mara decided to use his services, making sure everything was ready for the battle.

"There, your equipment should be ready to take on the Dark One," he told her.

"Thanks. You should get out of here. It's not safe."

Talon nodded. "I will, and good luck."

Mara left Talon and rejoined Aspen. She looked back to see the blacksmith packing up his things and leaving the abandoned town.

* * *

The two undying reached the port. The chancellors, guardsmen, and knights were already present. Both Davis and Evan stood before the small army they gathered. The light of the lanterns illuminated the faces of the two men.

"Thank you for coming," Davis began. "You've been called upon to assist Miss Ashwood with defeating the Dark One." He gestured to her. "You are to protect her and the Watcher from harm."

"We have provided Terra's government with our artillery," Evan added, "equipping four vessels with cannons and ballistas. Each ballista has a silver-tipped spear." He looked at Davis. "But I admit these armaments are ancient. Lady Isabella had these commissioned one thousand years ago."

"They should still be effective," said one of the guardsmen. "All supernatural are weak to silver. The Dark One should be no exception. I know this as a former Silver Thorn."

Everyone gazed at the guardsman.

Davis nodded. "Very well." Then he looked at the huntress. "We are ready to assist you, Miss Ashwood. If you would come with me, I will guide you both to your ship."

The chancellor guided the two women to a central ship, where it lacked any form of artillery. At least it had some lifeboats. Only Mara and Aspen occupied it, while twenty crew members went to the other four ships.

Mara gave a questioning glance at Davis. "You expect us to man this by ourselves?"

"With my powers, it shouldn't be a problem," the Watcher said.

Mara glanced at her. "Okay," she responded.

Davis gazed at the two undying while holding his hands behind his back. "I pray for your success and safety."

The two women nodded to him, then walked towards their ship.

* * *

They boarded the vessel by midnight. The night air was frigid. When they were ready, the eyes on Aspen's visor began to glow. The ship departed through her psychic powers. As soon as it drifted from the port, the other four followed suit.

Mara's eyes scanned the dark ocean, only to see the other vessels surrounding them. Some of the guardsmen and knights held lanterns.

Glancing down, the huntress noticed the Moon Lantern glowing brighter. Mara gazed ahead to see a great mass arising from the sea. The ocean swelled as waves caused the ships to rock and sway. The huntress almost lost her balance and fell, yet Aspen remained unfazed. The Watcher kept the ship stable while the creature emerged from the churning ocean. Mara looked at the other vessels. The guardsmen and knights took to the cannons and ballistas, getting ready for the inevitable encounter.

The light reflected from the blood-red moon shone upon the divine. Aazalith had seen better days. Much of her rock-like scales had rotted away as sparse flesh clung to her black bones. Beneath her decaying flesh, sparks of blue floated about. Her magic began to revive her flesh. A white glow within the rib cage caught Mara's eye. She reckoned this was the divine's core.

The head of the creature appeared as rotten scales came to life and covered the exposed skull. Six curved horns sat on her head, as well as several spikes along the ridge of the nose and above the empty eye sockets. The regenerated dark scales were like stone. Glowing blue spots graced various parts of her face and body. Fins and frills, once torn and decayed, repaired themselves.

Mara was stunned at the divine's appearance. "What the—?"

The reanimated corpse transformed into a large and majestic dragon, like the picture Mara once saw in Saskia's bestiary. A massive decayed bat-like wing emerged from one side of the divine. Another soon followed and stretched into the sky, blocking out the glowing moon. The creature released a roar while stretching her skeletal wings into the air. The sound Aazalith produced made everything shake. Waves of energy spread over her limbs, healing the rugged membrane. If she wanted to, she could fly away. She created powerful wind gusts with ease. The magical essence flowing through the great dragon could be seen beneath her scales, giving them a turquoise tint. The interior of her wings, frills, and fins glowed bright blue.

"Aazalith has fully regenerated," Aspen said. "It's possible the seals siphoned much of her power away in addition to restricting access to Amara's soul."

The guardsmen and knights held their ground, although they appeared terrified. The divine was massive compared to a single vessel. Only half of the dragon's torso was visible while the ocean submerged the rest. Her wingspan rivalled all five ships combined.

Aazalith gazed at each of the five vessels. She blinked a few times as a blue substance filled six empty sockets. Her eyes were the last to mend. The divine looked at Mara and Aspen and kept her gaze on them for the longest time. Her eyes were like glittering blue moonstones. As she roared at them, blue flames billowed in the back of her throat. Despite her restoration, Aazalith did not fly away. She was likely exhausted from using her magic to heal herself. Mara watched the rows of sharp teeth. The dragon possessed two sets of jaws, one inside the other.

A massive migraine hit Mara without warning, accompanied by a high-pitched sound. The huntress clutched her head and squeezed her eyes shut. After a few moments, her eyes shot open. A hand rested on her shoulder, and the migraine faded away. After removing her hands from her head, Mara glanced at Aspen. The Watcher gazed back with her hand placed on Mara's shoulder.

"What was that?" Mara demanded.

"The divine spoke to us," Aspen answered, removing her hand. "The Seven Divines are not only powerful but very intelligent. They can communicate with telepathy. However, most humans and creatures cannot comprehend or understand a divine due to the limitations of their minds. It comes off as a high-pitch sound and a painful headache. Only the most experienced Thoron Sages or kin can understand them without the risk of having their minds crushed."

Mara glanced back at Aazalith. The massive dragon was still while watching them.

"You can understand her?" Mara addressed Aspen.

The Watcher looked up at the divine. "She knows why we're here, but will not hand Amara over as long as she keeps her alive," she explained. "Aazalith demands her soul back. She wants the thieves responsible."

The dragon inhaled and exhaled. Glowing blue mist escaped from her maw. The divine's voice assailed Mara's mind, making her head shudder out of control. After the splitting headache stopped, the huntress looked up at the divine.

"Mankind is unworthy of existing," Aspen translated Aazalith's words. "For many years, humans have exploited everything around them, taking what is not theirs. They commit more atrocities to their kind than the monsters they fear. And it was humans who murdered her children and stole her power. She will never forget. She will never forgive."

Mara watched the divine. Knowing the great dragon could not be reasoned with, she unsheathed Nightingale. Actions spoke louder than words, and Mara refused to allow Ardana's destruction. The divine received the message and grew displeased. Aazalith slammed her arms onto the women's vessel. Judging by the sheer power and weight of the divine, the ship was bound to break in two.

However, it remained in one piece. Mara looked back at Aspen and saw her trembling. The Watcher had created a wall of light to protect the ship. But Aazalith refused to yield. Electricity surged around the divine's claws and Aspen. The Watcher raised her right hand, the eyes on her visor glowing brightly.

Suddenly, a booming roar came from the other ships. The guardsmen began to fire the cannons, while the knights shot at the divine with ballistas. The silver-tipped spearheads penetrated her flesh, as one bore into her wing.

The dragon screeched as she backed off. Aazalith grew enraged and turned on one of the other ships. A single swipe of her massive claws was more than enough to destroy a vessel on the left. No one survived the attack. The divine returned her attention to the two undying and attacked their ship again. Aspen kept her barrier up to stop the creature from destroying their vessel.

"Why is she attacking us?" Mara asked.

"We are the only ones who can kill the Forlorn," Aspen said between pants. "Without Amara, the divine is as good as dead." Then she cried out in pain. Electric sparks surged around her. The Watcher was being pushed to her limit again.

Seeing the divine's claws coming closer, Mara needed to do something quickly. She ran at the dragon's left hand and swung with Nightingale. Her attacks bounced off; it was like hitting a rock. She stopped, fearing Nightingale would break, but had to do something quickly. The huntress reached into her cloak. Taking her moonstone necklace, she inserted the gem into the pommel. Nightingale transformed into a Lord Slayer as the etchings glowed bright blue. She attacked the claws again. After a few strikes, the divine yanked her arm back. Mara watched the magical essence flowing through the blade and into the moonstone. Ignoring the divine's roar, she dashed to the other hand. The huntress struck a few times, cutting through the rock-hard scales. Aazalith pulled back and screeched.

Then the remaining three vessels shot at the divine. A cannonball hit Aazalith's right wing, producing a loud cracking sound. The creature unleashed a pained roar. If Aazalith wanted to fly away, it was now out of the question.

Mara turned her attention to Aspen. "Are you okay?"

The Watcher calmed down, though breathing heavily. Mara began to approach Aspen to see if she was okay, but the divine's roar drew her attention.

Aazalith took her anger out on another ship. She opened her jaws, unleashing a large stream of flames upon it. The artillery caught fire and exploded, engulfing the whole ship. The huntress frowned at the burning vessel, doubting that anyone survived.

"Mara, look out!" Aspen yelled.

Mara turned to see the divine's gaze upon her. Aazalith opened her jaws, then slammed her head forward, intending to devour Mara. The huntress ducked out of the way, but still felt the impact of the divine's slam. The ship gained a gaping hole, yet their vessel remained afloat. Mara hit the deck with a thud. That was very painful. Mara groaned as she tried to get up.

Then she noticed the Moon Lantern before her. It was separated from her person while dodging the attack. The lantern glowed brighter while lying on the bow of the ship. The divine took notice and lowered her head to investigate. When her mouth came close, the lantern unleashed a bright explosion of light.

Mara and Aspen covered their eyes. The lantern unleashed a force of energy, causing Aazalith to throw her head back. After the light faded, the two women uncovered their eyes. The divine remained stunned. Mara got up and approached the lantern. After picking it up, she looked at Aspen. The Watcher's eyes glowed again as she levitated from the deck.

"I can sense the Forlorn within the rib cage," Aspen said. "I'm going to slam the ship into Aazalith. According to my calculations, it should penetrate the divine's torso and stun her. You must break open any ribs and the sternum so we can get inside."

"What?"

Before the huntress could understand, the vessel backed away from the dragon. Once it was far enough, Aspen pushed the craft forward. Thanks to the Watcher, it travelled swiftly. The remaining vessels took notice and attempted to keep up. The huntress grabbed a rail and braced for impact. When the ship reached the divine, the bowsprit tore through abdominal muscles. Incapacitated and defenceless, Aazalith roared in agony.

Aspen's eyes remained glowing. "Fire the ballistas."

All of a sudden, the other two ships fired their ballistas at the divine. One of the spears hit Aazalith's face, dislocating her bottom jaw. Another penetrated her neck. Two were embedded deep in her torso. At this point, the divine was in no condition to do anything.

Mara recovered and dashed at the divine. Taking the powered-up Nightingale, she hacked and slashed at the dragon's chest. The scales and bones gave way, allowing her to cut a path. As soon as the huntress created an opening, the two undying fled into Aazalith's body.

* * *

Being inside the divine was like being inside a dark cave, albeit a very bad smelling one stinking of blood and guts. Mara took out the Moon Lantern and looked around. Black tendrils writhed and slithered about like snakes.

Magical essence flowed throughout the divine's body. Muscles and flesh formed a dark tunnel surrounding the two. A light emanated from one end.

Walking towards the light, the huntress had an uneasy feeling. She gazed at Aspen, who was beside her.

"Never expected you to do that," Mara grumbled.

The Watcher walked past her. "It worked, did it not?"

Mara gazed at Aspen until she heard a cry before them. Mara stared into the light. "Amara..."

"We must end this," Aspen said.

The two followed the sounds of the cries.

Eventually, they found the core. The two women stood before a great white sphere surrounded by dark tendrils. Attached to it was a woman with pure white skin. She resembled a statue with her hands in prayer. Only the upper half of her body was visible while white, long hair partially obscured the face. The Forlorn remained still, eyes closed as if she were sleeping. As the huntress watched her, she wondered what Amara was thinking. Did this girl still remember the pain she endured long ago?

"It is best to kill her now," Aspen suggested.

Mara nodded in agreement, then took a step forward with Nightingale in hand. Suddenly, the Forlorn's eyes flew open to reveal pitch-black orbs. A dark viscous ooze poured from them, contrasting with her white skin. The pain and rage radiating from the undying froze Mara in her tracks. The huntress could feel her heart thumping in her chest. The Forlorn looked furious as she stared at the two.

The unexpected cries of Aspen drew Mara's attention onto her friend. A tendril had impaled Aspen through her heart, blood pouring from her wound. The Watcher was heaving while looking at her injury. The huntress glanced back at the Forlorn, noticing her glare upon Aspen. The undying decided to take her anger out on the Watcher. It happened so fast. More tendrils burst out of the ground and pierced Aspen. One tore through the back of her head and out of her mouth. The force ripped off her visor. The Watcher twitched as blood seeped from her mouth and body.

Mara grew horrified. "Aspen!"

Before the huntress could do anything, a tendril struck her, sending her flying. Hitting the ground with a thud, she tried to recover but was too late. The tendrils tore off pieces of Aspen's armour. Several more tendrils wrapped around and crushed the Watcher's body. Aspen gave no resistance because she was already dead. The core absorbed her, her soul claimed by the Forlorn. The undying also sank into the bright orb. Mara glared at the pulsing sphere while struggling to her feet. She gripped Nightingale.

Intense rage burned within Mara, for Aspen's death pushed her over the edge. Rushing to the centre, the huntress avoided the tendrils, which the Forlorn controlled from within the heart. Upon getting close, the huntress slashed at the core with her sword. Mara then heard the divine's roar as her surroundings shook. Aazalith was displeased. More tendrils shot at her, forcing her back. Mara returned to finish the job, but more tendrils wrapped around the core, forming a shield.

Mara bashed her sword against it, yet it would not budge. The huntress backed away, heaving in frustration. Even with a powered-up Nightingale, none of her attacks had any effect. Looking around, she noticed four tendrils connected to the heart, where magical essence flowed through them. What would happen if she attacked them?

With nothing to lose, the huntress attacked the glowing tendrils. Upon severing the first one, the shield weakened. The Forlorn retaliated by shooting more tendrils at her. Mara avoided them while slicing another. Unable to stop the huntress, the Forlorn was losing her protection. Aazalith released a weak roar. With the core severed, the divine was dying. And the Forlorn was now vulnerable. Holding Nightingale in both hands, Mara raised the blade over her head.

Plunging the sword into the core, Mara saw the light pulsing a few times before going dead. The sphere split open, and a pitiful creature crawled out. The Forlorn began to change. Her skin became tanned as her hair turned dark. No longer were her eyes black, but a lighter brown colour. She wore tattered brown rags that were once a dress. She looked identical to Mara. The huntress knew what happened, for the rules of the undying applied to them all.

Amara whimpered while crawling away, though she wasn't going far. Seeing this defenceless creature reminded Mara of the helpless hare in the snare. She could have been a better person and showed mercy, but Aspen's broken remains were in the core. And her murderer was now trying to flee for her life. The huntress gazed back at the undying and followed. She only needed to walk to catch up. The girl began to cry.

It confused the huntress. "Why are you crying?"

Amara would not answer her question. She continued to crawl away while bawling her eyes out. Mara watched with glowing eyes while following her. A thought crossed her mind. Did Amara feel guilty? Mara had seen this before in children. Whenever they did something wrong, they would cry. Some claimed it was because they knew they did something wrong and felt guilty. Others would say they do it because they got caught, thus putting on fake tears. The huntress leaned towards the latter. Gripping Nightingale, she approached Amara and stabbed her through the back. Mara was swift, giving no second thought to her actions. The girl went as soon as the sword sliced through her heart. She fell to the ground and became motionless. She gave no resistance. Amara was dead within seconds while a pool of blood formed around her body.

Mara stood frozen, staring at the corpse of the first reincarnation. The quest Harold sent her on was near completion. According to Alkina, she only had one more to obtain. Mara was on the cusp of reaching her goal. But why were tears forming in her eyes? Why was she feeling guilty all of a sudden? This girl was a monster, or Mara kept telling herself.

However, the more she gazed at Amara's body, the more she began to realize this was simply untrue. Many people demonized this girl. She was a victim of Kallisto, who sought to prevent her rival's return. Lying priests had spurred a crowd who called for this woman's death. In the end, Mara saw no monster but an innocent caught in the crossfire. In some ways, she saw herself in Amara.

She now understood the nature of humanity and monsters. And why is it that people turned into creatures after death. Magic played a role, but there was so much more to it. Humans were monsters from the moment they were born. It did not matter if one was good or evil. No one was safe from the sickness. Mara heard it before from Lady Isabella. Even the alpha werewolf she hunted in the previous month told her this. Even Aazalith said it.

Mara snapped out of her thoughts when the soul rose from Amara's body. The huntress reached out her hand. It was the only thing she could do. After absorbing it, her body flared up in pain. The searing pain in her veins made her collapse and have a fit.

Chapter Twenty-Two

Innocence Lost

"Amara," Mara uttered.

Opening her eyes, she found herself lying next to the remains of Amara and Aspen.

At least she had honoured Khan's request, and his daughter no longer suffered. Gazing at Amara's body, Mara realized how dangerous magic could be. This primal force had twisted Amara's innocence, transforming her into a creature of pure rage and corruption.

Gazing at Aspen's body, Mara grew solemn. Their plan fell apart as she failed the Watcher. Aspen was to claim the Forlorn's soul. Then they would take on Kallisto and her followers together. Now Mara had to face them alone. How was she going to explain Aspen's death to James?

The huntress struggled to her feet. Her body protested, though there was a silver lining. If Alkina was right, Mara was now the last undying. Her attention was drawn to Nightingale, lying on the ground before her. She crouched down and picked up the sword. Thank goodness it remained intact. After sheathing her blade, the huntress removed the moonstone and put her necklace back on. She still had her crossbow and the Moon Lantern. At least she had everything she needed to take on Kallisto. Mara also noticed that she was still in control. She did not need to use the Binding Dagger, but it remained strapped to her belt just in case.

The sound of rushing water drew her attention as the blackened sea came in, filling the dragon's corpse. Mara fled back to the entrance she created earlier. Once outside, she discovered the bow of the ship already submerged.

The bowsprit remained firmly lodged in the divine's torso. And nothing could stop the great dragon from sinking into the ocean.

Then she spotted a lone lifeboat, which came with the ship. The huntress dashed to it. Unsheathing Nightingale, she cut the ropes, then pushed the small vessel into the ocean. Mara managed to get on while the boat drifted away from the dead divine and the sinking ship.

* * *

Mara reckoned it had been at least an hour since boarding the lifeboat. She laid in the boat as it drifted in the ocean. It was still nighttime as she gazed up at the darkened sky. No longer was the moon red, and the stars shone in the black velvet sky. Sitting up to a seated position, Mara scanned the dark sea. But no ship was visible. She needed to figure out how to get back to land. She could use the paddles, but it was very dark. The moon water was no help, and the Moon Lantern only lit up to Aazalith's presence. Now the lantern was dead. Maybe the current could push her in the right direction. Mara lay back down and stared up at the starry sky. Closing her eyes, the huntress wanted to rest a little.

All of a sudden, a bright light shone upon her face. It went through her eyelids, creating a red tint.

"Here! She's over here!"

She heard a man yelling but did not recognize the voice. Mara opened her eyes to see a large vessel near her little lifeboat. She did not see it before. A guardsman watched her from the ship's deck, shining a bright lantern in her direction.

"She's over here! She survived!"

Mara watched while the man continued to yell. She remained frozen and exhausted. Everything went dark as she lost consciousness. The man's voice faded away into silence.

* * *

Mara awoke to the frigid air. The huntress did not die, though surviving the ordeal was a miracle. Opening her eyes, Mara discovered two guardsmen carrying her on a plank of wood. Once they reached the port of Har' Yhan, the guardsmen lowered her to the ground and walked away.

Sitting up, Mara spotted the two remaining ships before her. She also noticed some damage to the port, with some fishing vessels knocked over. Other crafts became beached, likely from the churning sea. Despite Aazalith being nowhere near land, she was still able to cause some damage.

The guardsmen and the knights were busy retrieving the dead washed up onshore. Her gaze fell onto the sea. The vessel, shared by her and Aspen, sank further into the ocean. The divine's body dragged it under, producing loud cracking sounds as the ship gave way.

As Mara approached the edge of the port, a gleaming object in the water caught her eye. Taking a closer look, she found Aspen's broken mask. A remaining fragment of the Watcher washed up on shore while the rest sank into the ocean along with Amara. She stared at the visor before picking it up.

"Miss Ashwood?"

She turned to see Chancellor Davis accompanied by some guardsmen. Evan was also present, making a report of all the casualties. They had witnessed Aazalith's defeat, and they were not alone. Around twenty to fifty civilians anticipating the divine's awakening came by, despite being warned to stay away from Har' Yhan. But none could blame them for wanting to gaze upon a god-like creature who had slumbered for a thousand years.

Mara kept her gaze on the chancellors while approaching them. Davis stared back at her, looking as if he saw a ghost. The huntress figured he never expected her to survive the encounter tonight.

"Is it true?" Davis inquired. "Is the Dark One...?"

Mara nodded. "The Dark One is dead."

She heard gasps and murmurs around her.

"What about the prophecy?" asked a bystander.

The huntress wondered if she should speak the truth. She might upset some disciples in the crowd. But everyone had a right to know.

"There is no prophecy," Mara said. "Kallikratés was losing power in Ardana. They plotted to use the creature to destroy this land and their opponents. The Faith was responsible for most of the seals breaking, starting with Saskia of Ozin."

Everyone was gawking at her. Davis stood slack-jawed while Evan looked disturbed.

"What?" Davis questioned. He knew about the possible corruption within the Faith, but not its depth. It was one thing to arrest several women, then sell them to a rogue guild. It was another to hire the same guild to terrorize the people of Ardana. But now the Faith was responsible for the awakening of the Dark One?

"She is lying!"

A middle-aged man approached them, condescendingly looking at Mara. Judging by his fancy attire, she reckoned he was a noble as well as a follower of the Faith.

"If I'm not mistaken, that is the Cursed Herald from the prophecy," he said. "The one who broke all the seals to the Dark One."

Knowing this would happen, the huntress was ready to stand her ground.

"There was no Cursed Herald," Mara argued. "That was another thing made up by the Faith, so they could justify hunting and murdering innocent women."

Everyone glanced at her, then the nobleman.

"Aye, they arrested my daughter for no reason," said a middle-class man.

"More lies spread by the Cursed Herald," the noble claimed, ignoring the man. "She is wicked. A depraved soul who seeks to spread lies and poison the minds of anyone listening!"

"I'm wicked?" Mara questioned. "How often do you visit the temple?"

The nobleman gave a strange look. "Well, I go there often. It is a sacred place."

Mara folded her arms. "Did you even know the temple sits on a source of the magic blight?"

Davis gazed back at the huntress, sporting a puzzled expression on his face. "What do you mean, Miss Ashwood?"

Mara pointed at the dead divine. "That was Aazalith, one of the Seven Divines of Thoron," she revealed. "She attacked Ardana once before, seeking to destroy humanity. Thoron aided this land and stopped Aazalith by removing her soul, which is currently inside Golden Mountain." She shook her head. "Both the divine's body and soul were the sources of the magic blight. Not only does magic cause cadavers to rise as monsters, but it can also turn the hearts of the living wicked. So, if you ever wonder why your neighbour is an asshole, that's probably why!"

People murmured to each other.

"It must be true," said a lower-class woman. "No wonder why them nobles are so snobby and rude. Acting like they're better than everyone."

"Not all of us are bad," a noblewoman argued. "Though my neighbour is a devoted follower who travels to the temple often. He changed over time, and now I can't stand him."

The nobleman stood there, placing his hands on his hips. "Thoron is a land ruled by demons," he declared. "The Thoron Sages are nothing more than servants of demons!"

Mara glared at him. "If the divines are demons, then so are Kallisto and Kratés!"

Those listening responded with a gasp. Both Davis and Evan gawked at her.

"What do you mean?" Davis inquired.

"They served a covenant sworn to protect mankind," said the huntress. "But they betrayed their own by stealing the soul. That's how the Faith of Kallikratés rose!" She glared back at the nobleman, seeing his astonished face. "I know this because Harold of the Silver Thorns was part of that covenant, as well as my predecessor, Thalia. They were prisoners for a long time before escaping. Yet the Faith only focused on hunting Thalia."

"Why is that?" Davis asked.

"She was the only one who could stop their gods. So they began hunting us, starting with Amara. After Kallisto and her followers captured her, Amara escaped and awoke Aazalith by accident. She spent a thousand years fused to the divine's core. I was the only one who could slay her." She looked at Davis. "Did you know Aazalith was seeking her soul?"

"Is that so?"

Mara nodded. "She was after Kallisto and Kratés." She looked back at the noble. "Oh, and the Legend of Kratés is a lie. He never stayed behind to fight the divine. Kallisto murdered him."

After she finished, Mara glanced around to see everyone looking astonished. Davis was speechless, stunned by the revelation. The truth had arrived, and it was up to the people on what they wanted to do with it. Gazing back at the nobleman, Mara saw his face turning red. He looked angry to hear those words.

"How dare you speak blasphemy?" He pointed at her. "You should be arrested for slander!" The nobleman then addressed the other followers. "We shall take her to the temple for judgment!"

The other followers began to approach the huntress, only to be stopped by the guardsmen. Davis stood before them while the guardsmen held them back.

"You will not approach her," Davis spoke in a stern tone. He looked to a guard. "Take her back to Mirahyll. Make sure she returns home safely."

A guardsman beckoned her.

As Mara followed the guardsman to a coach, the followers glared at her. The nobleman chased after her. "Why are you defending her?"

Something in the huntress snapped. She turned around and slapped the nobleman across the face, knocking him down. Everyone froze like statues. Some stared with wide eyes while others had slack jaws. The nobleman sat there with a profound red mark on the left side of his face. He lifted his gaze to her and began to sneer.

"She hit me!" shouted the noble.

She reached over and grabbed his collar. Her eyes began to glow. She removed her mask, showing the dark blotches around her eyes and down the sides of her face.

"I lost everything," Mara hissed. "Because of you and your gods!" She glanced at the other disciples. "And yet, I chose to save your worthless lives."

Mara released his collar. She stood up straight and walked away, not caring if she offended. Chancellor Davis gave an approving look after hearing her words. She walked with Davis while the rest of the guardsmen held the crowd back. Looking out to the ocean, the huntress watched the last of the divine's body. Now void of magic, Aazalith turned into a black mass and sank into the sea.

She boarded the carriage to Mirahyll with the chancellor accompanying her. The horses galloped at a higher speed as the two rode back to the city. In Mara's hands was Aspen's visor. She held onto it, never letting go.

"Ardana and this world have no idea how much it owes you," Davis said.

She kept her eyes on the visor. "No amount of money will fix my problems or undo everything that happened," she murmured.

Chancellor Davis took note of the broken visor, growing aware of Aspen's death.

* * *

Within a few hours, Mara arrived at Mirahyll.

"Drop me off here," she requested. "I'll walk the rest of the way."

"Are you sure?" Davis asked.

"Yes, thank you." Mara then left the carriage.

The chancellor watched her. "Miss Ashwood, I want you to know that your actions will not go unnoticed. I shall make sure Ardana is aware of what you have done for her people."

Then they parted ways. Mara remained silent while walking to the Moen Residence. On the way home, she noticed several people surrounding the town crier.

"Hear ye! Hear ye! The Dark One is dead," the town crier announced. "Ardana is safe!"

Many of the city folk were surprised to hear this. They glanced at each other.

A lower-class man asked, "So, it's true? The so-called Cursed Herald saved us?"

"What? I thought she was supposed to bring an end to the world, not save it."

"I saw it with my own eyes," a woman said. "She and another woman went with an army to confront the Dark One in the ocean."

"That is not what happened!"

A nobleman stormed up to them. He was similar to the one Mara encountered in Har' Yhan but younger.

"Kallisto and Kratés defeated the Dark One," he claimed.

The huntress shook her head, for even the fanatics would say or do anything to discredit her role. It was classic damage control.

"Praise Kallikratés," the noble announced.

"Praise Kallikratés," a few other followers chanted in unison.

Mara rolled her eyes and turned away. At least the land of Ardana had been spared tonight. But Kallisto remained a problem. Mara needed to figure out how she was going to confront the goddess.

For now, she would go home to rest as this had been a long day. Mara saved Ardana but lost Aspen. She took her time, trying to think of a way to explain Aspen's death to James. Walking through the streets of Mirahyll, she saw people staring at her. By now, everyone learned what had happened. She ran to James' home. The door was unlocked, so she invited herself inside.

"James?" Mara called.

She found him in a chair. He dozed off while waiting for their return.

"James," she called again. Mara pulled down her mask to reveal her face.

James woke up, appearing groggy until he saw Mara. Then his eyes grew wide as his mouth dropped open.

"Mara, you came back!" James exclaimed. "Then it means…"

She nodded. "Aazalith is gone. Ardana is safe for now."

James looked astounded, for the plan had worked. "Then…" He paused and glanced around. "Where's Aspen?"

Mara gave a sad look while presenting the broken visor. Upon seeing it, his face dropped. He held out his hands to take it back.

"I'm sorry." Mara placed the visor in his hands. "Aspen was killed and absorbed by the Forlorn. Even though I killed the undying, I couldn't save her."

James gazed back at her in sorrow. "I hope Aspen didn't suffer for long. If Allen were here, he wouldn't have let her go."

"None of us would have, but she chose this." Mara changed the subject. "I intend to leave at sunrise."

"Why?"

"I'm going to confront Kallisto. If I need to bring the fight to her, then I will." He shook his head. "You can't."

"If I stay, they will come here. And I am not losing another friend."

James became silent, for she was right. They lost so much because of Kallikratés. There were so many more atrocities they committed. The Faith needed to go.

He gave a stern look. "Very well. Get as much rest as you can. Make sure you're ready to take them on!" His face softened into a smile.

Mara gazed at him, then smiled back.

She went to her room to prepare. After making her preparations, Mara collapsed onto her bed and fell asleep. The day had caught up with her.

* * *

"Mara! Mara, wake up!"

James' frantic voice jarred Mara awake. The first thing she saw was his panicked face, his eyes filled with fear. She then noticed a dark grey haze seeping into the room, accompanied by the familiar smell of smoke.

"James? What's going on?"

She thought she was dreaming, but the terror in his eyes made her realize this was real.

"The house is on fire!" James exclaimed. "We need to go now before the place collapses on us!"

She shot up from her bed and grabbed her belongings, including Nightingale, her crossbow, and the Binding Dagger. Mara had to leave some things behind like Dad's weapons after retrieving them from Edwin. After gathering her belongings, she followed James to the door.

He opened the door, and the roaring flames greeted them. The fire had engulfed most of the living room, except for a path to their escape. They needed to stay low to avoid smoke inhalation. Visibility was limited. While Mara followed James, she could hear loud popping and sizzling sounds from the back of the laboratory. The flames devoured all of Allen's work, including the Gateway.

Mara was the first to escape as the two made it out to safety. Black smoke and embers filled the morning sky. Gazing back at the burning building, the huntress knew someone was responsible. Her eyes scanned the streets, searching for the perpetrators, but could not find them. They might have fled as soon as they set fire to James' home. The cowards couldn't be bothered to face her. The city's inhabitants watched the fire devour the home laboratory.

"I don't see them," Mara said but got no response. "James?"

Gazing back at him, she found James frozen like a statue with his face contorted in pain. Mara was confused. What was wrong? When she took a step towards him, a red spot formed on the front of his clothes. The huntress stopped and watched as it grew bigger. He tried to speak, but only blood poured out. A steel and silver sword emerged through the front of his chest, slicing through his heart. James was dead within seconds. His body fell forward and hit the ground.

Mara froze while watching the last of her friends die before her eyes. Her breathing grew uneven as she stared at his corpse. She lifted her gaze to the one behind this atrocious act. The huntress recognized the dark grey garb, the golden plates of armour on the left shoulder and arm, and the red cape draped over the right side of his body.

Commander White stood between the burning building and the corpse of the man he slew. A blank expression decorated his face as he began to clean the Hand of Kratés. With a single swing of his sword, blood flew off and splattered onto the ground. He swung again to remove any more excess.

Mara could not believe her eyes. It was him! Why was he here? The Watcher had erased his memories, taking the commander out of commission and restoring Karl to his true self. He was supposed to be in Corlin with Mr. White, and away from Kallisto! Mara gazed at him in bewilderment, but he continued to ignore her. Taking out a cloth, he wiped the blood off of his sword.

The huntress reached for Nightingale with a trembling hand. He stopped cleaning his blade, yet he did not look at her.

"How could you?" Mara demanded, unsheathing her sword.

The commander lifted his gaze to reveal cloudy eyes. After he finished cleaning his blade, he discarded the bloodied cloth and strode towards her. Commander White possessed an emotionless expression on his face.

"For aiding an enemy of the Faith, his sentence was death," he spoke in a cold tone. Commander White paid no mind while walking on the man he just killed. He used it as a bridge to avoid the pool of blood forming around James' body. "You are under arrest for spreading blasphemous slander, endangering the land of Ardana, and conspiring against the Goddess."

Walking on the corpse, the commander shifted all of his weight on the head. Mara's blood was boiling. It was one thing to witness the death of her friend, but seeing his murderer show indecency was too much. He noticed her sword, then glared at her.

"Sheathe your blade before you hurt yourself," the commander said coldly.

She could not take it anymore. Mara yelled while dashing at him. The commander also closed the distance, his speed catching her off guard. He backhanded her in the face, knocking her to the ground. Nightingale fell beside her. She reached for it, only to get a boot to the stomach.

The huntress attempted to stand, but he kicked her in the head. She fell backwards in disorientation. The commander thumped his foot onto the undying's chest. She cried out in pain while trying to push him off of her. He shifted his whole weight. Then came a painful snap; one of her ribs had broke.

The Holy Blades stood back as the spectators froze in fear. None dared to intervene.

Looking up at the commander's face, the huntress saw something likened to a beast or a demon. Pure rage burned in his eyes as he clenched his teeth. She tried to say something, yet could not.

"Shut up, you stupid bitch," Commander White snarled. "Just shut up!" He stomped on her a few times.

Mara had no time to defend herself. She heard another painful crack from her chest, for he had broken some more ribs. Blood went flying as he attacked her. Even she never expected this level of cruelty from him. So far, Mara received a black eye, a cut on her right cheek, several bruises, and six broken ribs. Her left eye was swollen shut. She could feel a puncture in her right lung. Yet, by some fluke, Mara remained alive and conscious. The pain was intense, and the tears were beyond her control.

Seeing her battered face in tears, the commander grew agitated.

"Stop crying!" Commander White shouted. "You look uglier when you cry!" He raised his foot, ready to smash her head.

He brought his boot down, but something stopped him. The spectators gasped. The commander looked down, seeing Mara holding his boot. She was heaving as she glared up at him with teary eyes. She refused to allow this man to beat her any further.

A familiar sensation washed over her as her eyes glowed blue. Thalia was taking over. And Mara had no problem letting her. If it meant defeating the commander, so be it.

With much of Thalia's powers restored, she forced him off of her. Mara then felt her ribs mending themselves, as all of her cuts and bruises faded away. And her left eye had fully healed.

Mara watched as Thalia confronted the commander. Stretching out her right hand, Nightingale flew off the ground and returned to her.

The Holy Blades gasped as they watched her warily.

Thalia turned her gaze onto the commander.

"I don't want to fight you," Mara heard Thalia talking to him.

The commander stared back with a blank expression. Mara watched him, sensing something was not right. Dark fumes rose from his body. A dreadful sensation washed over her.

"His soul is completely corrupted!"

Mara was shocked by Thalia's words. What did she mean?

Commander White suddenly dashed at her with his sword in hand. Thalia was not quick enough to free his mind. She could only block his attack with Nightingale at the moment. He kept gazing at her with a hollow stare while their blades clashed. Looking into his eyes, Mara thought she saw Kallisto staring back at her. It seemed the goddess was controlling him as if he were a puppet.

The commander's eyes roamed up and down her body until they focused on a particular item strapped to her belt. Thalia glanced down and saw the Binding Dagger. Before she could do anything, he grabbed the dagger and plunged it into her torso.

"No!" Mara cried. She was in control of her voice.

In an instant, she lost Thalia's powers. The original undying had vanished like an extinguished flame. Mara sank to her knees with the weapon still buried in her body. She grabbed the blade and pulled it out, a black ooze seeping from her injury. The dagger disintegrated, crumbling away into dust. A horrible sensation washed over Mara. She wanted to stop Thalia from taking over, but not like this. And Thalia was not the only one sealed away.

Gazing up at the commander, Mara shook her head. "How could you?" Tears filled her eyes as she clutched her chest. "What about your wife, Evelyn?"

Commander White gave a cold stare. "I have no wife," he said. "Kallisto is my everything."

He then delivered a swift kick to the side of her head. She was thrown to the ground and knocked out cold.

* * *

She awoke in a prison cell. The first thing Mara saw were the chains and shackles binding her wrists. At least she did not die. A Holy Blade walked out of her cell, locking the door behind him. The huntress found herself in a dungeon. She recognized this place.

It was thirty years ago, after her transformation into an undying. Once, she attempted to escape. But the Holy Blades captured her and kept her here. She was later dragged out in chains to watch Dad die.

Gazing through the bars, Mara saw the commander on the other side. He had Nightingale. The Holy Blades took everything except her jewellery and the keepsakes. They probably thought her necklace was a useless trinket as well.

Commander White unsheathed the sword to glimpse upon its craftsmanship.

"This will make a fine trophy," said the commander. He looked up at her and gave a cold glare. "She will be executed tonight as well."

"Yes, sir," a Holy Blade responded.

Then they walked away. The huntress rose to her feet and approached the bars. There were four rows of prison cells stacked on top of each other. She was on the top floor. Others were trapped here—people who had offended the Faith and the gods. Some appeared to have been here for quite some time. She spotted an emaciated man with raggedy clothes, a long beard, and long fingernails. A few others shared a similar appearance like him.

"Mara," called an old man.

Mara glanced back and saw a small window with bars on her right. The voice was familiar. She approached it with caution.

"Mr. White?" Mara called quietly. She heard the older man whimpering.

"I am so sorry," he said as his breath hitched. "I never wanted any of this to happen."

"What are you talking about?" Mara gazed through the window and saw him huddled near the corner. He seemed very dishevelled and rough. "Mr. White?"

He looked up at the huntress. She froze upon seeing his face. No longer did he appear to be in his sixties. The former college professor looked as if he had lost twenty years of his life. More wrinkles were present on his face, his hair was stringier, and his beard was longer. His muscles had wasted away, and his skin was looser.

Mara gave an astonished look. "What is this?"

Mr. White appeared sorrowful. "I haven't been honest with you," he spoke in a weak voice.

"Well, that I can see!"

The older man slowly rose to his feet. He groaned in pain as his old bones struggled to support him. He hobbled towards the window. "Kallisto used a spell to slow my ageing. That was my reward for playing a role in your demise—to live long enough to see the Golden Age return. But I betrayed them."

"What happened?"

"The Holy Blades were waiting for us," he revealed. "Kallisto learned of my plan and ordered our capture. She undid the spell on me, reverting me to my true age. And Karl..." He paused briefly. "Upon discovering that he no longer remembered Evelyn, Kallisto completely took his mind and ordered him to capture you."

"I know," Mara said. "He murdered James and attacked me. I let Thalia take over so she could stop him, but Kallisto was in control. She saw the Binding Dagger and made him snatch it. He stabbed me before we could do anything."

The older man frowned. "Then, it is hopeless. Kallisto won. All the things that could've defeated her are now gone."

The huntress gazed at him. Should she tell him of the last remaining hope? But considering his circumstances, it was safe to say that he was no longer a member of the Faith. It had taken its toll on him.

Mara took a deep breath. "That's where you're wrong, old man," she said. "Godstruck was just an ordinary sword."

Mr. White's eyes widened. "What do you mean?"

"It was the moonstone. That's Kallisto's weakness." Then, "I know why Dad died. It wasn't just to trigger my transformation, but he knew how to forge a weapon like Godstruck. He made Nightingale before he died. It can take a moonstone." She gestured to her necklace. "I have one, but I need my sword back."

He watched her, then changed the topic. "So, you've killed the Dark One?"

"Yes, and no," Mara replied.

"What do you mean?"

"Still have to deal with Kallisto," she answered. "And I don't know if I can save Karl." Mara sighed. "If Thalia couldn't help him, what can I do?"

The old man said, "Defeating Kallisto might be the only option left." Then he sat down.

She nodded before turning away from the window. The huntress returned to the back of her cell. All she could do was think about her plan. It was risky, relying on her enemies' ego and pride. The commander would likely have Nightingale on his person to add insult to injury. She hoped he remained oblivious to the true nature of her sword.

Chapter Twenty-Three

The Execution

On the night of December 26, the Holy Blades dragged Mara into the throne room. Kallisto and her followers watched in anticipation. Mr. White was bound, awaiting his execution after they have dealt with her. Mara spotted Nightingale strapped to Commander White's belt. At least her plan might have a chance of working. The Holy Blades then forced her to a device, restraining her neck and wrists. Before walking away, they removed her hood and mask.

Kallisto stepped forward. "Behold! This vile woman tried to take my husband before," she announced, pointing at the huntress. "Now, she returns to tear us apart once more!"

The followers gasped while others roared out for Mara's execution.

The queen raised her hand to silence her followers. "She shall never return."

Mara frowned, wondering what Kallisto had planned. A male priest stepped forward with a golden box. He sank to his knees before the goddess and lifted the box over his head. Kallisto opened it. She reached inside to retrieve a green-bladed dagger. It was a basilisk blade, the same weapon used on several other undying. And now they were going to use it on Mara.

Kallisto looked to the commander and beckoned him. He obeyed and approached his goddess. Then he sank to his knees.

Kallisto gazed down at him. "Rise, my commander," she ordered.

Commander White rose to his feet and looked to his goddess lovingly.

She presented the dagger to him. "I shall give you the honour of dealing out the punishment. Send a message to those who would dare separate us."

Commander White lifted his hands to receive the basilisk blade. He gazed at it before looking to his queen.

"Yes, my Goddess," he said in a slow and deep tone. It sounded like he was in a deep trance. He then approached Mara.

Mara tried to struggle out of the bonds, but they were stronger than anticipated.

The commander stopped at least two feet from her. With a free hand, he reached over and tore her cape off. Commander White gazed at the open "V" shape in her shirt before raising the dagger to his face. Staring into her eyes, he pointed the basilisk blade at her.

She watched as he lowered the blade to her chest slowly and deliberately. When the sharp tip made contact, he did not stop. The commander continued to press the dagger until it broke her skin.

Mara screamed in excruciating pain. She renewed her struggling, yet the bonds held her in place. Commander White did not react. He kept pushing the dagger into her body. Kallisto and her followers only watched, showing no remorse. Mr. White could not stomach the sight. He looked ashamed that this was happening to Mara but was helpless to stop it.

"This will make sure you will never return," Kallisto hissed.

The commander pulled the blade out. Mara's body jolted in pain, though the restraining device did not budge. Looking down, she saw her veins turning black with poison. Her skin began to pale and decay. Seeing the stab wound made her think of Morgan in her last moments. She felt another sharp pain in her chest and screamed. Commander White stabbed her again, creating a new wound. Mara's hands tightened into fists as she pulled on the bonds. She tried with all her might to break free, but her strength was fading. He watched with no emotion while keeping the blade in her.

"Stop it!" Mara screamed. "Just stop! How could you do this?"

The commander was unmoved by her pleas. He remained silent, his face devoid of any emotion. Looking into his glazed eyes, she could no longer find the man he once was. With his humanity stripped away, only pure evil remained. Kallisto approached them.

"He is assuming the role Kratés failed to fulfill," the goddess claimed.

The commander watched Mara in disgust. "I must atone for the failures of my progenitor."

"Karl, wake up!" Mara cried, fighting back the pain and tears. "Why can't you see she's controlling you? She is using you!"

Commander White kept glaring at her. "Kallisto opened my eyes. You are the Cursed Herald. You are evil."

Mara clenched her teeth. None of her words reached him.

Kallisto sneered at her. "Admit it. You tried to take my husband and throne."

The huntress glared back at the goddess. "How could you call him your husband? You murdered him!"

The goddess frowned. "So, you know the truth?" Kallisto shrugged. "Not that it mattered. Kratés died because he was led astray by your progenitor. You and the other reincarnations must pay for her sins!"

Mara could not believe her ears. Even though Kallisto admitted to her crime, she still blamed Thalia for Kratés' death. Thus, her justification for murdering innocent women.

The goddess looked to her commander. "Come to me."

Commander White kept his cold stare on Mara for a while before returning to his goddess. He also left the dagger in her chest. She watched as he bent the knee before Kallisto. The goddess stroked the side of his face. The commander's head followed the motion of her hand.

Kallisto glared up at Mara while doing this. "Do you see? Kratés and all who come after him belong to me! I own his body and soul."

Mara could not speak anymore. The dagger embedded in her chest released more poison. She began to weaken as the pain grew more intense. She could no longer breathe as black sludge rose to her throat and out of her mouth. Decay spread throughout her body. Darkness claimed her while her heart desperately tried to keep beating. Then it stopped.

* * *

"Mara," a voice whispered to her.

Mara opened her eyes and found herself alone in the throne room. It was dark. Where did everyone go? Didn't her enemies want to see her die? She looked down again.

"Mara," a female voice called to her. It sounded familiar.

Lifting her gaze, Mara saw the Watcher standing before her.

"Aspen?" Mara asked in a weak tone. "What's going on? Why are you here?"

After being stabbed by the Binding Dagger, the huntress should not be able to see the Watcher, yet Aspen stood before her.

"I broke through the veil," said the Watcher, "so I could use my remaining time to show you."

"Show me what?" Mara looked down at the dagger embedded in her chest and frowned. "It is over. They won."

"No," Aspen told her. "It is not over."

"But, I lost Thalia's powers."

"You have something better," the Watcher claimed. "Only a few knew you had it." She took a step forward and raised her hand. "Let me show you."

As soon as Aspen touched Mara's head, memories flashed before her eyes.

Mara found herself strapped to an examination table in a sick room. She recognized the place as Hemal Clinic. It was the same night she killed Lady Isabella. No one was allowed in her room. However, Commander White ignored Dr. Simon's warning. She saw him towering over her. The huntress remembered breaking free of her bonds and attacking him. She sank her fangs into his neck and drank his blood. His screams echoed in her mind. After the attack, everyone looked at her in astonishment. Mara saw her reflection revealing a more human face.

Mara then found herself in a snowy forest in the dead of night. She was fleeing from Commander White and a group of Holy Blades. The huntress got him alone, and the two fought. She remembered this as the Black Smoke Incident. She was more than a match and defeated him. After impaling him into a tree, she approached and descended upon his lap. The huntress gazed upon his beautiful face as she caressed his flawless skin. She then ran her fingers through his thick hair before grabbing it and pulling down his collar. Exposing a spot on his neck, she sank her fangs into him. He screamed as she drank his blood. Then she saw her face in the commander's armour. Colour returned to her flesh while her face grew fuller. Mara watched as she became human in her reflection.

Finally, Mara found herself standing in Dr. Moen's laboratory. It made her happy to see Allen, even though he died earlier this month. Even the Watcher was present, observing the doctor's experiment.

Mara then noticed some flasks, filled with blood. One stood out, for it was as black as night. It was her blood.

Allen used a needle to extract a small amount. Then he took another vial with different blood inside. It had a label: K. White. Commander White's blood looked unusual, sparkling with tiny sprites. Allen's notes had mentioned the high amount of magic present in his blood. Upon mixing the two, the commander's lifeblood grew dull, bereft of magic. Both Mara and Allen were stunned.

"Mara, you can defeat them," Aspen called out to her.

Mara glanced at the Watcher, seeing the latter's gaze upon her.

"Wake up."

* * *

The tingling sensation touched every nerve, bringing them back to life. The tingle turned into a burning sensation. Fire rushed through her veins, pulling Mara back from the dead. Opening her eyes, she found herself still restrained. The basilisk blade remained in her body. She had revived but lost her human form. Mara renewed her struggling. Her bonds had weakened, allowing one of her arms to break free. Then she reached for her neck and pulled on the strap. Now free from the restraining device, the huntress slumped to her knees. She glanced down at the dagger and reached for it. With all her strength, she pulled it out of her chest. Mara groaned in pain, but she removed the basilisk blade. After throwing the dagger away, she began her slow recovery. The poison sapped much of her strength. The huntress looked back at Kallisto and struggled to her feet. Taking deep breaths, Mara limped towards her.

Kallisto's face twisted with fury. "You!" she raged. "How dare you defy me?"

The huntress kept staring at the angry goddess as she came closer. No longer did she fear Kallisto. Sensing this, the goddess grew angrier. She began to mock her.

"Look at her!" Kallisto announced. "Look how ugly she is!"

The followers murmured in agreement while others laughed. The commander folded his arms and glared at Mara. Ignoring their words, Mara kept limping towards Kallisto.

Realizing the huntress was coming closer, Kallisto lifted her right hand. "Begone!"

The goddess unleashed a powerful force, knocking Mara down. The huntress cried out in pain as she hit the ground and skidded several feet away from them.

However, the huntress remained alive. Mara coughed up some blood and got up again. Everyone was surprised at her resilience. She should have been dead, but she refused to give up. After struggling to her feet, Mara began to approach the goddess again. Her body was in pain, yet she kept going.

Kallisto was furious. How dare this lowly creature defy the goddess? Insulted by Mara's insolence, Kallisto raised her hand again, releasing another powerful attack. The force threw Mara against a wall.

The huntress shouted in pain while colliding with the wall. The impact was strong enough to cause damage; cracks formed on the ivory surface. Mara slumped to the ground, though remained alive. Everyone was baffled. Despite everything done to her, she was not dying. Mara watched Kallisto and took deep breaths. She was in more pain, for one of her ribs broke, and her fractured right leg left her unable to stand. Still, the undying kept going. On her hands and knees, she crawled towards them.

The goddess was losing her patience. Even she could not believe Mara withstood so much. Kallisto approached her until she was ten feet away from the undying. Determined to finish her off, the goddess raised her hand again.

"I will strike you down again!"

Mara glared at her with glowing wolf-like eyes. Opening her mouth, the huntress launched herself at the goddess. Before Kallisto could unleash another attack, Mara vanished in a wisp of black smoke. Then she reappeared right in front of Kallisto. With a wide-open maw, the undying aimed for the goddess. Before anyone could react, the huntress clamped her jaws on Kallisto's right arm.

The followers stared in shock, their mouths agape. None could believe their eyes. Mara bit Kallisto! The queen watched in horror as this raggedy undead creature took a massive bite on her arm. The huntress held on tight while her canines penetrated the goddess' flesh and drew blood.

"How dare you? This blasphemer assaulted me!" Kallisto yelled, trying to pull her arm away, but Mara would not let go.

Enraged, the goddess began to hit Mara with her left arm. With a tightened fist, Kallisto bashed her face, bruising Mara's skin. But the huntress refused to let go.

Mara responded by strengthening her bite. Her canines dug deeper, going down to the bone. They tore through veins, causing the goddess' blood to pour down her throat. Her blood was in her mouth as well, mixing with Kallisto's. The magic coursing the goddess' veins flowed into Mara's stomach. Every cell came alive. It gave her the strength to heal. Every passing second, Mara felt stronger.

Kallisto kept hitting Mara until she noticed her arm. It began at the spot where the huntress bit her—the radiant beauty was fading as her skin withered. The goddess was shocked to see old age spreading to her hand first, then the rest of her arm. Kallisto cried out in horror as she changed. Her luxurious blond hair grew thin and white. Deep wrinkles appeared on her smooth skin as large bags sat under her eyes. Her nose grew wider while her skin became looser and hung from her face. Within seconds, her youthful beauty had vanished.

The goddess switched her gaze onto the one responsible for changing her into an old crone. Mara's face began to transform. The black scars closed up while her face grew fuller. Her skin went from a greyish tint to a healthy tan. She regained her human appearance, although she still looked like a beast with glowing eyes, dark blotches, and elongated canines.

Mara gazed upon the false goddess, now siphoned of all magic. Kallisto released a loud cry, wrenching her arm away from the undying's jaws. Mara stood up straight and watched her handiwork.

Without any magic, Kallisto was unable to heal the massive bite wound on her arm, let alone undo the damage the huntress did. The goddess felt her face, becoming aware of her loose and rough skin. Kallisto gazed back at her followers, seeing the shock decorating their faces. None had expected this transformation.

Even Commander White was shocked, his face contorted in horror. It was an expression Mara had never seen before. After witnessing his goddess' humiliating defeat, he looked mentally broken.

Speaking of mental breakdowns, Kallisto turned to the huntress with shock and horror.

Mara gazed back with wide glowing eyes. Blood painted the huntress' lips and chin. Still, she could not get over what just happened. All that youth, beauty, and god-like powers—gone in seconds! To be honest, it was satisfying to see her enemy like this.

Kallisto's loss had not only taken a toll on her body, but also her mind. The goddess looked daggers at her and began to hyperventilate, her face twisted in rage. Without warning, she lunged at the undying and screamed in her face.

Mara was startled by the sudden outburst of raw anger. What did Kallisto hope to achieve by screaming in her face? Then she realized this was all the so-called goddess could do.

"You bitch!" Kallisto crowed. "You fucking bitch! What have you done?"

Scowling at the old crone, the huntress' hand tightened into a fist. In one swift motion, she slapped Kallisto across the face. The impact knocked the crone down.

The disciples gasped in distress. The Holy Blades looked apprehensive but remained still.

Mara would know better than to harm an older woman, but this was Kallisto—the same one who caused all of this. Mara looked down at the old crone while the latter glared up at her. The huntress tilted her head to the right. Lifting her right arm, Mara wiped the blood from her lips and chin. Her face reverted to normal.

"Such ugly language," Mara said in a cold tone. "Then again, ever look in the mirror?"

Kallisto frowned at her. "What did you do to me?"

"I siphoned your magic by drinking your blood." The huntress gestured to Commander White. "I did it twice before on your commander."

Everyone was astounded. Even Kallisto gave a bewildered look.

Mara noticed her gaze. "You didn't know? It's one of the three ways to regain my human appearance. His blood is less effective due to the tiny piece of the divine's soul. But you have a much larger portion, making you replete with magic."

Kallisto kept glaring at her.

Mara smiled insincerely. "Thanks for your help." Then, "Oh, and my blood can also siphon magic. I had some in my mouth. It's likely in your system, extracting every bit of magic from you."

A horrified look formed on the crone's face, for she had no power. Kallisto had lost.

Turning around, the huntress saw the commander approaching her with his sword drawn.

"How dare you hurt my Goddess?" Commander White raged with burning fury. He trembled, tightening his grip on the Hand of Kratés. He intended to fight her.

The huntress frowned. "I hoped to free you from her control." Mara saw the darkness rising out of him once again. Then she glanced at Kallisto. "But I see you remain devoted to her."

Kallisto laughed. "He loves me and only me! He will always be devoted, no matter what!"

"Even after you're dead?" Mara questioned.

Commander White stepped in between them. He made it clear he would never allow any harm to come to Kallisto. If what the fallen goddess said was true, then the huntress had no choice. Looking back at him, Mara noticed Nightingale strapped to his belt. At least her plan could go through.

The commander slashed at her. While stepping to the side, Mara grabbed Nightingale by its sheath. Reclaiming her weapon, Mara unsheathed her sword. She did not hesitate to slash at his neck. He jumped away from almost being decapitated but suffered a nasty gash. The commander stared at her while holding his wounded neck. Blood poured out for a few seconds before his wound closed up. His classic glare returned to his face as he gripped the Hand of Kratés.

"How dare you?" Commander White slashed at her again.

She took a step back and got into a stance. Mara gripped Nightingale with both hands, ready to fight him.

Commander White scowled at her. "You dare fight me with that sword? Are you stupid? That blade cannot kill me!"

Mara reached into her cloak and pulled her necklace out. Upon inserting the moonstone into Nightingale's pommel, the etchings glowed bright blue. Everyone stared at the blade in shock.

"It's like Godstruck!" Mr. White exclaimed.

Mara watched Nightingale, then looked back at Commander White. Her eyes began to glow.

"You shouldn't have stabbed me with the Binding Dagger," the huntress hissed.

Then she did battle with the commander once more. Commander White was fast and powerful but was no match for the huntress' restored powers. She teleported around him, then slashed him on his right arm. He winced and grasped his arm in pain. Blood seeped from his wound. The notes from Dad's journal were right—her moonstone was more than enough to defeat him.

Commander White lunged at her. Mara sidestepped, then she gave a quick punch to his back. He recovered and swung at her again. His arrogance was his undoing as the huntress used her left arm and parried his attack. She struck his right hand, forcing him wide open for the finishing blow.

Commander White froze as bright red blood erupted from both sides. Her sword plunged deep into his torso; the crimson-stained tip emerged out of his back. His dark grey coat turned red. The commander was speechless while staring into her eyes. Blood poured out of his mouth.

Mara gazed back at him in silence. Sometimes, the right choice was not easy or obvious. Once, she wanted to save him. Even after learning the whole truth, she would have freed him from Kallisto's control. Yet this man caused so much pain to her and others. Mara did this, not only for herself but for all the lives he ruined.

He sank to his knees while the divine's soul rose from his body. The tiny flame floated before the huntress. She stretched out her hand and absorbed the soul. The huntress felt nothing, for she consumed such a small shard. Turning her attention to Commander White, Mara pulled the blade out. And he fell to the ground defeated.

The Holy Blades were mystified to see their commander fall. The thought of attacking his slayer did not cross their minds at the moment, which was good for Mara. She focused her attention on the fallen commander.

Unlike Kallisto, who changed back to a bitter hag, Commander White did not show any signs of ageing. Yet he was in grave condition than his false goddess. He struggled to breathe. The commander fought a losing battle to stay alive while a pool of blood formed around his body. The commander's gaze remained on Mara.

"Kallisto…" he whispered with his dying breath. Then the light faded from his eyes.

In silence, Mara lowered herself to him. With her left hand, she closed his eyes. It was the end of Commander White.

Mara stood up and turned to Kallisto, knowing she had unfinished business. She remembered Morgan's advice to reclaim Aazalith's soul. The huntress already obtained the late commander's fragment. There was one last thing to do. Mara began to approach her, gripping a powered-up Nightingale. The old crone might have known what the huntress had planned. She had seen what became of her commander and was not going to give in without a fight.

"Kill her!" Kallisto ordered her followers. "I order you to kill her!"

All of a sudden, the Holy Blades surrounded Mara. They stood in her way, keeping her from her intended target. They drew their weapons and watched her with dark expressions.

Mara could not believe what she was seeing. Despite exposing Kallisto, her followers still defended her.

"No!" Mr. White shouted.

Mara turned her head and noticed the dreadful look on the older man's face. Then she looked in the direction he was staring.

Some priests ran to help their false goddess. On Kallisto's orders, the group fled through the door on the left side of the stairs. She gave Mara a sinister glare while fleeing. The huntress didn't know what they were doing at first but had a revelation. Mr. White watched her with a grave expression. He also knew what was happening. Mara wanted to get to the door, but the Holy Blades stood in her way. Soon, she realized something.

"You knew!" Mara scowled back at the priests and followers. "You knew she's not a goddess. You knew all along!"

Their cold eyes confirmed her fears. After all, they stood above the remaining source of the magic blight.

"So what if we knew?" asked one of the priests. "This power allows us to shape the future we desire. It is ours to take!"

Mara shook her head. "How could you say that? How could you be so willing to allow millions to die?" She glanced at everyone. "I saved this land from the monster you awoke. The same monster who is trying to reclaim the power your "goddess" stole!"

"And you are a fool," the priest berated Mara. "The last thing we needed was you playing the hero!"

Mara stared numbly at the priest.

The priest issued an order to the Holy Blades. "Kill her!" Then he glared at Mr. White. "After we deal with her, we shall execute you for your treachery."

The older man's face turned pale while two followers grabbed him.

Mara frowned as the Holy Blades surrounded her. She never wanted to fight them but had little choice. To stop Kallisto, Mara would have to go through her followers.

A loud thump on the main entrance drew everyone's attention as if from a battering ram. After a few knocks, the doors flew open, and a large crowd of people charged in. The Guardsmen of Mirahyll stormed the Temple of Kallisto, outnumbering the Holy Blades. Even the followers were surprised by the sudden invasion.

One of the priests stepped forward. "What is the meaning of this?"

A female guardsman with pale skin, short black hair, and steel green eyes walked forward. Her garb looked similar to the commander's, but with silver plating, and the greyish-blue coat was shorter. She appeared to be the captain.

"By order of Chancellor Davis, we demand your surrender," said the captain. "Your crimes include conspiracy with the Blackthorn Guild, damage to the city caused by your fire, and murdering the Moen Brothers. If you refuse, we shall use force."

Mara looked back at the priests, seeing how unhappy they looked. The one priest, who made the order to kill her, just stood there and clenched his teeth. His hand tightened into a fist.

He looked to the Holy Blades and shouted, "Kill them!"

The captain shook her head. "Then you leave us no choice."

She drew her blade. The guardsmen followed suit.

Madness ensued. The Holy Blades, guardsmen, and even some of the followers and priests fought each other. Within seconds, it became a bloodbath.

With no one paying attention to Mara, she managed to reach the door where Kallisto fled through. Before leaving, she looked back at the battle.

Amidst the chaos, she saw Mr. White cowering in the corner. An armed Holy Blade approached him. Mr. White tried to flee, only to be grabbed by his collar. The older man was thrown down with force as the Holy Blade intended to execute him.

While watching, Mara realized he was different from the others. The older man did not appear to be affected by the magic in this mountain.

Something in Mara changed. Even though the former college professor played a role in her misfortune, she didn't see the entire picture before because she refused. Mr. White was an unwilling pawn, forced to do unspeakable things. He always appeared to be remorseful of his actions.

Gazing at the commander's body, the huntress soon realized that there was another life worth saving. Mara returned to the older man. On the way, she spotted her cloak. The huntress retrieved it while traversing past the combatants.

The Holy Blade never saw it coming while raising his sword above his head, ready to execute Mr. White. In a flash of gold and silver, his sword suddenly fell to the ground behind him. The Holy Blade lowered his arms to find both of his hands cleanly sliced off. He stared at his arms and did not react until being stabbed in the back. The tip of Nightingale emerged through his chest.

The older man stared in shock while blood splattered onto him, staining his clothes and his right cheek. The huntress looked over at him with glowing eyes. In one quick motion, she moved Nightingale upwards. The Holy

Blade made loud gurgling sounds while being sliced in half. Mr. White sat frozen. Mara leaned over, cut his bonds, and grabbed his left arm. She pulled the older man to his feet.

"You saved me!" Mr. White cried. "After all the things I've done."

The huntress dragged him to the door. On the way, she glanced at Commander White's corpse. The pool of blood surrounding him spread further. Mara looked away and guided the former college professor to the door. She saw a few more priests fleeing through it.

"Where does this go?" Mara asked him as they approached the entrance.

The older man snapped out of his shock, then cleared his throat. "Ah, this leads down into the Dark Labyrinth, where the soul of Aazalith resides."

She stared down the dark pathway and took a step forward.

"Find somewhere to hide," she instructed him.

Mara ran down the path and entered the Dark Labyrinth.

Chapter Twenty-Four

The Twisted Divine

Mara followed the priests deep into the depths of the mountain. She came across a narrow bridge and watched as they crossed it. A terrible tremor bellowed from below, causing all but a few to fall to their deaths. The others paid no mind and fled into the darkness. The huntress waited for the tremor to end, then crossed the narrow bridge. To her luck, the bridge didn't feel her weight. After crossing, she felt another tremor. She reckoned the earthquakes were caused by using the soul of Aazalith. She needed to hurry.

She arrived at a large chamber, where an immense blue flame sat atop a pedestal. It was the soul of Aazalith, in which Kallisto was bathing in its power. Mara stepped forward with Nightingale, only to be halted by the Holy Blades and some of the followers.

"You are too late!" shouted a priest. "The power belongs to her! No one will interfere!"

Mara could only watch as the soul enwrapped the old crone. Within seconds, the flames faded, revealing a revitalized Kallisto. Upon claiming the whole soul, Kallisto returned as the powerful and beautiful goddess, undoing all of Mara's efforts.

The followers fell to their knees and bowed.

"Hail Kallisto!" announced another priest. "Our glorious Goddess has returned."

Ignoring her followers, Kallisto gave a smug look at the huntress while lifting her arms. A powerful aura flared up around her like blue flames. She was merely demonstrating her power.

Mara glared at her while gripping Nightingale. After absorbing the entire soul, the huntress speculated that Kallisto was even more powerful.

All of a sudden, the blue flames dissipated. Kallisto froze, then began to tremble. One of the priests lifted his gaze and noticed the goddess was shaking.

"Goddess, what is wrong?"

The other followers took notice and rose to their feet.

Kallisto buried her face in her trembling hands. The shaking did not cease. As she breathed heavily, the magic flowed out of her lips.

The disciples looked concerned. One of the priests stepped forward.

"Goddess," he addressed her again. "What is wrong?"

Through her fingers, Kallisto gazed up at the priest. Mara noticed her eyes were glowing blue. When the goddess lowered her hands, everyone froze. Six blue eyes sat on Kallisto's face. No longer did she appear human. To the huntress, she looked more like a darkling. The followers seemed baffled, unsure of how to react to their goddess' transformation.

Kallisto lifted her right arm to the priest. Black tentacles burst from her arm and bore deep into the priest's face, gouging his eyes out. He had no time to scream as the appendages tore through his skull and brain. Then Kallisto pulled them out. The priest was dead before he hit the ground. The rest of the followers stood like statues, their mouths agape and eyes wide open. None expected this to happen. Even the huntress did not see this coming.

Glaring at everyone, Kallisto roared as more tentacles shot out of her body. Magic billowed out from her wide-open maw while cracks formed on her face. Unable to contain the immense power of the divine, Kallisto's body burst into flames. The goddess screamed as she became charred beyond recognition.

Another tremor caused the chamber to partially collapse, taking the pedestal and Kallisto along with it. Plumes of smoke and ash rose from the chasm. Then, from the chaos, a dark creature emerged. Tentacles wrapped around the false goddess' remains, reshaping into a huge grotesque monster.

The new monster appeared female with transparent skin as several tendrils formed her skeleton. Within her bosom was a glowing white core, like Aazalith. Gigantic tentacular sprouted from her torso while she was visible from the waist up. With six lustrous blue eyes, she cast her gaze upon everyone. It was Kallisto, who had somehow transformed into a divine. The creature released another roar.

Mara gripped Nightingale, knowing that she needed to slay this horrible monster, or else the rest of Ardana would be in danger. However, she would find no help. Most of the followers either died of shock or fled for their lives. The remaining became paralyzed with fear. Kallisto raised her right hand and blasted them with powerful magic, striking them down. Mara survived but wondered if she was fortunate to be alive. While struggling to her feet, the huntress glanced around. No one else survived the attack. She gazed back at Kallisto. Could she do this alone?

"What? Don't tell me you're giving up now!"

Mara heard a well-known female voice. A woman appeared before her, donning Silver Thorn armour and red braided hair. The red-haired woman turned and smiled at Mara. The huntress saw her steel-blue eyes and immediately recognized her.

"Saskia? How? Why are you…?"

"We have been watching you," spoke a familiar male voice.

Mara looked to her left and saw Harold, who appeared as he did before dying.

Khan, Isabella, Anna, and Heru also appeared by her side.

"You're all here." Mara glanced at each of the six heroes who defeated Aazalith long ago.

"If you think we came here to give you a pep talk, you are mistaken!" Isabella chided.

Mara identified Hema's former ruler by the ivory and dark purple dress with jewels sewn into it. She still wore her white pearls and silver jewellery, as well as her matching crown. Isabella was once a vampire who lived for eighteen centuries, but her eyes were now pale green on a slightly fuller face. Her skin remained pale, though her long blonde hair seemed to possess more colour. Mara suspected this was the queen's human form. The huntress looked at her face. Isabella remained sour for what Mara did.

Lady Isabella placed her hands on her hips. "I would not mind if such a creature destroyed Ardana. Perhaps humans will learn how to be appreciative for once!"

"Would it not be better to have her stop the ones who caused our misery?" Heru questioned.

Everyone watched him.

Heru noticed this and scratched the back of his head nervously. "What?"

Mara knew the tall and muscular man by his tanned skin and short silver hair. His shaven face remained the same. He still wore his leather armour, decorated with metal plates and a wolf's pelt. Heru was an ancient werewolf, though he looked no different as a human. Never once did his dark eyes fall upon Mara. He likely remembered that incident.

Isabella raised an eyebrow. "Never thought a mongrel could still desire revenge."

"Well, you were not the only one targeted for assassination!" Heru scowled at the former vampire.

"True, very well." Isabella turned to Mara. "If you know what's good for you, you will defeat this creature once and for all."

Lady Isabella and Heru faded away after imparting their final message.

"It's time for the world to know the truth," Anna said.

Mara looked at her. At first, she did not recognize Anna, the darkling formerly sealed within the Black Tower. Anna now possessed red hair like Saskia, but it was in a neat bun. The young woman appeared to be in her early twenties with pale skin and dark brown eyes. She wore ancient robes, matching her role as a scholar.

"The veil Kallisto and Kratés created must fall." Anna then joined Lady Isabella and Heru.

Khan walked up to Mara. Unlike the emaciated man encountered in the labyrinth, he looked much better and dignified. His skin was brown, and he possessed short black hair. Khan wore brown and white robes and held a wooden staff. His dark brown eyes gazed at Mara with respect and admiration, for she reminded him of his daughter.

The wandering monk placed his left hand on the huntress' right shoulder. "I've been waiting for this day," he told her. "As the reincarnation of my daughter, I have faith in you." He also disappeared before her eyes.

Mara was left with Harold and Saskia as the three watched the colossal creature.

"Any advice?" Mara addressed Harold.

He studied the monster. "Kallisto has become like the divines," he told her. "She will be a great foe but is not without her weaknesses. Behold the core in her chest." Then he gazed at Mara. "I am sorry."

Mara looked perplexed. "About what?"

Harold sighed. "I believed only Thalia could stop her, but you have proven me wrong. Despite not having the original undying's power, you were able to defeat the goddess and her commander on your own. So, I know you shall prevail." With that, Harold faded away.

Saskia looked at Mara and shrugged. "See? No pressure. Just remember to keep your sword up and don't get hit." She waved goodbye to the huntress, leaving her alone to face the twisted divine.

As Mara watched the monstrous entity, she sensed a presence nearby.

"Mara… Remember…"

In the darkness, she saw the seven glowing eyes of the Watcher.

"Aspen?" Mara asked.

Aspen's eyes remained on her, gazing into her mind. The Watcher broke through the veil one more time. All of a sudden, Mara saw the images of the White Lady, the Siren, and the Marionette.

"Each undying had a place of power," Aspen said. "The White Lady had Misty Valley. The Siren had the waters around Har' Yhan. And the Marionette had her home near Haranta Village. Each place holds a significant meaning to them. It is where their power was at their strongest. You have the Dark Labyrinth. It has been your domain for the past thirty years."

Then the Watcher's eyes faded from her view.

"You have the power to end this," Aspen said.

Now alone, the huntress gazed up at the twisted divine. She could sense the magical essence flowing through the Dark Labyrinth. Tiny sprites appeared before her. Just a fleeting thing, but Mara walked through them, absorbing them into her body. She stopped and raised her arms. The magical essence flowed into her. When she absorbed enough magic, a dark aura burst forth and flared up around the huntress. Her eyes glowed yellow while the dark blotches reappeared on her face. She gripped Nightingale. Storming over to Kallisto, Mara knew she could defeat her.

The twisted monstrosity released another roar as she unleashed powerful magic from within her core. It nearly knocked Mara over while it surged throughout the Dark Labyrinth. A light moan drew the undying's attention. Looking behind, Mara saw five Holy Blades and two priests rising to their feet. Their faces were pale with white eyes and grey lips. Kallisto reanimated the corpses of her followers. The undead took notice, then shuffled towards the huntress.

At first, Mara believed this little undead army would not be a threat. But soon into the fight, dark red fumes burst from the Holy Blades' bodies. Their eyes glowed red as a black ooze seeped from their eye sockets. They suddenly came after her with ferocity, speed, and strength. Then she noticed the priests, who were droning incantations. She could not understand them, for it sounded like jumbled words. Like the Holy Blades, a red aura surrounded them, hinting to Mara to take them out.

At least the priests were easy to kill, which their deaths dispelled the enchantment on the Holy Blades. Without the priests, each Blade took a few hits before falling. While dealing with the last one, a dark shadow loomed over the huntress. Mara turned to see a giant tentacle falling towards her. She dodged out of the way, but the Holy Blade was not so lucky. Blood gushed from his flattened body. Mara's attention fell on to the divine, who appeared unhappy. Kallisto raised another tentacle and tried to hit her, but the huntress dodged her attack.

Looking at the core, Mara dashed towards it. She intended to end this now. However, the divine released another magic blast, knocking the huntress down. She cried out in pain while hitting the ground with a thud. While recovering, she saw one of the tentacles wrapped around her left ankle. The divine pulled the huntress up into the air, and she was hanging upside down.

The monstrosity shook Mara like a rag doll, trying to make her drop her sword. Though the huntress held on. She glanced down and saw the divine looking up at her with a sinister smile. Kallisto opened her maw. Mara looked back at the tentacle and saw it uncoil, releasing her ankle. The huntress screamed while falling into the void.

* * *

Mara opened her eyes. She was still alive. The huntress glanced around but did not recognize her surroundings. Black tendrils surrounded her, writhing like serpents. Mara was now inside the twisted divine. At least Nightingale remained by her side. If Kallisto thought this was going to get rid of the huntress, she was mistaken. Mara rose to her feet and glanced around. She needed to find the core and destroy it.

All of a sudden, an arm grabbed her right leg. Startled, the huntress slashed at the hand with Nightingale. It eventually released her. Then another one appeared and snatched her left arm. As Mara pulled away, she saw the angry face of the false goddess.

"You will pay for your insolence!" Kallisto yelled.

Mara struggled out of her grasp, then stabbed the goddess. Kallisto did not appear to have much of a reaction and dissolved into the ground.

The huntress looked disturbed. "A manifestation?"

Whatever it was, it was not the real Kallisto. Mara looked ahead and saw a light shining at the end of the tunnel. She ran in the direction of the light.

Soon, Mara found the core, comprising of Kallisto's remains. Several fractures decorated the sides of her face. The eyes and mouth were black as if burned from the inside-out. There were even more cracks present on the body. Black tentacles, stretching in various places, replaced both her arms and legs.

Mara gawked at Kallisto before glancing down at her chest. The soul of Aazalith pulsed within. Magic flowed out of her body, unable to be contained. The huntress gazed up at Kallisto's closed eyes. She appeared to be unconscious. Mara looked down at her sword before returning her gaze onto the enemy. Once Mara took a step, Kallisto's eyes flew open. A black ooze poured from her eye sockets, similar to what Amara had. Realizing the huntress was standing before her, the goddess glared at her.

Kallisto roared as blue embers flared up around her. Mara took a step back and raised her left hand to shield her face. As soon as Kallisto stopped screaming, the flames dissipated. The huntress lowered her hand and gazed back at the goddess.

Mara shook her head. "How the mighty have fallen!"

Raising Nightingale, Mara stabbed Kallisto. The goddess released a loud gasp as she looked down at the sword embedded in her chest. Then she glanced up at the huntress. Kallisto's face twisted in horror and agony. Her skin began to crumble as her eyes bulged from their sockets. Engulfed in the fire, she released a final screech. The bright glow blinded Mara as the flames engulfed her as well.

* * *

Mara awoke to the burning pain rushing through her veins. The huntress had never been so grateful for being cursed, even though it was always her goal to lift it. Considering what happened, Mara doubted she would have been successful as a regular human. She opened her eyes to find her vision blurry. The haze eventually cleared, and the first thing she saw was Nightingale by her side. At least the sword remained intact, but her attention fell onto the pommel. Sparks came out of the moonstone. Deep cracks formed in it, then it shattered into a fine dust. Mara frowned upon losing a keepsake of her father.

After gripping Nightingale, she rose to her feet. Her body ached in pain. With her hand on her head, the huntress began to remember what happened.

A deep rumble bellowed within the depths of the Dark Labyrinth. She turned her head and saw the divine. The monstrosity was already dead, burnt from the inside out from the explosion. Her corpse had collapsed, hanging over the abyss. Body parts fell off and crumbled away as black fumes rose from the remains.

A terrible stench filled the air, making the huntress cringe. When the black smoke lifted, she found what remained of the fallen goddess. All that remained of Kallisto was a blackened skeleton with organs. She was barely recognizable, save for her head and the upper part of her chest. All of her hair had burned away. Blood and fluids oozed from various sores on her burnt face and scalp. Her organs liquefied, turning into sludge as black ooze seeped from her eye sockets. Mara stared at Kallisto's decomposing face and shook her head.

"How the mighty have fallen indeed," she murmured to herself.

The cost of vanity and greed led Kallisto to an ugly end. It was over. The huntress watched while the rest of the false goddess melted away. A healing stone was left behind. Very convenient for Mara, considering that she risked her human form to defeat the twisted divine. She crouched down and claimed her prize. The huntress decided to use it later in a safer place.

After putting the stone away, a glowing orb surrounded in blue flames drew her attention. Mara lifted her gaze to Aazalith's soul. It looked much smaller, making her believe that Kallisto had exhausted most of its power. She was unsure about absorbing the soul after witnessing Kallisto's transformation. But Mara remembered Morgan's advice. It seemed to be the only way to get the Thoron Sages to help remove her curse.

Reaching out her hand, Mara watched as the orb flowed into her. She could feel the immense power of the divine's soul as it began to spread through her entire body. A tingling sensation overwhelmed her. After absorbing the soul of Aazalith, the huntress passed out.

Chapter Twenty-Five

Flight of the Nightingale

"Can you hear me?"

Mara's eyes fluttered open upon hearing an older male calling to her. She recognized the short and round man with white hair. Mr. White looked rougher with his clothes appearing dirty. His hair also had some dirt.

"Mr. White?" Mara could not believe that he came all this way down here to find her.

He looked relieved. "Thank goodness you're alive!"

She watched him and frowned, wondering why he did not express revulsion at her undead appearance. Reaching for her face, Mara noticed the lack of scars. Her face felt fuller. She regained her human form, but how? The huntress glimpsed into her pocket. She suspected the healing stone and its fragility, but it remained intact. Then she realized what happened. The huntress absorbed the soul of the divine. Feeding on Kallisto or Commander White's blood also yielded a similar result. However, she felt no different than before.

Glancing back at the older man, the huntress noticed a group of people behind him. They were walking away. Six of the seven heroes, who defeated Aazalith a thousand years ago, left this world. With their tasks completed, their spirits could finally rest. They faded away into the darkness of the labyrinth.

Mr. White watched her in confusion. He glanced at whatever she was looking at before returning his gaze to her. "Mara?"

She looked back at a very concerned Mr. White. Tears welled up in her eyes.

"It's over." Mara broke down and sobbed.

The former college professor gave a sad smile and placed a hand on her shoulder.

Without warning, the ground shook as a roar bellowed from deep within the earth. Mara shot up to her feet, realizing it was another earthquake. Rocks fell from above as more of the chamber gave way. Knowing they were in danger, the two fled back to whence they came. At least Mara knew her way around the Dark Labyrinth.

* * *

The morning sun greeted them as they left the labyrinth. Mara found herself in a familiar place. She and Mr. White ran down the mountain trail overlooking Ozin Village. They were not out of the woods yet. Looking back, they watched the mountain falling. The Temple of Kallisto was rocked from its foundation and shattered into several pieces.

While the two ran down to the village, the older man could not keep up. Mara grabbed his arm and pulled him along as the rocks fell near them. He screamed, but the huntress could not hear what he was saying over the roar of the earth.

Upon reaching Ozin Village, a few people saw them. At first, they were wondering what they were doing here but noticed the roar growing louder and the mountain coming down.

"Evacuate this village!" Mara yelled over the earthquake.

Without hesitation, the villagers went to every household, making sure everyone escaped the cataclysm. Even the huntress and the former college professor helped out. Checking the last house, she spotted Alderman Nigel trapped below a fallen bookshelf. She remembered him as the one who ordered her execution after Saskia's murder. Mara grabbed the bookshelf, then lifted it off of him. Nigel was mystified as she helped him up to escape.

Mara, Mr. White, and the villagers got to safety and not a moment too soon. Golden Mountain came down and crushed everything in its path. Nothing remained of Ozin. It was very fortunate there were no casualties, though many were unhappy about losing their homes.

* * *

Mara stayed with Mr. White while waiting for a carriage to Mirahyll. She wanted to leave Ozin as soon as possible, thanks to her previous experience with the former village. Glancing around, she noticed the lack of Holy Blades. Ozin decided to use them after Nigel deemed Saskia to be useless. Now it seemed the former village was without any form of protection. For how long, the huntress did not know. As far as she could tell, they were not around to help with the evacuation.

It did not take long for Mirahyll to learn of the cataclysm and send carriages, supplies, and doctors for the displaced inhabitants. The convoy arrived within a couple of hours. Much to her surprise, the chancellor was among them.

Davis saw Mara and approached. "Oh, you're alive. That's good."

Then he glanced up at the mountain, or what remained of it. The unexpected cataclysm took him by surprise. The villagers approached them, seeking answers.

Mara lifted her gaze to Davis. "Kallisto is dead."

Her words surprised the chancellor and anyone who heard.

"Is that so?" Davis asked. "The guardsmen told me that the followers of Kallikratés went mad and attacked them. They had no choice but to engage them in battle. We lost quite a few of our own, yet were able to arrest a handful of followers and retrieve the dead."

"It was a good thing you sent them." Mara looked at Mr. White. "If not for them, we would not be here."

The former college professor nodded in agreement.

The chancellor held his hands behind his back. "I am glad you're okay." Then, "Considering recent events, Evan and I have decided to hold a referendum. The people of Ardana shall vote on whether to keep the Faith of Kallikratés or not."

Mara figured this would happen, but was still surprised to know many more people are standing up against Kallikratés. Not only did it fill her with hope, but it also made her proud of her home. Ardana's governments were finally listening to the people.

"Might as well dismantle it," she said. "Not only were Kallisto and Kratés false gods, but several followers had been aware from the start."

Everyone stared at her in shock. Davis' jaw dropped open.

"Yes, everything she says is true," Mr. White confirmed. "I was there when it all happened."

Chancellor Davis cleared his throat. "We shall consider it," he said. "Regarding Kallikratés' dealings with the Blackthorn Guild, we have testimony from Father Vernon. He might have confessed to save himself. Still, the vandalism to the city and the murder of the Moen Brothers was the breaking point. We could no longer allow the Faith to do as they please."

"You managed to arrest some disciples?" Mara inquired.

"We did." Davis gave a strange look. "Though something strange happened. Some of the ones we arrested fell into a catatonic state. It's as if they witnessed something very horrific."

"Their goddess transformed into a horrible creature," Mara said. "Many died of shock." She stood up and changed the subject. "So, what's next for Ardana?"

Davis pondered this. "The Holy Blades are no more. Most of Kallikratés' disciples are gone. If we decide to dismantle the Faith, we must figure out what to do with the Grand Cathedral. Most of the other temples and buildings can be torn down or repurposed. Still, there are a few who remain and must answer for their crimes."

The chancellor eyed Mr. White, knowing he was a member of the Faith.

She took notice and shook her head. "He wanted to leave and have nothing to do with Kallikratés ever again."

"Oh, I see." The chancellor watched the former college professor. "Speaking of which, I thought you were leaving for Corlin. Weren't you looking for a doctor for the commander's amnesia?"

"We were," the older man answered. "But the Faith captured us, and brainwashed Karl." He gestured to Mara. "We tried to save him, but he died."

"I am sorry," Davis said solemnly. "It will be impossible to retrieve his remains now. We don't know how unstable the cataclysm has made the area. As of now, Golden Mountain is off-limits except for those who have special permission." The chancellor switched his attention to the mountain ruins. "Now, if you excuse me. I must survey the damage."

As he was about to walk away, Mara followed after him. After hearing about Ardana's future, a thought crossed her mind.

"Sir," she called.

Davis stopped and looked back at her.

"Will travel to Thoron be possible?" Mara asked.

"Since the Faith is in no condition to impose those laws in Ardana, making contact will be possible," Davis explained. "It will take a while, considering the damage to Har' Yhan's port. Once we cast the referendum and repair the port, then we shall attempt to open a peaceful dialogue with Thoron. Why do you ask this?"

"I'm leaving Ardana. The answer to removing my curse is in Thoron."

The chancellor nodded. "Very well. As I've said before, it'll take some time. But I have reason to believe travel to Thoron will be possible." With that, Davis left to look over the damage caused by the fallen mountain.

While watching the chancellor walk away, Mara could sense Mr. White approaching her.

"Mara, please return to Mirahyll with me."

She looked back at him. The older man froze as soon as her eyes fell upon him.

"Why should I return with you?" Mara asked.

Mr. White regained his composure. "I don't have much time left, but I need to go home and make some changes. I had Karl's name in my will. He was to inherit everything upon my death. Now he's gone. And I wish to add yours instead."

She shook her head. "You do realize he's dead because of me."

"I don't blame you for his death. You did what you had to do," he said. "After all that happened, this is the least I can do to apologize. Everything I have shall belong to you. I also offer my home for the time being."

She was surprised by his offer. Then again, the huntress no longer had a home.

"Please, come with me," the older man pleaded again.

Mara sighed. "Fine," she said, "but I hope I can still trust you."

Mr. White nodded. "I promise I won't let you down again."

She stood there for a while before striding over to him.

* * *

The two boarded an available coach for a return trip to Mirahyll. Gazing back at the ruins of Golden Mountain, Mara noticed something unusual. A lone figure stood before the collapsed entrance to the Dark Labyrinth. Possibly a survivor, but after what happened, the chances of finding any more survivors were slim. No one else seemed to notice the person, and only she saw them. Stranger still, the figure was staring right at her. She could not look away.

"Mara?" Mr. White called.

She snapped her gaze away from the mountain ruins and glanced back at him.

The older man watched her with concern. "What is the matter?"

"I thought I saw someone near the entrance."

The older man looked out the window and gazed to where the huntress claimed to have seen the figure. He squinted. "I don't see anything."

Confused, Mara peered back to where she saw the figure. It was no longer near the entrance. She examined the mountain to see if it moved, but could not find the person. It was as if it had vanished while she turned away. Maybe it was a ghost? It would not be the first time Mara saw one. Nor would it be a major surprise, for several people died on that mountain. While searching for the ghost, Mara heard Mr. White whimpering.

Gazing back at the older man, Mara saw tears flowing from his eyes. Mr. White's face was red from crying.

Mara watched him in concern. "What's wrong?"

He looked back at her. Despite his tears, a sparkle remained in his eyes.

"Oh, I'm sorry," he sniffled. "I can't believe it finally happened."

Mara understood him, for it had to be a burden to serve the Faith of Kallikratés, and hide Karl's dark secrets. Looking at him now, the huntress saw a different man than before. He was happy knowing he no longer had an obligation to serve the Faith, Kallisto, and Karl ever again.

With tears still falling from his eyes, Mr. White smiled at Mara.

"After all these years, I am finally free."

About the Author

Born and raised in Edmonton, Alberta, Canada, Rina S. Mamoon got into writing at the age of fifteen. Her favourite stories include Hans Christian Andersen's *The Snow Queen* and H. Rider Haggard's *She*. A fan of fantasy movies like *The Lord of the Rings*, *The Hobbit*, and *The Mummy*. She's also a lover of video games such as *Demon's Souls*, *Baten Kaitos*, *Bloodborne*, *Dark Souls*, *BioShock*, *The Witcher 3*, and *Fatal Frame*. In addition to writing, she's also a digital artist and a photographer as a side-gig and hobby.

On August 5, 2013, she embarked on a personal project using a first-generation iPod Touch. It was from there *The Dark One* was born. The original story and the first remake, which became *The Lost & Cursed* and *The Cursed Herald*, were written almost exclusively on that device.

www.ingramcontent.com/pod-product-compliance
Lightning Source LLC
Chambersburg PA
CBHW061228170626
46809CB00007B/2571